Familial Tears.

a novel

Enbe Cee.

THROWN FROM NOWHERE.

- Ha, ironic reversal!

The guard tried to focus on the path, but his gaze strayed to the headstones.

- A cemetery to a morgue.

The steeple clock glowed in the moonlight. It had stopped with both hands pointing at four. He paused to look around; there was a bench a few yards ahead. Although the clock was no help, he knew he was early. The bus driver had been a maniac, foot down all the way. As the guard sat, he stretched his arms along the bench then stared at the stars. His journey and the embarrassment of being caught staring at fellow passengers came to mind. First, at a young couple, flirting. The young man appeared to be touching the girl's hair and face whilst whispering; her gaze darted between the floor and her boyfriend's face. The guard had become hypnotised by their actions. He longed for what they had, the joy of sharing, even though he knew that their relationship was doomed. It became evident to him that the young man was playing route one. His goal was physical, hers not. The girl had caught him staring, although he was unaware of how long. He had turned away ashamed, then remained head down until they got off the bus. Another couple boarded who looked to be in their fifties. They were flirting too, but she was playing to an audience. Her lover was looking deep into her eyes, but she was looking all around as he spoke. On the odd occasion she looked at her companion, she would raise her head, flicking her hair and look around to see if she had gained attention elsewhere. She caught the guard's eye, then keeping her gaze on his, smiled and winked. It appeared to be a knowing smile, knowing he was lonely, alone. He wanted her. Not forever, but just long enough for her to understand who he was. What he had become. She could comfort him, Mother him. Make him feel wanted - then in the morning, he'd be gone. It had happened before.

- Is no one happy with their lot? He bayed.
- All I want is what they have.

The moonlight revealed an eerie skyline from where he sat; shapes and angles drew his eye along until they focused on a family plot nearest to him, the name McBride carved into the wedge stone. He scanned the names and death dates; one of the names made him smile.

- How do you do, young Willie McBride…?

He laughed.

- Bet you've heard that a million times. I hope you died well, and I hope you died clean.

He hummed forgotten words, then remembered…

- Or was it slow and obscene?

He paused.

- Does it matter? - You are all together now. Something I've never had; I wonder if I will? Did you grow up in a close family; share each other's thoughts and dreams? Fought and forgave within minutes and never thought of leaving the fold. I never had that. I never grew. I was always treated as the same age by those who ran my life - leaving age. All I wanted was what you had. I'm not jealous; I'm talking. Not talking about anything in particular, just talking. I need to speak and read. It distracts me from the loneliness of my family less world.

He put his head between his knees, took deep breaths, and then sat upright.

- Words carry too much baggage; they make me feel forgotten.

He smiled.

- It's times like this that memories stream. I remember the faces but not the name; then the name - not the face. Countless faces are flashing through my brain, like a one-armed bandit. It's stopped at a guy I worked with in Wales; he confided in me that he "Was born a bastard". He found it necessary to tell me as a friend; I never told him I was an orphan – perhaps I should

2

have; it might have made him feel better about himself. I have to
McBride family. Be on my way, or my brain will never stop
rehashing old memories trying to make sense of something I'll
never understand.

He pushed himself up off the bench, looked up at the clock and
whispered,
-    Let me let myself be loved.
As he reached the churchyard boundary, he noticed steps up to the
vestibule entrance and a large wooden door. The guard took the steps
in one bound and stood with his forehead pressed against the flaking
varnish.
He thumped the door with the heel of his clenched fists and shouted.
- WHY – WHY?
He laughed as he skipped down each step, ran out the gate then slow
stepped towards the hospital lights.
-    Always wanted to do that.
The signs directed him towards the staff entrance. Approaching the
gate, he noticed the CCTV cameras panning within their arc of travel;
the lens was now angled toward him as he pressed the bell.

✳   ✳   ✳

The control room manager scanned the bank of monitors. A refresh
line washed over the image as she scrutinised the identity card then
pushed the entry button which recorded the timeline - 15-10-
2012@23:55. She flicked then released the camera control lever,
forcing a nodding movement of recognition. As the gate opened, the
solenoid's noise buzzed his cue to flash a false smile at the camera
and make the gesture of tugging his forelock. Stifling a sigh, the
manager looked down at his face and smiled; the guard continued his
journey, unaware that the voyeur knew more about him than he did.
As he lifted his hand to close the door, the cold of the steel caused
him to pull it back and lick his fingers; this drew his eye to his watch
and made him wonder why any sane person would arrive at work five
minutes to midnight on a cold Sunday evening?
This was his first shift in a medical facility; he had never been offered
anything this grand in the many months he had worked for this
security firm. The order had come as a pleasant surprise. He smirked,
knowing he would spend the evening alone.
He preferred that.

On most occasions, the guard enjoyed being with fellow employees. The random assembly of these others irked him; not being able to pick with whom he had lived or worked had been a life pattern. His usual working remit of shopping centres, industrial units and the occasional museum had resulted in being alongside various characters, none he had ever felt any affinity. It was the same as his upbringing. The thought of being alone in a mortuary frightened him. This was good.

Over the years, he had mastered a procedure that revealed a mind map of his perceptions. An intuitive function telegraphed current events, forecasting an outcome of a shift of eventualities. This internal defence mechanism evolved from the only school subject which had inspired any interest. Countless schools he attended had differing names for it, but the fundamentals of programming were the same.

An intuitive decision-making flowchart.

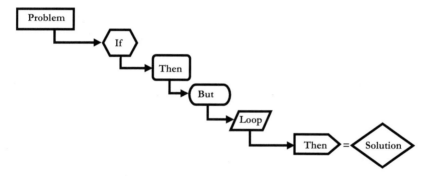

It was a recursive process that helped him understand and accept the unknown. His experience of being thrown into many different homes, schools, environments, situations and jobs had made this an instinct to be trusted.

The guard was not an anxious type. It was not his nature to physically and psychologically react to non-existent threats, but fear and apprehension initiated the process. He fobbed it off and patted his satchel. The process confirmed comfort.

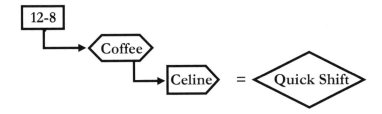

His eyes acclimatised to the white-walled corridors. The flickering frequency of fluorescent light produced the illusion of shadow movement. The floor, smeared with the rubber of many trolley journeys, painted the path of the dead delivered to their holding area before release. He was unsure of the route but followed the confusing colour coded path. It was getting colder too. As he walked, he read the instructions and standing orders. It was simple; there was no handover, no contact with others; he maintained a presence to prevent break-ins from removing cadavers. Highlighted in faded yellow was a paragraph on the importance of maintaining the temperature with a diagram, displaying the control mechanism alongside the location of thermostat and thermometer.
 - If they want them - they'll get them.
The words resonated through the white space.

Opening the lab office door, he felt the unease of a trespasser; he might have been entering the gates to heaven or hell. The silence scared him, but he told himself it was a shift like any other where loneliness would make time drag. The smell first encountered in the corridor was now at its strongest, stinging his eyes. A mix of vinegar and gas; that smell of propane had haunted him since childhood. Cheap heaters had fused this smell, along with that of damp rooms and adolescent sweat, to transport him back to an unhappy time. Memories of his orphanage upbringing and what he considered to be the smell of the doomed. For a second, he wanted to leave this job then, cursing his melodrama, cleared his mind. He'd spend the evening reading, enjoying the anticipation of where thoughts would take him, a ritual instilled through years of institutional upbringing. First off, there was a routine to follow: check the function of allocated equipment, monitor check, pan and zoom features of cameras, then check in with the control room that operated the camera scanning the office—watched on watch.

He followed the camera's arc and saw a desk under a massive window looking out into the large holding area where the bodies were stored; he stared through the glass.

Black, white and grey out there – oblivion.

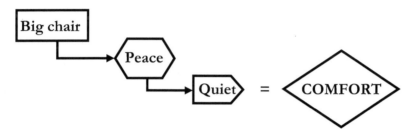

Opening his satchel, he removed a large flask of strong blue mountain coffee then poured a shot.

A rare treat; a bag of beans was three hours pay!

Inhaling the aroma, the guard savoured the flavour. He sat back in the chair imagining the first time someone had tasted it - and the euphoria felt when the caffeine did its work.

Relishing the moment, he reached for his book then cursed, realising he'd left on the bathroom window.

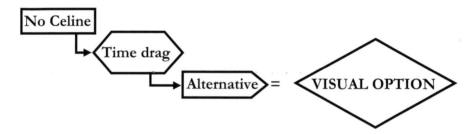

His thought pattern arrived at the solution when he looked at the screen; he had tested both cameras but not viewed the holding room. As he manipulated the camera, it shuddered as it scanned the area to reveal five bodies. One camera directed onto the head end whilst the other was on the feet. There was an area of intersection where both cameras showed the same image, like a Venn diagram. There did not seem to be any blind spots to his trained eye.

Driven by morbid curiosity, he viewed each face in close up. Something far back in his brain or superego prevented him from going any further than their faces, and he remained unaware of the gender of each of the deceased. The camera made each face appear larger on screen, which created nausea coupled with a strange sense of inner tranquillity. It reminded him of an exhibition he had worked where monochrome photographs of life and death masks were on display. The figures lying prostrate in the holding room, soldered to the stainless steel beds with the air's cold flux, created an eerie beauty. Their faces portrayed an intent expression, screwed up eyes portrayed the distinct impression of them being deep in thought. The guard became transfixed. He closed his eyes to pull out the trance that the two-dimensional images and caffeine had lulled him to. Looking over the faces, he counted three men, what looked to be a teenage boy and a lifeless face whose gender he could not readily identify.

One face in particular caught his attention.

The recognition made his body tingle, an older guy who used to play the local comedy venues. His name was Jeff Plant, but he billed himself as "The Baron" – a real thought-provoking comedian. He laughed, recalling the ranted routines that were not a conventional comedy. They questioned attitudes and social behaviour through what appeared to be drunken allegories to make the audience feel that they were laughing at themselves and their petty ways.

Looking over the desk for reading material, he noticed the in-box tray contained several pale buff-coloured folders, the contents described on the remnants of sticky labels torn off then layered with another bearing a scribbled name. All had been repaired and now framed with a yellow aged sellotape edging that had lost its adhesion. He poured another shot and opened the first: he began to read out loud, his voice quivered…

The following is a transcript taken from a digital voice recorder compiled by the deceased. He requested a bound copy sent to those mentioned in his will.

"HELLO, HELLO, is this thing on? The voice recorder has arrived, a new toy and no one to nag me about it. If I had a pound for every time I'd heard 'boys

and their toys', I'd have a fortune and… I'd spend it on more toys! My family, who were my life, did not realise that in the end, tongue in cheek, it is the one with the most toys that wins.

This machine is easy to work, so I will use this from now on. I started writing my last testament, but it was tiring me out. It is on my computer, on the desktop named 'The End'. I thought about using video as a living will but let me assure you, I'm not a pretty sight. According to the instruction manual, I have many hours of recording time so it should last; ha - more than my lifetime. I wish that what follows is to go to a transcript by designated Solicitors who are also the executors of my will. They will send a copy is to my family. The coroner or autopsy can use it or wherever needed as my remains are to go to medical science if they'll have them; if not - cremate. I'll switch it off when the pain comes. Let me tell you; the sound belies its intensity.

About twenty years ago, I mentioned at a table of friends that dying in pain to be the ultimate end of life experience. If, as life intended, the full gamut of human emotion had to be endured by the fate of being involved in family and friends - then the final chapter had to be extreme physical pain. They all laughed it off as one of my irreverent quirks, but my mind was firmly set; I would take the opportunity if it ever arose.

When I started to feel breathless, tired and dizzy, I put it down to being overweight and unfit. The lump on my right testicle set my mind straight on that, significantly when it enlarged and became painful, along with a constant ache in my lower stomach. Also, I was having difficulty starting and stopping peeing, there was often blood in the flow, and the pain was like the proverbial barbed wire. I stopped getting hard-ons which caused no end of aggro with my wife of forty-odd years. Later, there was blood and sometimes mucus in my stools which I knew was not a good sign either. I had seen my parents and my older sister decimated by the disease and reduced to skin and bone with the treatment - and for what - a few extra months.

Not for me.

I decided then to by-pass the N.H.S. Too much waiting, false hope and misinformation.

I alone was the one who knew there was something wrong, and that was the way it was staying. So rather than hide from it - I embraced it.

The recurring thought of Plant's face and fate distracted him as he attempted to absorb the story. He closed the file and replaced it on the desk. Plant had been a tall, grey-haired man with a certain elegance. His rakish smirk made others think that he had life sussed.

There was an enthusiasm in everything, from an ordinary greeting to ordering a drink. He always made a big thing about everything. Now he was a small, shrivelled up, a white-haired ex-man with a skin pallor similar to the gurney on which he lay. A chameleon on a dull mirror canvas. He opened the file marked PLANT.

Steadying the camera over the face, he centred the image on the monitor. The serene look was nothing like the madman he had known. Opening the file he thought of the evenings spent with him. It had been fun until that final evening, the best nights he could recall. Laughing and joking with a crowd, none of whom he knew. Their common bond was "getting Planted".

Strangers thrown together in the same city.

The file contained little information. A doctor's certificate stated that cirrhosis of the liver was the cause of death. Another form confirmed there were no known next of kin or funds for burial or cremation. The guard stared at the file. He'd never had anyone close to him die; he never had anyone close to him at all. He pondered Plant's past, the little known gleaned from what would have been an acquaintance for six weeks and compared it with his own.

The thought had occurred many times before; perhaps Plant had been his father.

Who could tell?

He could have been; those thoughts had come and gone many times over the years about many men. Plant told him he had kids never known. Once, when they were drunk, Plant had confided that he hoped all his children would meet one day. He wanted them all in one room so he could play "A boy named Sue" before suffering the onslaught expected. When Plant confessed to fifteen potential offspring, the guard had mentioned that his stage name should be "The Inseminator".

He had enjoyed that company, learned a lot too. They shared an interest in philosophy, talked about what they had read, liked and collected from Socrates to a shared dislike of B.H.L. Plant was well versed and had recommended a title that could be life-changing. The guard had found the book and devoured it; it had become a treasured possession. Plant believed it contained a sentence that solved all of the issues life threw up and challenged the guard to find it.

The guard had become aware of someone staring through the glass. He jumped in shock before realising it was his reflection. The face staring back had adopted the greyscales of those beyond the window, mirroring his own death mask. He composed himself and laughed. The phone rang, and he jumped.

It was the control room. The guard could hear the sniggering in the background, asking if he had been stung by a bee. He made a single finger gesture towards the camera then hung up.

JAY TEE SQUARED.

In the control room, an audience was gathered around a monitor, mocking the guard as they watched his fright. Jay Thorpe-Tracy shouted,

- Enough.

That snapped them back to reality; she gave them a look that had them scurrying back to their seats. She knew it was good for morale to laugh together to break the monotony, but she needed to flex a verbal muscle to maintain discipline.

She watched her charge retake his seat.

For the past hour, Jay had not taken her eyes from the monitor trained on the morgue office. The others had noticed and were nudging each other. None would say anything as they were where she wanted them. They knew some of her story and fast track promotion—an ex-Military Officer who had been around and not to be messed with. What they could not understand was why she had taken this job. She had spent many years in the Military Police and considered herself a career soldier until that innocuous paper trail exposed a part of her life she never knew existed.

Transferring her eyes from the big screen, she opened her laptop and refreshed the H.R. file on the object of her fascination.

Ben Black; DoB 16-10-83.

She knew his history verbatim: foster care, care homes, a variety of schools, attempted further education, series of dead-end jobs in different locations then this, back in the city of his birth. At least he had held been with this security firm for eighteen months working at various sites. It was then she realised he had never worked in a hospital before and could question why someone gave him this shift.

She could see his eyes were green; they looked strange on his face.

They gave him a warm and vulnerable appeal. Returning to the big screen, she could see him seated and drinking from a small cup. He was reading aloud.

* * *

Ben Black composed himself. He caught his reflected smile and thought about what had just happened.

Knowing no one would hear, he shouted.

-     What a tee-double-you-aaa-tee.

Scanning the desk and noticing the scattered folders, he gathered them up in a deliberate fashion placing Plant's on the bottom, patting them all square on the desktop. The top file read in red pen GERRY BROWN. Hoping it would calm his nerves after the scare, he sat back, opened the flap and pulled out the loose-leaf document inside. It was entitled Police Statement #1250001.

He started to whisper the words.

I cannot recall a time when I did not sport a bruise of some sort.
About six months into us living together was when it started, a nip here and a nudge there from minor interaction - an affectionate punch as Mr McKenzie put it. There was never a full-on blow nor anything aimed. I used to wonder where it came from and why it happened. Everything seemed so trivial to me. Moving a jar or book or leaving foodstuff in the wrong place. These misdemeanours resulted in low-level physical retribution, which some may interpret as tactile interaction, and although wary of it at the time, I thought nothing of it.
*   When we first got together, we had talked about our past relationships. I married for ten years, then we divorced, my fault according to the daily put-downs. Thank Christ no children - I was too selfish and not responsible enough - or so told. I met up with a few friends from my past that I thought would be good to see again. Lessons learned by the bucketful and the realisation that the grass was never greener. I met with an exact opposite, a real reverse role model if ever there was one, and lived together ten years. I left everything behind to get away from that destructive world of spiteful anger, snobbery, jealousy & bitterness. Then I met Gerry, and my life changed.*

Gerry also married once, lasting 30 years. Incredible. They had met at 17, then married at 21, first love for both. The obligatory gentleman's family of two kids, one of each and a typical struggle to make a happy family life. They had been part of a community, siblings and parents lived nearby, involved in all social events at the golf club, church and local council, viewed by their peers as pillars of local society. A concept so, so alien to me. There was physical conflict, but it understood, by themselves, to them knowing each other so well and became part of resolving issues. Could be that village life is like that throughout the country. Blows came from both sides, but it was taken as the norm. I had never gone through anything like that and am at a loss to understand that being a part of life. Domestic or aggressive behaviour was alien to me, but aggressive sexual behaviour was even stranger. After our tiffs, there was real aggression in bed towards me. I felt sometimes I was an object reclaimed. Pinned down and branded. It was simultaneous stress relief and exercise. Strange because in the beginning, it was gentle, loving, peaceful, fulfilling and mutual.

Having had time and space to reflect and I know this will sound clichéd but bad things happened cyclically. Like the moons pull on the tides, the ebb and flow of good times and evil were in direct proportion to when the red mist descended, as we used to say to each other. This was when the raging bull appeared. It worked on both sides, though. We used to laugh about it and christened the impending menopause, the "switchover". It seemed to make it feel as it was something we could face and chart through together. We laughed together, but at times I noticed I would laugh and she a second later. It was something I was uncomfortable to discuss—the last taboo. My introduction to the physical discomfort I felt at the age of thirteen was the words "Welcome to the Sisterhood" from my forward-thinking Mother. Followed by "Have children by the time you are 30 otherwise you will dry up, inside and out".

I recall feeling very uncomfortable when we attended an art-house cinema where there was a retrospect on Sam Peckinpah movies. The discussion after by the self-styled expert was that it was menstrual envy portrayed by the director as he was the first to show blood flying at all angles out of the shot or stabbed victim on the big screen. I remember thinking at the time what absolute garbage. I can never watch these types of movies now without feeling uncomfortable.

- Enough – does no one lead a comfortable life!

Ben shouted, then, realising where he was, lowered his head beneath window level as an act of apology.

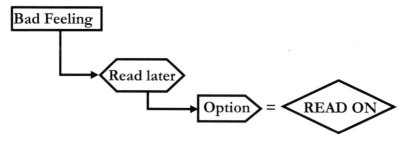

He picked up the Gerry Brown file again, hoping for the best, knowing it wouldn't be...

On the day in question, I was chopping and slicing vegetables with a cleaver we had bought earlier in the Chinese Supermarket. It had started as a nice day, awoken with sunshine through our windows, nice easy lovemaking with quiet smiles and glances. I recall an excellent breakfast with us both knowing what to do to make the table a perfect setting to enjoy our food, coffee and conversation. A well-practised routine could have been scripted, and we performed it to perfection. We had a slow drive into town along the coast with the top down, then parked in the shaded part of the high rise for the dog. As usual, we had to leave the dog in the car. Poor thing suffered from separation anxiety, could not bear to let Gerry out of its eye line but forgot this when left alone in the car. It could have been a result of feeling isolated after Gerry's divorce and was out of sorts. I know Gerry felt guilty about this and in all probability, made the dog worse by pandering to its affliction. It was deaf, suffered from haemophilia, and was on steroids, but it was calm, gentle, pretty and made it an ideal pet, but as soon as it saw another dog, it transformed into vicious attack mode.

That makes me think. Is a pet shaped in the way of its owner?

We had a nice lunch and strolled about the shops buying odds and ends. I always thought a cleaver was a kitchen essential after watching Chinese Chefs, so we purchased a small, good quality one along with other "nice to have but not needed" items. A favourite derogatory quote I often heard, generally after I had done the food shop. I noticed the tone and atmosphere changing. We drove home in silence, and I suggested I cook a noodle dish courtesy of our current favourite T.V. chef. Gerry suggested a Hendricks and fever tree as a sundowner, and the situation seemed resolved.

I had finished grating the carrot and was chopping the shallots using the cleaver when I heard the angry tones. It seemed that the purchasing of unnecessary items had been simmering and had manifested itself into this swirling cauldron of expletives and accusations I could hear behind me. I never moved; I stared out of the kitchen window and faced forward. It is difficult for me to remember how long this all went on, but the next thing I remember was a sharp pain at the back of my neck. It must have been a punch. Aimed and directed with full body weight behind it and launched with precision and venom. I was shunted forward with the pain unbearable. I turned around in an instant and instinctively put my right arm up to prevent the next blow from reaching its intended target. The cleaver was still in my hand.

I could not stop the blade slicing through the right-hand side of Gerry's neck and watched as the look of shock came over her face. I have never seen anything like it before. Horror and realisation. Blood seemed to be pumping out everywhere. Everything was in slow motion. The chord sequence and structure of "The Gift" and John Cale's incredible voice came alive in my head as if I had picked up some wayward broadcast. The final words of the piece repeated over and over again in my head, "which split slightly and caused little rhythmic arcs of red to pulsate gently in the morning sun…"

I had let the cleaver go as soon as I had made contact and the noise of it clattering against the tiled wall seemed to be the cue for everything to speed up. I watched her fall.

As I watched the blood flow slow, my thoughts led to Peckinpah's menstrual envy. She had bled out. There was nothing left, a body devoid of life, anger, pain and love.

Ben became caught up in the moment. He could not take it all; he re-read the confession.

- Gerry's a woman!

Ben looked at his feet then shook his head.

It occurred to him that all a person wanted was to head through life, like everyone else, and get happiness from that. That couple was matched after finding each other, especially what they had both been through, but then something uncontrollable put an end to that.

Thoughts abounded now, how Gerry's children must be feeling, and worse still, the lasting memory they had going through their lives.

Grabbing the joystick, he moved the camera until the young man's face appeared on the screen.

The boy's name was Jamie Farr; he would forever be fifteen years old. There was not much data in his file other than he had been found hanged in his bedroom.

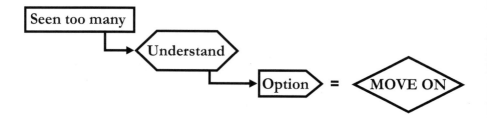

Ben was now fighting back a wave of emotion that came from his toes and engulfed him in a mix of rage and fear.

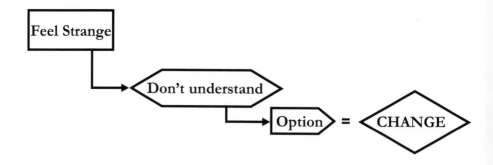

He decided to give Conrad's tale another go. Pouring the last of his flask, he laid the file flat on the desk and looked over it with his hands supporting his head.

* * *

Only I knew there was something wrong, and that was the way it was staying. So rather than hide from it - I embraced it. My wife knew I was hiding something, and the relationship started to breakdown. The kids had left home years before, and, as my thoughts began to drift towards my death, we ceased to communicate as one. I had been losing weight and was starting to look brighter than before. It was all my fault what transpired, and I may have engineered it somewhat. Accused of having affairs etc. - never denying it was the start, shutting down communication and, in general, being a grumpy old git that wanted everything done my way. It wasn't long before she left and started divorce proceedings. I agreed to all her terms, did not even bother getting a lawyer, and was happy to take the deal. She got the lion's share of pension, savings, house etc. I was pleased that a lot of the burden that might happen later was off. Also, her grieving process of us splitting gave her a live target, so to speak, something to blame. I had cash to buy a flat in a run-down area of our city, with the rest calculated to last as long as I did. I sold my car and all my other belongings and locked myself away. I never needed a television; radio was the best company. That's where I am now.

In hindsight, my life was never to be a special one.

We hoped it could be so; two seventeen-year-old virgins attempting coitus in a B&B in Berwick on a warm summer evening. I'm smiling as I remember the love we felt and how happy we had been that day. We had known each other from school, I was an apprentice plumber, and she had started nursing. The only thing planned was the day out. At the time, it was an essential thing in our lives. I lost sleep waiting for her to tell me she was "on", but it never came. It was the first time we had ever rowed. Parents were sat down together and informed, and we had to suffer the barrage of terms like, ruined your life; struggle ahead and even the term bastard, which now seems tame but was a real blow to me then.

We had been married on my 18th birthday. It was a shotgun wedding. As the song played at the wedding disco, everyone that mattered to us danced and laughed at the irony and futility whilst the bitter oldies sat in the corner tutting and scolding at the folly of youth. Now I can see their point.

We had twin girls. They were a joy; I was overcome with emotion and loved them so much it hurt. We had bought a two-bedroom flat and were both hard working. I loved my life then. The term back then was a nuclear family, and we were happy to be part of it. The wife worked hard in her nursing, becoming a Sister very soon, and I was now in the Fire Service. Our shift work pattern helped us stick together as there was always someone there for the girls, and we also had our family support group around. We worked hard, had our share of ups and downs but sailed through them together. Promotion at work came for us both, and we used our new-found prosperity to fund what some considered affluent in the years of "That grim E.E.C. hag", we took holidays abroad, drove nice cars etc. All the material crap. The girls grew up to be spoilt, got all they wanted and was not a good grounding for future life as they came to expect and demand rather than enjoy. As time passed, I needed more to occupy my mind. The Fire Service funded an M.B.A. course for me, so I achieved a goal after years of part-time study. Although, what good was a forty-year-old fireman with a master's in business administration. I stuck it out until I retired at fifty.

The girls had left home, and my wife had her own life that I was not part of. She had told me, in bed, after her 40th birthday bash that she no longer wished to have sex on all fours. I found this a bizarre thing to say. It was because it was demeaning to women and made her feel subservient. As we were both drunk, I told her I didn't know why I would not find her sexually attractive then. After a long pause, she said that was the end of it all, and we were both now responsible for our orgasms. For the next ten years up to my retirement, I became marginalised within the household, barely tolerated, my opinion not required on any topic. The girls, when they visited to ask for things their partners could not afford for them, and my wife were now a coven and banished from their world. I took up golf, went to the pub, and went on tour for Grand Prix, rugby and football matches and all the things that I thought men in their twenties would have done, including sleeping with other women whilst on tour. I learned then that I had missed a lot in that department!

I had never missed this form of entertainment in my youth and did not enjoy it now.

Over the next ten years up to my sixtieth, I tried many things. Boardgame ideas dispatched off to an agent, then rejected, competitions entered. I tried to learn guitar, then clarinet, all without lasting success. I tried writing poetry, then took up fishing, tried boating and loads of other stuff that I have now forgotten. Of course, all this fuelled the flames of mid-life crisis accusations — the truth was, I was an unfulfilled person put out to pasture by work and family.

Ben took a break to reflect and compare. He stood and stared out through the glass, then talked at his reflection.

- Have I wasted all these years waiting to be part of something?

He saw the glint of a tear reflected in the glass.

- Have all the books I've read trying to make sense of myself been futile?
- Illusory correlation or society?

Ben stared into his eyes.

- What the fuck have I done?

Ben screamed his revelation.

- This is metanoia!

He smiled at his reflection, content in the fact that some good had come of reading Jung!!

- This is no crisis though; it's confirmation bias!!! Ha, something's become clear, but I don't know what. All I have to do is understand.

Ben sat and faced the monitor; he zoomed the camera out, so all bodies filled the screen.

- All of you out had what I thought I needed — to be part of family life, to be adopted. But you were not happy. You wanted to be; you don't seem to be the bad one. You are victims too, victims of the wrong choice perhaps. Victims of fate, of trying to do good. Victims of the search for happiness.

He sat back, put his hands behind his head and shouted.

- Listen. What I've read about you has shown more about family life than living it. It's a mask, a façade hiding your inadequacies.

I've been the lucky one and understand it now. If my Mother walked in here, I'd tell her she did the right thing.

Ben became aware of the silence; he sat for what felt like an eternity listening to nothing. The office phone ringing broke this concentration. He snapped it up so as not to, as he thought, disturb anyone else.

-    Hello…Hello

Silence, followed by a click, then a loud high tone that reverberated and filled the room's emptiness.

Ben looked at his watch, turned and looked straight at the camera.

He mouthed "Assholes" and then returned to his seat.

 - 03:00; not long to go now.

Then the paranoia came.

THREE NAMES IN ONE.

Jay Thorpe-Tracy paced the control room with a manner that could be interpreted as arrogance. Focused, the last thing on her mind was to be friendly. She may have appeared aloof, but inside, she experienced a strange sense of not being in control of her emotions. As she entered the manager's annexe, the neon buzzed into life, illuminating the glass-walled office that created an artifice within. All was now either shadow or reflection. She picked up the phone at her desk and dialled the morgue extension; after a few moments, she replaced the handset without speaking. One of the dual monitors displayed the camera feedback. She froze the frame as Ben mouthed his profanity. With the image full screen, she hissed at the low quality of the bi-level resolution but took heart that she had heard his voice for the first time; she still had no idea how he looked in the flesh. This notion forced her to switch the image to real-time to pan and zoom the hardware to its limits and display the back of his head. The cold lighting created an awkward visual effect around him, that of a phantom aura. Intuition made her feel that she was under scrutiny, but a look of disdain directed at those on the other side of her office soon had their prying eyes returning to their own business.

Her fingers undid her wristwatch then caressed the skin where a tattoo outlined in coloured jigsaw pieces in the form of a bracelet circumnavigated her wrist. One more piece would complete the band.

She whispered… "Soon".

Again, she lamented the quantity of CCTV in the morgue office. Her investigations over the past year had revealed much of what was going on inside his head, what made him the person he was, his weaknesses, history and abilities, incomplete in isolation. She coveted full knowledge of his life and being. On the other screen, she called up her report. Scrolling to the end, the odd word flashed and subliminally confirmed that her life training, from adoption until this moment, had been geared towards what was to happen over the next ten hours.

Jay Thorpe-Tracy was the epitome of the Middle England new order: the fusion of working-class ambition and values with failed upper-middle-class old money. Her adoptive parents could be described as opposites, at least socially. Through her parents' hard work ethic, her Mother had managed to escape the rigours and insecurity of factory life that many endured during the nineteen sixties and seventies. She studied hard, her efforts rewarded with a red brick university scholarship which led to a passion for chemistry. Within three years of gaining a hard-earned Doctorate, she took her research into hazardous atmospheres and joined the laboratory board located on Harpur Hill in the Peak District. She had met her future husband through colleagues. His family had been farmers and abattoir owners for generations, but their businesses became decimated through E.E.C. regulations, foot and mouth, bovine flu, and ironically, Health and Safety requirements. Their marriage brought respectability and pride to her Mother's family and a financial regularity to her father's.

What was missing was a child.

Salvation came in the form of the adopted Jay, nicknamed $JayT^2$ by those close to her. This was not the orphanage's name, and, unknown to her, there was another on her birth certificate.

Three names in one year.

A lesser person would have been in counselling for years to cope with that lack of identity.

Her parents began to plan her formative years and education as soon as the adoption papers came through. Her name, nickname, home ambience, pre-school and environment crafted to suit their perfect childhood perception. They enrolled her in Repton as a boarder, even though her home was thirty miles away in the Buxton hills. She was encouraged to enjoy both lives—education and study during the week, then a weekend for family time.

Several career options became available through her success within the structured private education system. Her parents tried to guide her into the legal or medical professions, but the single-minded Jay had her mind set on a career in the Armed Forces, although it was unclear in which capacity she would excel. Much to her parents' chagrin, she took up the commissioning course at Sandhurst. Passing out at the Sovereign's Parade as the first to win both the Queen's medal and the Sword of Honour. Considered a dedicated and organised individual, she was offered an assignment to the Special Investigation Branch of the Royal Military Police, which she readily accepted. Previous research revealed this was a department in which she could thrive. She had termed it' investigative psychology' and revelled in its stimulating effect on mind and body. This empowered her to understand what her life wanted.

The job was a perfect fit for her, and she for it.

Solving simple and complex cases with the same methodology developed from training courses, intuition, planning and attention to detail, she had encountered every type of personality that the Army had recruited, trained and then left unused. Tick-tocks she christened them, time bombs that sometimes needed a release. Then, at twenty-eight years old, she encountered the case that brought the transformation. As she reached the end of the document, it struck her that she had forgotten the last time this report was updated. She checked the index created to project manage her investigation. It read,

- Dead P.M.T. website investigation.

- Discovery of abandonment.

- Discovery of true identity

- Discovery of birth parents.

- Ben Black. Uncovering history and location.

- Meeting Plant.

- Entering Ben's flat.

- Get a job.

- Engineering Ben's work schedule.

Jay's cheeks flushed, recalling her lack of self-control when she met Plant. During the time spent tracking Ben, she had seen the pair of them talking and drinking and was curious to know what part Plant played in Ben's life. She returned to the comedy venue the following evening to watch Plant's routine and source information. Jay realised that Ben was becoming an obsession and was willing to do anything to find out everything. Plant's interest in himself was her route into gaining his attention. She had introduced herself as an entertainment reporter for a national magazine and was compiling an article on Edinburgh's comedy circuit. Tricking him into the belief he was interesting her, Jay tried to appear hesitant when Plant invited her for a meal after last orders at the venue.

Throughout the next few hours, Plant's ego led the conversation to disclose Ben's information that Jay required freely. Jay enjoyed the company; it was a release from the past few weeks' emotions and the monotony of tracking Ben. Unfazed by the reality of Plant's arrogance, she accepted his offer of another drink in his hotel room. Handing Jay the glass, he took advantage of the closeness and kissed her. Jay let him believe that he aroused her and pulled him onto the bed. He removed her underwear and tried to kiss her once more, but she guided his head between her legs for her pleasure.

The epiphany that engulfed her was still a vivid memory. It was as if all the pieces bar one had come together at orgasm. There was no doubting, the man had a talent with his tongue, and as he licked and teased, her muscles tightened, feet stretched, and toes pointed to their extent. The flood culminated in her brain with all the knowledge gained about Ben revealing itself in a circular pattern: a whirlpool of enlightenment that showed what was needed. She remembered the look of disbelief on Plant's face when she did not reciprocate the pleasure. He remained speechless when she got up, dressed, then stared into his eyes. Jay looked down on the man on his knees, shook her head, then walked out of the room.

Then she recounted breaking into Ben's flat.

Finding the place was easy: just follow Ben. Thanks to her training, access to the studio flat was simple too. The real struggle which caused the hair on the back of her neck to rise was the first tentative step across the threshold.

A STEP TOO FAR?

Once in the main room, her emotions changed to astonishment. She had never seen such minimalist living. The kitchen cupboards contained coffee beans and a few small jars of dried spices. The fridge housed eggs, tuna, cottage cheese and beetroot.

- Who the hell ate that combo?

 The only visible items were a coffee machine and a battered leather-bound radio. She noticed that piles of books were furniture. A makeshift table of a cube of books with a recess scalloped and draped with a table cloth of sorts. Another block of books adjacent to the table functioned as a seat. A futon, surrounded by three walls of books about a meter high, split the room in half. Facing the bed was two life-size black and white photographs of the faces of older men. One had a round, balding head with a large white moustache; he had an eastern European's appearance and was staring into the camera. The other was in the classic American pose, sideways on, looking into the distance. She recognised neither. As she tiptoed through the sparseness of Ben's life, she had to steady herself. A feeling of dizziness and nausea came over her with a flush of panic. Her thoughts raced and, as she considered her actions, it occurred to her that this entry into Ben's innermost life was as a form of rape: an unknown perpetrator violating the innocent, exploring a stranger's being for her gratification. This adrenalin flow overloaded her nervous system, and she felt an urge to defecate.

 With a gut-wrenching feeling of shame, she rushed to the bathroom and reached the sink just as the bile welled in her throat. She felt weak as she tried to open the cold water tap. An inner strength help overcome this, and she felt relief placing her wrists under the running water; the sweat on her forehead ran into her eyes but was washed away by the back of her wet wrist. She controlled the gag reflex, rinsed her mouth and patted cold water on her face. Lifting her head, she caught her reflection to see the matted hair and red eyes. As she shook her head, the uncontrollable urge returned.

The perspective from her seated position revealed that this room was also devoid of any personality. A pack of disposable razors sat alongside a cash and carry size box of single-use ready-pasted toothbrushes. The plastic shopping bag hanging on the door handle testified to the use of these products. It was overflowing; through a hole in the bag, she could see several single-use razors, shower gels and broken toothbrushes. She poked the bag with her finger, and the settling noise of the plastic components made a strange manufactured wind-chime. She decided to get out, but panic returned as she realised there was no toilet tissue. Looking around, she thanked God as she spotted a box of moist wipes by the door.

- What way is this to live?

As she removed all traces of her being in the flat, she pondered that this must be institutional functional living personified. Everything was unemotional; nothing was personal or owned. Within that entire living machine, it was the only the radio that could have had any history.

Ensuring there was no one about, she left the flat, bewildered but convinced that Ben Black's character traits had been shaped by his upbringing rather than nurtured from family life.

BRYCE.

Captain Thorpe-Tracy listened to the presentation whilst reading the supporting documentation from the Police Central e-Crime Unit and the C.I.D. She absorbed the salient points in seconds, leading to understanding what happened but not the reason why. When the civilians had finished, she paused before responding. Not for effect, to remind her of the stupidity of squaddies with too much time on their hands. Even Sergeant Bryce, whose face looked up at her from the files - twenty-eight years' service and active duty in every conflict - was a fighting machine with not one ounce of common sense.

- Leave it with me. I'll use your case files then investigate and interview Bryce. When we get all the facts, then we can meet again and make a joint decision on how we will progress this. What is your feeling towards a resolution?
- We respect his record and service, but we will have to evaluate if he is a threat and act accordingly.
- We are agreed then. Who's the point of contact?

One of the men who had not spoken piped up.

- D.I. Lambert, my contact details are in the file.

Escorting them to the exit, she pulled Lambert aside and asked.

- Any thoughts?
- All we want is it resolved. Get it off the desk, tick the box and set a precedent.
- I'll get onto it. These guys trip themselves up. I doubt if he realised the consequences of his actions.

Returning to her office, she sat down, flashed up the monitor and called up Bryce's detailed file. As a career soldier in the Infantry, he had seen more than most. Considered an excellent combatant, he had commendations and glowing service reports. He had the genetic make-up of the ideal soldier and had managed, so far, to keep out of any reported trouble. With his image on the screen, she asked

- What are you playing at, Bryce?

Bryce stood to attention and saluted as the Officer entered the interview room.

- Sit down, Sergeant, she commanded

Maintaining full eye contact, she laid the folders on the desk in front of him.

- Any idea why you are here?
- None, Ma'am.
- Dead P.M.T.
- How do you know about that?
- You set up the website on a laptop whose I.P. address is within the Barracks. It's flagged as a threat by the civvy e-Crime Unit, and they want to ream your ass with a dick the size of an elephant's.
- There's nothing illegal about it.
- That may be so, but some might see it as tantamount to treason.

At this point, he seemed to enter a state of shock. His face drained of colour.

- You cannot run a sweepstake on when an ex-Prime Minister will die.

He looked up at the ceiling, his eyes darting all over as if searching for a response.

She continued.

- You know the divide of feelings her name causes.

- Have you been on the site? Have you seen how many hits it has taken?
- Bryce, I've been through everything, as have the PCeU. Your problem is that the taglines used, specifically, "Ruined more lives in this country than Hitler" and "Celebrate her death", do not stand in your defence.
- Have you read the forum comments where the contributors share how she affected their lives?

- Right, it's interesting reading, and that is where the threat lies. That plus the sweepstake to guess the date and time of her death.

She paused.

- Did you consider that some nut might take it upon himself to win it by making it happen?
- What do you mean?
- You never thought this through, did you, never considered that you'd be traced?
- No, Ma'am.
- Think about it, Bryce. Some other idiot will pick a date and time, make it happen. You are aware that anything anyone posts on the internet will always be available to any investigators.
- No, Ma'am.
- Pay attention now, Bryce. I don't believe that you created this with any malicious threat. Due to your record, I will make a case within those confines. I need you to explain, in full, what the hell you thought you were doing. The video has been running since you came in, so all this will be your statement. Okay?
- Yes, Ma'am.

He looked around the room for a minute; he started to speak, then stopped. Taking a deep breath, he exhaled in a slow, precise manner.

- I created the website last year after my father died. I was in Helmand when I got the news and granted leave for the funeral.

Then in a lower voice, he continued.

- No one told me he had been ill. He wanted it kept from me. On my way home, all I could think of was his life. He had been a miner since he left school; McGregor and Thatcher took his and other people's dignity and pride. They broke us all to satisfy their ambitions. Divided and conquered to pave the way for financial institutions to hurt us all again 25 years later.

His speech became animated, and he tried to regain composure.

- My father knew the solution to unemployment was to go back to college and retrain. He had a strong sense of survival and knew that it came from education and knowledge. So he did and suffered the indignity of being in the same year and class as my younger brother – his son! I knew it was demeaning for both of them, but they fronted it out. They both finished and got Technical certificates which got them into Nissan. Strange how it took a nation, defeated in a world war, to understand the value of a loyal and proud workforce that existed in Tyneside. He worked on the assembly line until he died. He likened his working life to that of a sheepdog and joked that at least he had not been shot when he outlived his usefulness. He never blamed Thatcher. He knew none of her policies was her own, all ripped off from '"The Road to Serfdom", he would say. I never knew what he meant. Even her bollocks speech about "may there be harmony etc." was ripped off from some Saint or other. He knew she was a puppet, a Judas goat, and would reap all she had sown. Everyone today knows who she is... except her!

He took a long pause, then sat up straight,

- The bottom line is that I set up the website as a memorial to my Dad and those others whose spirit became broken at that time.

The Officer looked into the Sergeants eyes and asked,

- So, Bryce, if he never blamed her – why do you?

Meeting her stare, he answered,

- It's a focal point. She made herself the target - so in true Military fashion, if you live by the sword...

The room went quiet. Staring at Bryce, she held his gaze for several seconds and then broke the silence.

- Okay, Sgt, you have two options. The website is down already, and I need the email address details of everyone who has contacted you. In short, I need all the information you have. Your first option is simple. Co-operate, and we can limit any damage to your career and your pension. The other option is to treat you as a subversive, stripped your rank,

31

cancel your pension and sack you with a dishonourable
discharge, which will then clear the way for civvy criminal
proceedings. I don't know what they can get you on, but they
intend to put you away for something.
- First option, Ma'am.
- Right Sgt, you have two days to get everything to me. I mean
everything. Don't try to be smart now. Do you understand?
- I understand.

She gathered the folders, stood, then left as he snapped to attention
and saluted. Closing the door behind her, she thanked the patron
saint of Army training for not developing a squaddie's brain.

Two days later a package was delivered by hand. The contents looked
unorganised: one CD and various printouts that showed names,
addresses and email testaments praising and thanking him for the
website. There were also many cursing him, with threats of court
action and press exposure. This thing had gone way beyond her
expectations; it was national. Local groups formed with the express
intention of celebrating on 'The day that Thatcher died' and further
suggestions that it be a yearly commemoration, an unofficial Bank
holiday.

Bryce had created a stir. How had civvy law had not picked up on
this before it went viral. Shutting down the website was not going to
stop it; it was a catalyst to encourage localised debate and discussion
between the politically disenfranchised. One folder contained
additional information that needed scrutiny. Judging by the un-
moderated forum uploads, there was ill-feeling breeding.

It was out of Bryce's control. She opened the spreadsheet showing
the details of all the subscribers to the website.

One surname caught her eye; her own.

Stranger still was the location, a hamlet situated a few miles from her
family home just outside Buxton. She believed she was the last of the
Thorpe-Tracy's' and told the name would die with her. She had never
questioned her parents - perhaps now was the right time.

She decided to inform her superiors that a field investigation was
required to expedite the Bryce case.

DEAD P.M.T.

Many thoughts preoccupied her, making the drive pass quickly. She had been aware of her adoption at an early age, had never questioned her previous history and had assumed her birth parents were dead or had just not wanted her. There was never any thought of tracing them, but now, she needed to understand her genesis with her family world expanding. Approaching the peak district, Jay acted out the expected. She would go to the hamlet first, identify herself without the hyphen name, then use a fear tactic to glean whatever information she could. It was a real one-horse town. A village green, church and a few cottages scattered along a narrow road. No pub, shop or any sign of life. She drove through, parked up in a layby, and then walked back to the village. Knocking on the door, she felt a tingling sensation.

She might find out things she was not supposed to.

A woman in her late fifties answered the door. She had the whitest skin Jay had ever seen. It was no pallor, more a blue-ish white that gave the illusion of transparency.

-    Hello, are you lost? We often get that with ramblers.
The woman stared at the uniform.

-    My name is Captain Tracy; apologies for the intrusion. Perhaps I should have telephoned first, it's nothing to worry about; I'm researching a list of names from a website. Do you have time to talk?
-    That's okay, dear; I have only free time these days. What website?
-    I'm here regarding your sign up to the Dead P.M.T. website. She displayed her warrant card. Are you Mrs Thorpe-Tracy?
The woman looked over Jay's shoulder and appeared to be considering her options. Jay's nerves were jangling now, making her hands shake.

- I am Miss Thorpe-Tracy. Ah yes, the Thatcher thing – I think it's a great idea- don't you?
- I'd like to ask a few questions about it.
- Nothing wrong, I hope.
- No, it's routine. We are trying to gauge the interest. There are a fair few members in this area, and I'm talking to each about it. Do you know any of the others locally?
- Yes, I do. We meet to laugh at some of the forum posts. Come in then, would you like tea?

Jay felt a shiver as she walked into the low ceilinged room.

- Come through to the back, and we can sit outside.

They walked through to the small garden and sat on a worn wooden bench.

- I've just made a pot; I'll get another cup.

Jay surveyed the surroundings.

She had never been to this part of the peak before and was curious why people chose to live in such an isolated spot. Maybe they were all hiding from something or someone. One town here was much like another, and there were so many that no one could know them all. This house looked comfortable, picture postcard, the perfect idyllic retreat for those who could afford it—the last place for a militant stronghold.

The lady returned, sat down, poured tea and gestured towards the milk and sugar.

- My name's Melissa.
- I'm Jay.
- I know who you are.

Jay felt her face flush.

- You are a Thorpe-Tracy too. I've not seen you for many years, but I used to spot you when you returned from school.

Then, turning her head toward Jay and with the faintest of smiles,

- You are my brother's adopted daughter.

Jay remained silent.

- What's wrong, my dear? Surprised at me knowing who you are? Or are you surprised at finding me?

Pulling herself together, Jay straightened up and asked,

- Why join the website?
- Just a bit of fun, my dear. There is no harm in adding one's voice to something that one believes in. I did it for moral support. The miners were not just in the North East, you know.
- I know that. Derbyshire had it worse than most.

Jay turned full on to face the woman.

- Who are you? What do you mean, brother? Who, who are you?
- I'll tell you. I'll let you know everything if you want; are you sure you want to know, my dear?

Jay dropped her guard.

- Please tell me. I thought I was the last of the Thorpe-Tracy's. Why has my father not mentioned you to me? Why have I never met you?

The woman's tone changed.

- What do you know about your grandparents?
- I know they were kind, loving people who helped my Mother and father when they were younger.

The face of the woman reddened, and her chin quivered as she spoke. She raised her voice then lowered it after the first word,

- YOU know nothing.
  They all disowned me when I was sixteen. Farmed me out here to the sticks and set me up with a trust that is just enough to keep me here and prevent me from leaving. It was made clear that if I ever interfered or got involved with the family, I would lose everything. Not easy for a single Mother with an Asian baby. Racist bullies, the lot of them. Your so-called father was the worst.

She took a sip of tea, then asked,

- Have they told the truth about you?
- What truth? I was adopted when I was six months old. What truth could there be?

35

- Did they tell you that your parents abandoned you outside a Post Office? Did they tell you that you had a twin? Did they tell you why they did not adopt the two of you? Why they chose only you?

Jay was reeling now. She felt dizzy; the tea calmed her.

- Why are you telling me this? What am I supposed to do with that information? Hate my dead grandparents and question my father's decisions? What is it you want?
- I don't want anything. It was you that came here, remember.
- I made a mistake. Curiosity got the better of me. I saw your name on the list, and I had to find out more. It's what I do – piece things together to make sense of ridiculous situations. All I've done is open old wounds and came off worse. Now I will have to dig deeper. Maybe I should thank you.

Jay felt a hand on her thigh; the mood had changed, and the woman's tone warm.

- Perhaps something good will come of this. Maybe I should never have told you those things. If you uncover bad things, don't let the bitterness eat you up. Come, I'll show you out.

Jay walked through the village, her mind swirling as she tried to make sense of what had just happened. Jay had organised to meet her parents that evening in Ashbourne at the pre-booked hotel; she had no qualms telling them a half-truth about working and staying for one night in the area. They had tried to persuade her to visit and stay with them, but Jay insisted they meet. As Jay drove to the hotel, she considered her actions. She had never been flustered like that before. She was proud that she could keep her emotions under control. She had worked hard at that; detaching herself had come easy due to lack of parental love and boarding school isolation. She had understood at an early age she had no love for her parents, no emotional attachment. She provided them with a successful child and, for them, the means for her to achieve. Perhaps they loved her in their way, but Jay had no emotional attachment to them. Through Army training, Jay knew any close relationship was a weakness that clouded vision. Jay was proud of her stoical attitude; it was an asset that solved cases.

Soaking in a large bath, she formulated a plan. They would eat together, and she could tell them what had happened, then perhaps they could clarify the situation. Jay booked a table in the restaurant and ordered a bottle of red on room service.

She lay on the large bed, sipping the wine and feeling relaxed, the embarrassment of her flustered mind from earlier in the day forgotten.

Good knowledge, she thought, as she fell into sleep.

The bedside telephone woke her. The receptionist asked if Jay still required the table. Looking at her watch, Jay realised she had been asleep for about three hours. Had anyone asked for her at the reception? No.

Something was wrong.

She switched on her mobile and called her Mother.

A female voice answered, but it was not her Mother.

There was a strange background noise, an industrial whirr she at once recognised as a helicopter.

- Who is this?
- W.P.C. Marr, who is calling?
- That's my Mother's phone; what's going on? Where are my parents?
- There's been an accident. We did not know who to call. Are you nearby?
- I'm in Ashbourne. Where are you? Where are my folks?
- Airlifted to Derby. It seems the car left the road.
- I'm going to the hospital now.
- I'll inform my colleagues and make sure they meet you there.

Jay left the hotel and drove to the A & E in Derby, her emotions in check. Jay focused on the future. She knew others would think it harsh, but there was an inconvenience here. Jay would not be able to get the information needed. She shook her head as she cursed her lack of emotion or concern.

Announcing herself at the hospital desk, a police constable notified Jay that her parents had died and the crash's details and what they thought had happened. After taking her details, they gave her names and addresses to contact, including a bereavement counsellor.

Jay turned and walked away. Striding back to her car, she sensed a betrayal; they had left her. Abandoned again. How was she ever to find out the truth now? She had lived a life without parents; this would make no difference to her.

Random scenarios raced through her brain. She had to stop to regain composure. She had to find out the truth.

THE ERRATIC.

Ben was getting bored; he looked at his watch but did not register the time. Picking up his bag, he removed the contents and placed them next to his flask. An old Tupperware box, frayed and scuffed with age, contained his food for the shift, a fork, a pack of paper napkins and a worn graffiti decorated folder. As he selected the folder, several papers fell to the floor. He placed each face-up on the desk, each with a crossword skeleton on each page. The layouts varied; a few were eight squares by eight, some ten by ten and the majority twelve by twelve. Some partially complete with forenames horizontally and surnames vertically with shaded squares separating them. Others had the surnames vertically and forenames horizontally. Two had a mix of both, but the majority of the sheets showed empty grids. Ben stared at them, trying to fathom the logic. He sighed with frustration as he returned them to the folder.

He poured a fresh coffee. He placed his nose in the cup, filled his lungs,

-    Ah, Moroccan

He had spent an hour making this from Arabica beans and a variety of spices. Savouring the cocktail, he reached for Conrad's file, opened it and reclined in the chair. Finding his marker, he shook his head and shouted at the top of his voice,

-    I know how this ends!

I had anticipated the pain and had stocked up on all forms of over-the-shelf medication to combat it. What I did not grasp was the intensity. At first, it came in waves, starting at one point then pulsing out to the rest of my body. I could control it with the pills, but soon I was eating them by the handful, like sweets. One of the local Neds who got my shopping saw the state of me one day and asked if I want something stronger. I'd never thought of that. Self-medicating on what I always considered to be the scourge of the communities I'd fought fires in, I'd seen charred junkies along with the devastation and desperation of their lives.
On the other hand, I'd seen melted bodies in affluent areas, one lawyer had set fire

to his home when freebasing, but that was many years ago. So, I started on the weed. That dulled my brain; it felt coated in cling film, and no thoughts were getting out. It controlled the pain though. The Ned sold me anything he could get his hands on. I had no clue what I was taking and got used to the names he called them. Eckies, jellies, goofys, I had a go at them all. They dulled the pain, but it never went away. The waves were coming more and more often, and I could not control them. I had spells of struggling to breathe. I could not swallow, and the pain in my throat was intense.

Many times I thought of getting the Ned to call an ambulance but never did. Once, the Ned saw me doubled over in pain and was going to call for help. I had to remind him if he did, there would be no more cash. I knew he'd looked around the flat for anything to steal, but when he realised there was nothing, he stuck to his promise of getting me the gear. Crack was a revelation. I have never felt anything like that in my life. No wonder it is so addictive. That sensation is like nothing on earth. Not even the smack, which I tried once.

Never injected, burnt it on silver paper and inhaled it through a plastic pen casing. The pain in my throat doubled with this stuff added. I was sick and lay there in a dwam. Still, it numbed the pain. I don't know for how long; I have no concept of time any more. The pain became more and more intense. It felt as it if was coming from inside my bones. Once, during an acid trip, I saw my skeleton when I looked at my arms and legs. I was strange, the bones were transparent, and I could see what looked like piranhas, swimming in the cavities, devouring the marrow and eating me from within. That was a terrifying experience

That's the cure, you know, a skeleton transplant.

I stopped taking the drugs after that. That was when it struck me; they were anaesthetising my death, and that's not why I was doing this. I was here for the hurt experience – that was the whole point.

To feel pain before death.

Then I met the pain.

It is nothing like a short sharp external blow but the real deal; it comes from within, from your very being. Almost as if it is the soul that is hurting. The question is how to be deal with it. I discovered its enjoyment. The endorphins that came with the pain released a euphoria that outshone the human-made narcotics I had been consuming. The pain became addictive; I wanted more. Pain drives the world out. It is a torture that gives you a kind of peace of mind that you cannot find anywhere else, and believe me now, I have tried. It starts in one place then washes over. I could feel it only at the source, but its radiance throughout my being became addictive. I wanted more and more. The pain surges became more frequent; they were extreme, penetrating, and powerful, followed by a shorter concentrated

staccato throbbing, like an earthquake aftershock. The agony has made me so weak it is a struggle to move. My skin is hanging off me.
I took a piss the other day and noticed something peculiar. I was circumcised when I was eight, and now, because of the way my skin hangs, my foreskin seems to have returned! That was a strange image.

I set the bathroom set up for my last days—heating on full and radio set to my favourite channel. The bath is lined and channelled with a waterproof fabric angled to the drain. I have set up levers to operate two shower heads, one above mine and the other at my groin. I can wash away detritus and keep myself clean, plus get water in my mouth. I cannot eat anything, and the protein shakes are running dry.

I'm in the bath now and can still move, but I don't know for how much longer. The voice recorder is nearby to pick up my musings, but I'm worried it may pick up other sounds. The neighbours bang on the wall when I'm screaming, but what can I do. If it's heard, omit them from the transcript to keep my tone positive.

Send my apologies to those who find me. I'm in my mess, not eating or drinking, and I'm weak and tired. I know it won't be long;
I need to sleep..."

END OF RECORDING.

Ben put the folder down and stared into space. As he tasted the last sip of coffee, he wiped a tear.

Taking a deep breath,

- All stems from domestic distress... why bother?

Back in her office, Jay watched Ben pick up a folder then put it down again. He appeared to stretch and lean forward with his elbows placed on the desk, and from her angle of vision, his nose looked to be touching the screen, Jay realising he was talking, flicked the switch on the telemetry software to activate her speaker.

She heard his voice once more.

BYBLOW.

Ben's face twisted as he thumbed through the file labelled JAMIE FARR. Forgotten memories flickered of a similar confused state at fifteen.

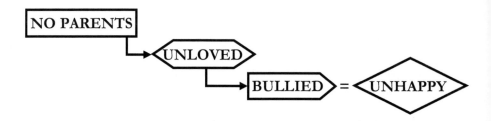

These reminiscences unsettled Ben. The agitation made him stand up and pace the office's length; he stopped, stared at the wall for a few seconds, and then returned to his seat. A morbid fascination goaded Ben to recognise what he must do. He did not want to look at, nor think about, the life the file was portraying, but some deeply rooted instinct to aid the vulnerable caused his brain to whirr into overdrive. He could feel the caffeine rush and tried to calm it by sitting back to inhale deeply. He raised his arms to shoulder height, stretched both palms and fingers as far as they would go, then exhaled, simultaneously lowering both hands until they were splayed flat on the desk. Leaning forward, he forced himself to look at the young man's face then, grasping the telemetry stick, made the image pan up and down, then zoom in and out in a futile attempt to slap life into the face.

Ben initiated a conversation with the monitor framed image.

"Jamie Farr".

Ben took a deep breath, then paused; his mind map was running amok as it tried to manage his thoughts.

- I'm a lot like you were

- I'm not a sentimental person. Sympathy to me is a word that comes between shit and syphilis.

As a numbness descended, he rubbed his sweaty palms on his trouser leg before continuing in a low tone.

- *I never cared for any fellow traveller to the grave. You remind me of all the others who cut their journey short - I need to tell you how selfish you were.*

You, Jamie, are the tenth person I've encountered who has taken his own life.

I remember the names but forget their faces. They'll never age in my mind, lost boys that became Peter Pan. I've found two, seen a number cut down and smelt the room afterwards – it's not nice. I've seen the uneducated hand-scribbled notes, trying hard to get their last desperate words to make sense. One guy - Hook, whom I knew reasonably well, killed himself because he couldn't go on wearing the hand me down clothes we shared.

Can you believe that?

Another boy, name of McKay, couldn't explain. His words.

'I cannae say why' – Not a fitting epitaph to a young man's life.

I remember the daftest, Billy Potter; he attempted to murder himself countless times; a serial victim, always teased in the home about it. His claim to fame was that a famous newsreader had abused him but could never recall if the abuser appeared on television or radio. One time, when the taunting got too much, he grabbed one boy by the throat and shouted, 'I'm going to kill you'. We all laughed and shouted,

'You can't even kill yourself!'

The guard sat back for a second and stared at the ceiling. Why were kids cruel?. He felt ashamed; he knew that incident would haunt Potter.·

- He had a breakdown after that and got sectioned. One of the real badass bullies sent him a letter and wrote his name on the address as B_l_y P_tt_r

and drew a picture of a gallows from the hangman game on the envelope. That was a step too far. We never saw him again. I learned that he had trained as a psychiatric nurse. He was wiping arses of those similar to him.

My first experience of a funeral was a victim. I didn't know what to expect. I asked my supervisor if we should get dressed in our best clothes for the occasion and the reply was,

 - Why? - He won't care.'

The image of that supervisor's face flashed for an instant in Ben's mind. He was a miserable man with a miserable life who needed to make all around him sad too. Ben smiled in the knowledge that the guy was a lost cause and remembered as such.

 - That lack of compassion still irks me. He chose me to be one of the mourners, a cord holder at the grave when they lowered the coffin. I can even see the small business card that the undertakers handed out; it had an outline of a coffin printed on it and the position marked with an X at where I should stand. The carer had taken me aside and explained that the priest would offer the prayer, and then before the coffin became lowered, would finish with…

`In the name of the Father, the Son and into the hole he goes.'*

I looked at him and asked if he did not mean the Holy Ghost. He slapped me around the head, told me to stop being cheeky and that I knew nothing. The perverse and twisted individual that he was, taking delight at messing with a fourteen-year-old boy's head. I waited for the words from the Priest. As I did, the man to my right at the head of the grave was sobbing uncontrollably. I didn't know who he was; he must have been a relative of the deceased. I didn't know what to do; do I drop the cord and comfort him? – If I did, would the coffin become unbalanced and fall? I was lost. Out of my depth on a solemn occasion with no one to help me.

Once again, Ben had to look away from the monitor, this time shaking his head and exhaling loudly. He pulled a sheet of paper from his bag, checked the printed grid was blank, and then wrote the names of the boys he remembered, surnames first, as in a roll call. Once they were all documented, he resumed;

 - I doubt anything like that ever happened to you, Jamie.

So, what could have been so wrong in your life that made you do this?

You had a home and loving parents - isn't that all any kid needs?

Did you have problems with identity or sexuality?

There is no problem with that. In the homes, no one cared about that. We were all orphans: the whole spectrum of colours and racial mixes. There was even one red-headed Jamaican kid.

We were all defined and judged as equal by society.

If you were gay, that was your issue and yours alone. Everyone else got on with life and felt no sympathy for whatever struggle. It was seen as a weakness to seek attention. What could be a worse struggle than being parentless? In this hetero-phobic, post-modernist, post-feminist and post-apologetic, self-opinionated world, most people are up their arses. They have no care for who is up someone else's. You are the selfish one and should have overcome any insecurities rather than expect others to get over them. The stigma of being different is nothing compared to the stigma attached to a parent whose child has taken his own life. Perhaps you were a rebel with nothing to rebel against and nothing to rebel with.

Ben was becoming anxious. He curbed an urge to punch the monitor and then quelled the need to test the primal scream theory. He had used this therapy many times before and instead soothed himself with deep breaths before continuing. Some of it was starting to make sense in his head.

-    *I found redemption - in reading. I don't understand all I read, but I try to understand why when I do something.*

I know the reason I'm talking to you.

Foucault wrote, 'Western man has become a confessing animal' - and that's what's driving me to talk at you.

That! - And the fact that I am spending eight hours alone. Usually, when I talk like this, I am told to shut up. People get bored with the things that fascinate me; if I do find someone who shares the same interest, they think, due to self-education, that I cannot justify my arguments—a lose-lose situation.

I'll try to explain how I see the concept of where we are tonight.

Ben sat back. He understood what he wanted to say but was struggling to get his point over.

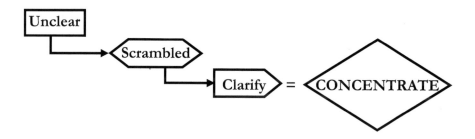

Emptiness came as the thoughts started to make sense. A moment of serenity encouraged him; he began to speak in a slow and methodical tone.

- *I'm in an office overseeing you on a screen through CCTV. I'm observed through the same medium. Those watching me are also monitored. You are the bottom of the ladder, as you do not know you are. Foucault resurrected the panopticon idea; a prison where all inmates are under view from one central point – without knowing it. He believed that our lives and behaviour have evolved and dominated by the fear of being observed. What society expects is decreed from school-age, where we are conscious of our visibility. The camera trained on you – and me - is a visible panoptic device, but many are invisible. Through social network sites and internet data gathering, those who want to can collate information on our individual preferences and bring the gaze of a superior into our daily lives. We think it new but delude ourselves. Bentham invented the idea, George Orwell made us all aware of it in 1984, and then Foucault rolled it into philosophy. Others have moved it on since. If we want to avoid this, all we can do is make it difficult for anyone to track us. I have no mobile phone, no computer, and no email address. I have a National Insurance and tax reference number. A bank account but no loyalty cards, no credit cards – nothing to make me visible. I am a marketing man's nightmare: a lost demographic—the last underground.*
  There is no underground anymore—no music, poetry, or political affiliation that can grow and gain momentum. No free-thinking. We are

not allowed. If something becomes trendy or cult, it's snapped up by marketers and wrung for every penny by the smart money - THEN they get out and leave the dregs to the masses who think they will benefit from it. Hyenas that pay the price. It has happened since the eighties - pension, property, stocks, shares, and all points in between. Profit and Greed will always encourage the suckers. I'm ranting now, Jamie, being carried away with my thoughts. That's what happens when there is no one to shut me up.

He realised his tone was becoming desperate and shouted the last few words.

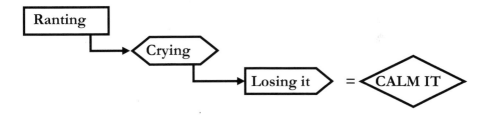

Content in the knowledge that he was making sense to himself, he considered the effect on someone overhearing him and suppressed a growing embarrassment. Catching a glimpse of a few words in his notebook, he toyed with the idea of getting those emotions out and then started to talk again in a calm and modulated manner.

- You could have enjoyed filial piety. The white-haired arsehole lying next to you put me on to it. He yearned for it all his life but never knew how to gain it, even though it was right in front of his face. He was the antithesis of family life and any form of moral or decent standard — now, he was a waste of energy, a man who hated himself for what he had become. The other lady and gent lying beside you appeared to have a beautiful family life, but, reading between the lines, history and indulgence conspired to take that happiness away. The difference was that they both had worked at it and tried.

They were parsecs adrift from that fossil of a philosopher Plant and his outdated and outmoded outlook on life.

I never knew my parents but would have loved to have lived within that philosophy of Confucius - but never had that good fortune. It made me think about all the others in the homes where raised. They might have had the chance but either never considered it, or they were selfish — like you. It suggests that we be useful to our parents; to take care of them and engage in good conduct not just towards family but also outside the home to maintain a good name. I don't get it, like the part that suggests we perform the duties of our job well to obtain the material means to support our parents: but the obvious makes sense, do not be rebellious, show love, respect, support and display courtesy. Some are not of our time, such as the need to ensure male heirs, uphold fraternity among brothers and wisely advise our parents on moral unrighteousness.

Ben covered his head with his hands and put his elbows on the table. He felt drained. His shoulders dropped, leaving him weak and without energy. This melancholy initiated an uncontrollable shudder throughout his being, which shook off the gloom. This was not the first time this had occurred, and instinct took over to free himself. It was as if his body knew how to react to compensate for the brain. He stretched his arms as high as possible and brought them down to the desk in an arc. He continued…

-    *If we'd met before you died, I'd have made a bet with you that you could recall more laughter in your life than grief.*

Up to the age you reached, I never knew what it was like to feel at home anywhere - I never knew what home was. Home became prefixed by the words Care or Foster - and that hurt.

But I do know the pain you felt, and I know where and how you thought it. It was as if a pair of condom thin hands had crept and slipped in between your skull and brain and clasped around your very being, those gloves squeezing out all the joy then massaging in darkness creating the dullest feeling you have ever experienced. At night, it was as if they enveloped the full surface area of your brain and replaced all the hope and good you had ever felt with fear and self-loathing.

I've felt that I've had all the imaginary conversations.

That's despair - pure and simple.

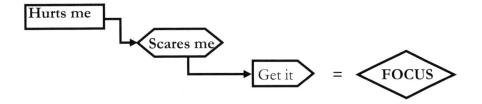

Ben felt uncomfortable but could not work out why. Something within made him stand up and scratch his back. As the ambient temperature in the room became unbearable, he removed his jacket. The recollections had overpowered him. He stood behind the chair, swinging it in an arc. He glimpsed the screen, threw his head back then laughed out loud at the futility of it all. Ben ran the length of the room towards the corner where the camera was and jumped up at it, contorting his face into a silent scream, hoping those watching saw him. He strode back to the chair, sat down, and then took a few seconds before raising his head and talking to the screen again.

- *You need a healthy mind to escape that covering grip Jamie, especially when there is neither support nor relationships around to inspire hope and effort. You were lucky enough to have parents, and for whatever reason, you thought they did not care.*

Let me tell you - they care now.

Your action has led them prematurely to discover that the secret of life is learning - to cope with any tragedy.

I've been there; tied the slipknot in the wire, opened the bottle of pills, stared at the Stanley blade - looked out over a motorway flyover and gazed at railway lines. I even tried religion as an escape from my crap life - but the priest was too creepy. He harped on too much about my soul rather than the reasons. Believe it or not, I found it overly dramatic! Even more surprising than the fate I contemplated.

It doesn't make it go away. The problem with pain is it's felt in one place. So, the pain that drove you to the ultimate sin could have gone by seeking more pain - I found salvation in reading. Reading, but not understanding. It was like a drug. My need was insatiable, and the diverse quality available inspired the need for more. I was devouring stories about how adult authors perceived youth development or child death: Garp, Earthly Powers, A Prayer for Owen Meany, The Fixer, Brighton Rock, Easter Parade, Rumblefish, Catcher, Mockingbird *and many, many more trying to make sense of a life I had no idea where was going. The only one that came near was* The Bell Jar, *but that was way beyond me — as most meanings were. I wanted salvation from these adults, but none was forthcoming. I read and re-read so hard I never forgot anything, and I learned a lot. I would never have otherwise. I was a youth, trying to find out about childhood from those who had lived it - best of it was they never captured it. They had forgotten the essence; they had discounted despair. The despair was in them, but they did not understand what it was to be purposeless and alone.*

Then for no other reason than school, I read Hamlet. None of the deviant subject matter that unfolded when reading that story was new to me. I experienced the entire spectrum of inhumanity within the home.

It was then I discovered intelligence was a fraud.

When the story introduced pirates as the catalyst for Hamlet's return, Shakespeare brought them from nowhere. His imagination created that random scenario. I realised then that nothing was ever as it appeared, and anything introduced to help existence on its way.

A real-life McGuffin.

He adopted a harsh voice as if trying to convince himself.

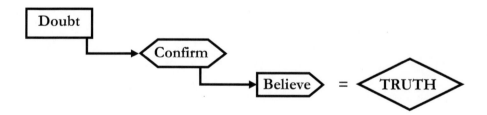

- *Intelligence is not always a survival trait. Less intelligent people live with the hand they are dealt with. The more intelligent may just give up. It*

didn't take me long to work out that smart people are more likely to kill themselves if their lives lack sense. People like me detached from their families and communities, people with few relationships. I had always been lonely, or at least was still reminded that I was a loner by headmasters, social workers, carers or whoever else thought it was helping a career path by helping me out. That was my situation, and I did not know any other. I was at odds to understand what improvements to my life these custodians wanted to make for me. Deep down inside, I knew something was missing, but had, and still have, no idea what it could be. My history had never been revealed, and I never questioned who my parents were or what became of them; I had conditioned myself to live in the now and take all that life threw in my stride. Other than that, I enjoyed a hedonistic teenage life. I enjoyed being seduced by those who tried to Mother me, and I had the measure of the male groomers; I used them for material gain without letting them abuse me. I enjoyed booze and drug usage on a singular level and could control it; I never dropped my guard nor laid my stall out too quickly. At sixteen, I was out of the system and on my own. My only regret was that I was never able to find in these formative years anything at which I excelled. I was an individual, un-calibrated in the ways of domesticity, with no sense of either being or family life.

No history. A non-person.

The experience of watching fellow orphans adopted, and so accepted by society, removed any hope from me.

I believe that I have inherited nothing spiritual and so can never impart anything similar. I've thought long and hard about my situation, which has led me to understand that my birth Mother's lack of closeness is the root of my inability to show or feel any emotion. My belief system limited by many factors — snippets of information taken from all I have read. The only genuine emotion I feel, which weighs heavily on my being, is when I imagine myself as an infant, lying alone crying, with no Mother to pick me up.

I long to have been comforted by her, and this has held me back in many ways. I understand why I had never experienced the thrill of ambition fulfilled; only the agony of purpose frustrated. This is directly related to what you had and now thrown away.

So Jamie, if we had met - would you have listened to me?

We will never know.

Ben poured a small coffee; the first sip took him into a happy inner moment that created a tremendous sense of futility. Oblivious to surroundings, he smiled and stared into his cup, as a fortune-teller would into a crystal ball. Jamie had lifted a significant burden.

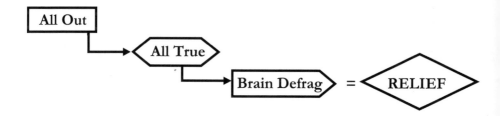

Jay stood away from the desk and paced office, touching the walls at both ends, quickening her tempo, as the thoughts created by Ben's words flew in and out of her head, causing uncontrollable anxiety.

A few calming breaths allowed her to regain composure. Listening to Ben had created an overwhelming adrenalin flow.

He needed to know all she did - that would calibrate him. Why had he used that word? Did he want to be aligned with family life? It was a strange observation on his part. She must explain what had made her the way **she** was, as **he** had to the monitor.

Why would he talk to himself like that anyway? Who the hell was Jamie Farr?

Could Ben see his reflection on the monitor? Was he talking to himself?

More thoughts raced around; she needed to help him, make him understand. She wanted to Mother him, smother him with love and protect him from himself. She was worried about what he would become. This thought pattern threw her into a state of mild panic. She had never experienced this behaviour before and did not understand its root. She needed advice but from where? Did she need Ben?

He certainly needed her. Only she - his twin being - could make him whole as a person and help him unlock his true potential. Her brain was racing; she had never felt such an emotional response. Calming down with deep breaths, she made an effort to think straight.

She must finish her report then let him read it. That was the answer, or perhaps it might be better to tell him the whole story face to face. She could post it to him. That would be the easiest way, then offer to meet up if he wished, or they could arrange a meeting to introduce herself. Jay stopped her confused state by banging the desk.

As she picked up the phone, Jay decided to finish the report by the end of the shift, then arrange a meet to give him the packaged item with minimal explanation.

Ben answered tentatively, expecting another wind-up;

- Hello, morgue office; Ben Black speaking.

Jay was in a state of panic when she heard him talk. Her mouth became dry, and trying to reply seemed to take a lifetime

- Hello Ben, I'm Thorpe-Tracy, the Control room Manager. We need to talk. Are you free after your shift?
- Why do we need to talk?
- Nothing to worry about, I have a report that concerns you, and I'd like your comments.
- Is it a complaint?
- No. Your work is acceptable. Can we meet after the shift, around eight-thirty in the café in the hospital foyer?
- It's my birthday, and I'm meeting with friends.

Ben offered, not wishing to get involved in Company politics.

- It could be beneficial to you, Ben.

Wincing and shaking her head whilst silently mouthing the words 'beneficial Ben."

After a pause of around twenty seconds, he replied;

- Okay then, I'll be there. How will I know you?

\- I'll recognise you - you're in uniform – right?

- Okay. I will be there around eight-thirty.

- See you then, Ben. Coffee's on me. She said, cringing at the childish rhyme.

HAMESUCKIN.

Jay studied the index. The report was in a healthy state, and a spell check reminded her how much of the information she wanted to convey. There was probably as much to leave out as to retain. She fingered the wrist tattoo as she picked up her watch. It was 04:00, halfway through the shift; the deadline was achievable by applying quick-reading techniques. She read then re-read the work, which kick-started her idea of what was required. Jay thought of the funeral portion of Ben's speech and his confessional method; this was her starting point.

"It took around eight days before my parent's burial; the police had to prove it was an accident. Evidence demonstrated that my father had suffered a subarachnoid haemorrhage, which led to a coronary whilst driving; the car had been on cruise control at the time. They established that my Mother was trying to phone emergency services as the vehicle went out of control: her fingerprints were on the steering wheel, indicating that she must have tried to wrestle control. Her last few moments must have been terrible. The car left the road and hit a telegraph pole at the passenger side. My Mother died instantly and, although my father was alive at the time of impact, he died soon after.

I've never understood the need to use the word "massive" as an adjective when used in conjunction with a heart attack; it's not the magnitude that kills.

I discovered more about myself in that period of mourning than in the whole of my twenty-eight years.

I must have been in shock when I left the hospital the night they died. I drove until dawn, ending up on Clee Hill, where I watched the sunrise. I remember a group of hang gliders setting up their kit. I watched them take such care and time in assembling their crafts, each safety checking the others, creating a unique bond of trust. It was a surreal experience for me as an observer, like watching migratory birds checking each other before becoming airborne. The silence of the morning coupled with the fog stretched out for miles beneath the hill, bestowed an eeriness soundtracked with the shrill of curlews, male voices and the clanging of steel assembly. The hang gliders took off simultaneously and then disappeared from the top of the hill. Something in my head jolted me back to reality. I knew I'd never see them again, just like I'd never see my parents. I had no one and was close to no person. I was on my own now — an orphan. I headed back to Buxton to what had been my home.

My Commanding Officer was a saving grace. I telephoned him on my return, and he arrived around four hours later with another Officer I had seen but never introduced to; she was of similar rank to me. She was a bereavement counsellor by the name of Brown. It felt too clinical, even for me. Brown had a wrong look for the job, too tall with a massive shock of black tightly curled hair, almost afro in style, and her demeanour was that of an undertaker. Her skin was pasty, and a poorly shaved upper lip took away any faith I might have in her professionalism. She had experience in coming across as friendly, but I could see through the façade.

I decided to stay on my own and would return to my post when the funeral was over. My C.O. sanctioned bereavement leave and, at my request, left me alone. For the first three nights, I cried. The grief enveloped me, and when I tried to eat, food was tasteless and alcohol bland; even making tea or coffee was a struggle. Family friends visited, sympathised and asked what arrangements had been made. The Police came and went. The family lawyers and doctor all rallied around and helped me come to terms with what had happened. It was a true communal spirit through a genuinely caring and supportive unity. I could understand Bryce's dilemma; what had been and what had gone. I could feel his uselessness in the part he was to play in the death of his father. I understood why he needed to atone.

I was the sole beneficiary in both wills. To finalise everything, the lawyers needed paperwork relating to stocks and shares plus my adoption certificate. They had been family friends for many years and had retained as executors. I was never involved in my parents' affairs but knew that everything was in the study so, when asked for information, I approached the intrusion apprehensively. It was easy to find what the lawyers wanted; everything categorised as was my life, in a filing cabinet in reverse chronological order. It was more of a documentary than a scrapbook, there were plenty of lucid memories but many more forgotten or not remembered. The investigator in me decided to re-live my life through the paper trail never before encountered. I opened the first file. There was a photograph of two doting parents smiling at a baby in a pram. It was my father's face that brought back the tears. He had a look of contentment that personified happiness.

Then I saw the first document.

It was the adoption paper bearing the name Penny Black.

I cannot remember how long I stared at the name, it could have been minutes, but its effect was profound.

I could not take it in; I was a void space; those two words had falsified my presence on earth.

Uncovering your history is a strange experience. I doubted if the army had a counsellor for that. It felt as if I had no memory, and I was starting anew. The documents showed I had been found at 2 am, alongside my twin, outside a post office in Edinburgh's Bruntsfield area, by nurses who lived in the flat above. One was from Simpson's Memorial, a children's hospital. She managed to raise our body temperatures before calling the police. She named us Benny & Penny Black due to the post office connection. There was no birth certificate in the file, only the adoption agency's name and the persons involved. The sole witness was a drunk heading home. His recollection of events was vague, but he did see a car in the vicinity and heard babies cry. The documentation was incomplete, but I made up my mind to find out who I was. I started to cry again at the realisation that I was not alone.

I had a brother.

Over the next few hours, I sensed all my feelings moving over my face, like clouds scudding across the sky. Joy turned to pride, then to embarrassment and finally, grief as I re-lived my life through my parents' eyes.

They had been immensely proud of me, and it showed in the contents of the files.

Photographs, letters and testimonies from school and army were lovingly preserved. I spent a day reading the files. It was incalculably therapeutic. Bryce had said that the playing of "The Living Years" had created an emotion and believed many things that should be said never were. That sentiment now appeared to be self-indulgent folly; some things should never be told. If Bryce's father had wanted to, he would have shared his emotions long ago.

The following day was the eve of the funeral. I awoke invigorated and with a mission. It was a strange feeling that I was over the grief, but more importantly, I realised and accepted that the generous couple who adopted me had reaped joy from me, and I, in turn, had benefitted from their selfless actions. I realised too that they were dead and that I would never again see or hear them. I had never been one to live on memories; this defined my stance now to cut a non-existent cord. I decided not to attend the funeral. My grandMother's, the last family one, was beautiful; her illness had kept her a prisoner for a long time, her death was a release, almost reason for joy, buried on a marvellously cold but sunny day in February. All funerals should be like that; I have happy memories of her funeral.

This action might appear bitter, but I realise when writing this to you, Ben, that I feel no bitterness; I'm not clouded with emotion.

Collective grief may or may not need someone to blame, and my non-attendance might deem me a natural candidate for the vacancy. I am, as I always was - better off out of it. As Oscar Wilde said: "There's only one thing worse than being talked about, etc. etc.".
All the dignity and grief at a funeral and the possible tut-tutting at my behaviour and lack of attendance carries no weight. I have no choice, but I see it as a matter of doing what is right – a point of pride. Most who attend funerals will grieve; they will feel tribal grief. Without sounding callous, if I had participated in my adoptive parents' funeral, it would have been as a mark of respect. For me to grieve further would be hypocrisy of the highest order. I consider respect far more meaningful than grief. They deserved and always had my love during our time. They did not need my grief and probably would not have even wanted it. One day, I'll go to their grave; I'll place some laurel leaves there and say goodbye. I don't need anybody to see me do that, nor anyone to know who put them there. It's between them and me. No-one else. That's the way it always was.

The lawyer was speechless when I told him that I would not be attending the funeral. I gave him written instruction that I wanted all the property and assets bequeathed sold and the proceeds deposited in my bank account. He had my contact details if anything else was to be signed. I left Buxton that day and never looked back."

Jay sat back in her chair, read her work and was pleased. It was detailed and had unfolded the way she wanted. She decided to reward herself with tea, and as she rose, she saw Ben on the monitor; he looked pensive as he stared out into the large office window.

She watched with growing interest

- What's going on now?
- Does he think about our meeting? - Better get on with it. This part is going to take some explaining.

My first task on my return to base was to wrap up the Bryce case. I had thought long and hard about Bryce and what he had done. I respected his loyalty to his father's memory and concluded that he would have been in a great deal more trouble if he had more brains. It was not difficult to persuade the C.I.D. to concentrate on the potential issues that the website raised and forget about one squaddie who was back on duty. The negotiations with D.I. Lambert had lasted around one week, which gave me time to settle back into my routine to focus on the new task. Lambert and I had a good working relationship. He had kept me informed of updates into my parents' case, and mutual respect was growing. I confided in him that I might have to do a bit of private investigation due to a rumour I had heard back in the Peak District, and he offered his services to help in any way he could.

I had shed a skin.

The next step was to be the longest. I had no idea how to trace my roots, origins, and parents – my history. Luckily, I had useful contacts within Army Legal Services, and one of the Officers who attended Sandhurst with me was in the Advisory Branch. We met for lunch, and I explained what had happened and what my intentions were. Apparently, under the 1976 Adoption Act, I could access my adoption file with details of parents' surname, Mother's maiden name and current address at the time of registration, but this applied to England and Wales only. I showed her the papers that the lawyers had returned, and she confirmed they were incomplete. She would introduce me to a colleague, Rory Glenn, who had been a Scottish Advocate before Sandhurst; he would be able to offer the correct advice. Another week dragged by, and my patience was running out. For the first time in my life, I wanted to cut corners, to reject compliance out of hand, but common sense prevailed. I just had to wait. The Army formalities of being introduced to a fellow Officer are outdated, outmoded male traits that irk me beyond belief. Imagine a workplace scenario where no one could speak or approach any other human being without being formally introduced. Anyone doing so would be considered an oik, an upstart and not an Officer.

The wait during the obstructive procedure was worthwhile. Introductions over lunch to a charming, pleasing on the eye, forty-ish

Scotsman revealed a few interesting facts that gave me the starting point. Original birth entry could be traced at the Adoption Unit at General Register House in Edinburgh. They were obliged to supply an original extract, and if I provided details of adoptive name, date of birth and full postal address, a declaration form would be sent. Further information might be available: place and time of birth, the original name under which registered, Mother's and father's name, and, more importantly, the name and relationship of the person who registered the birth. These details might also give a lead into Adoption or Agency records and the location of Court records. It transpired that older records were in General Register House.

The memory of that lunchtime meeting caused Jay to sit back in her chair, stretch out her legs, put her hands behind her head and gaze into space.

It was a fond recollection that generated melancholy. Rory had been the perfect companion. He had waited until she was seated before joining her at the table. Jay smiled and brushed her hair behind her ear, waiting for him to speak. His eyes had appeared to brighten, and this enthusiasm forced him to babble.

- Jay, we're on the right track, I've had communication, and the documentation will be available to us through the Jockanese new order!
- What new order? She had asked, trying to hide her laugh behind her hand.

Rory had smiled back then talked with an authority of slow, deliberate speech.

- Our new Scottish regime of leading politicians in Scotland, a fucking parcel of rogues.

He had continued to tease her.

- You have a burden now, thrust on you for being born north of the border—a responsibility to vote in the upcoming referendum. "The Tartan Curtain" is almost here, which will

create an enclave to dissolve the U.K. I've heard it rumoured that there would be border patrols if the vote is YES.
- Border patrols? – You're kidding.
- No. I don't, kid.
- Do you remember studying the Parsley Wars at Sandhurst?
- Of course. Brutal, tactless and indiscriminate murder.
- A proposed methodology to stop the influx of migrants post-referendum. Border patrols will hold up a spring onion, and if the potential migrant cannot reveal its Scots name, then-No Entry to Alba.

It had taken a minute for Jay to realise Rory was toying with her.

- Well, Rory, you almost had me believing you!
- Now you're getting it. That Scottish School of Common Sense that the bairns of Jock Tampson can only understand.
- Who?
  Rory had been silent after that question, then, after a few seconds, came back.
- Ah, you got me there, Jay.

The mutual flirting and laughter had brought them closer. A few moments of silence as they finished lunch had been enough to convince Jay that Rory was the right man to help her find the answers. The turning point that instilled confidence in completing her task. The recent deaths and discoveries had caught her unawares, and, for the first time in her life, she had been able to realise and confront her frailties. Rory had been the perfect gentleman, and as he talked and flirted, albeit subtly, she considered a future with him. He had known when to stop the mockery, which impressed upon her that he understood her situation. She never believed herself being involved in domestic bliss as her Mother had. The notion struck that she had never deliberated her happiness before, only what others thought would make her happy.

As they parted, he suggested they complete the necessary forms, and he would help with the follow-up. They had met again for lunch during the days awaiting the return paperwork. When it did arrive, a note was attached stating that the Data Protection Act prevented all information held under her adopted name from being released without a court order. Rory had calmed her fears; it was procedural when a third party was involved. He assured her that he would make it his priority to fast-track the court order's paperwork using the Army as the requesting party. This would ensure no further obstructions, and he included the possibility of a twin and access to all adoption paper and files within the brief. The wait was unbearable. The court order granted with a proviso that required Captain Thorpe-Tracy to be present at Edinburgh offices. Rory had offered to accompany her and offered her the use of his flat. They had enjoyed each other's company for two weeks but had never spent an evening together; this had weighed heavily on Jay's mind as her fondness towards him grew.

The following day they drove to Edinburgh, and in a small room in General Register House, two Officers laid out the beginnings of her history.

Her birth name was Mary Lister; Jay's birth parents - Robert and Mary Lister. The fact that they had been married came as a relief. They had lived in the Tollcross area, and both worked in Edinburgh Royal Infirmary Adoption paperwork confirmed the dates previously uncovered. A document noted a law firm had instigated a search at the birth Mother's request. It was dated 2003 but rejected by another law firm – a name she recognised from Buxton. Also included was an extract copy of her father's death certificate. He had hanged himself whilst on remand in Saughton in 1984. Jay's gaze focussed on the stack of paperwork. Imaginary scenarios played in her head. She asked Rory to listen and confirm what she had gleaned.

"I was born Mary Lister on 16/10/83. My father hanged himself in prison whilst on remand when I was four months old. Worse still, my Mother tried to trace me ten years ago."

He tried to hold her hand, but she pulled away.

She considered her options. The information on her father would not be a problem—a phone call to D.I. Lambert would ensure a copy of his file would be on her desk on their return to H.Q. She also requested any files on her Mother and brother. Crooks, in her experience, rarely worked alone.

The next visit was to the Adoption Office.

Her state of mind was not good as she and Rory marched in step along the adjoining corridors, the click-clack reverberating throughout the stone walls. All recent events and the growing emotional attachment towards Rory manifested in what she now considered a mini-breakdown. Stirring feelings of anger, acceptance, denial and despair ebbed and flowed in inconsistent waves. The receptionist, her back turned as they entered, greeted them cheerily with a diluted West Belfast accent. Her demeanour became tainted on seeing the Army uniforms. Her body tilted towards them in an aggressive pose as she asked what they wanted. Her curt tone added to the intended obstruction. After a brief explanation of what they required, she informed them they could not just walk in and expect to access sensitive information without prior approval. She took no heed of the court order and confronted them in a belligerent manner. Jay's shoulders dropped. She turned with her head down and walked towards the exit, stopping when she saw the toe of her shoe touching the closed door. Turning back to stare at her nemesis, a surge of anger and power snapped together within her. It was as if ten years of dealing with petty bureaucrats had synchronised into one moment. Faces and situations flashed into her mind of doctors and dental receptionists, gossiping shop girls, bullshitting estate agents, traffic wardens and every hush-puppied and high-heeled Hitler she had ever encountered was about to incur her wrath.

Rory, recognising her potential meltdown, interjected just before she erupted. He reminded the clerk that they had a court order, it was Army business, and she might be liable for obstructing the course of justice charge. If she did not give full co-operation, one phone call to her department head would be all it took to create an awkward situation. Startled, she sat and offered to assist in any way. Rory decided that reading the office material may be too much for Jay and requested paperwork copies. The receptionist copied all documentation, then handed over the folio with a forced smile.

At his flat, Rory suggested that she relax in a bath before going through the documentation. Revived by the vapours of the hot water, she visualised a strategy to seduce Rory that evening. Playing out the daydream made her self-awareness and confidence return. She became conscious that she had developed a way of carrying herself that could make men both embarrassed and afraid, knowing how to arrange her hair so that men would gaze at it rather than look her in the eye. Jay relished catching men stare. It made her feel desired, entrap with imagery.

Drying her body, she looked in the mirrored wall and cupped her breasts, wondering how Rory would react to her body. Who was she going to be that evening? Tra-la-la or Tinkerbelle? A combination of both?

She pulled on a light dress, bunched up her hair and entered the dining room. Rory looked up from the paperwork and watched as she closed the door with both hands behind her back.

He paused; she looked different, at ease, sexual and vulnerable.

- You have a twin - Robert, named after his father. You were both considered for adoption by the Thorpe-Tracys, but they decided to take you alone. No reason for that decision. Your birth Mother attempted to find you through her lawyer, and there is no contact address for her. It was your adoptive parents who put the block on the action. You had not reached eighteen, so this was a point of law. We can make inquiries through her solicitors if you wish.

Would you like a drink - tea, coffee…?

She nodded and smiled.

- All in due course, I'll get myself and all the data together back at H.Q. Thank you for helping me today.
- I'm happy to help. It can't be easy.
- I'd love a glass of wine, she replied, pointing to his glass on the table.
- Red or white?
- White to start. She paused for a couple of seconds and then followed with;
- White wine makes me think of things I want to do – things I do without thinking when I drink red.

He smiled, put on some slow jazz and poured the wine.

She took the glass, sat on a sofa and relaxed. Rory moved to sit next to her, but she stood up. What a dilemma. Her first thoughts were mercenary, if it all went wrong with Ben, she could quite happily live with Rory for the rest of her life, but emotional greed was the wrong path. She could nurture this relationship and be happy and not lonely for the rest of her life. Would he find out one day what she thought she was? And then it would be back to square one.

- Thanks for all your help today.

She moved towards him and stroked his hair.

- We did it together, Jay. It'll all come together.

It was as if she had stepped out of her body and was looking down on two individuals. One was sitting on a sofa looking up and the other looking down. She had the illusion of circling them and seeing it all from 360 degrees. Thoughts darted in and out, but a sip of wine brought her back to reality. She pulled him up to dance. Enjoying the selfishness, she prickled with the sensation of human touch. Goose pimples rose on her bare arms, and the feeling of closeness made her want the euphoria to last. She anticipated his next move and manoeuvred him, so they were cheek to cheek. Sensually swaying, aware her groin was pressing into Rory's, he turned his face to hers. Their eyes displayed mutual lust. Sensing his thoughts, Jay smiled at the transparency of the male species. She was in control but did not want to be. Once again, her brain ran through a million random thoughts and images.

The morning rays shone through the bedroom shutters, lying in his arms, she felt peculiar contentment that created a natural high. Jay could not remember the last time that she had woken up next to another person. It had been a while since she had experienced lovemaking. Rory had been a considerate lover; gentle to start, then physically passionate and consistent enough to satisfy. She had found her thoughts were on herself, which had aroused her fervency to achieve orgasm. Looking at his sleeping face, Jay considered her future. Rory enjoyed what he wanted out of it without realising, but she had got a hell of a lot more. She had let him take her and had played the vamp to perfection.

Back at the barracks, D.I. Lambert had left a voicemail suggesting they meet at a pub the following evening and requested she bring all documentation; in return, he would get relevant files from police records. From the outset, he made it clear that she could not look at the files, but he would read the information to her so she could take notes. The process took around four hours as she quizzed him on every paragraph. His documentation consisted of three parts. The first contained the information regarding her father's crime and untimely death, the second the report from the Procurator Fiscal into his hanging and the third, a statement made through a firm of solicitors explaining the disappearance of Mary Lister and the reasoning behind her abandoning her children.

Snapping to the present, Jay returned to typing the report.

"Our Mother abandoned us outside the post office in Bruntsfield, Edinburgh. Our parents were John and Mary Lister, both from broken homes and put into care as out of control children. John's family were from Falkirk, Mary's from Portobello. They met in Quarriers' homes and became a couple from the age of fourteen; they left the home at sixteen, had a quiet wedding and moved to Edinburgh, where they rented a tenement flat in the Tollcross area. Both worked in the Edinburgh Royal hospital, him a porter and her an auxiliary nurse. According to the police report taken from neighbours at the time of his arrest, they lived quietly and kept to themselves. They appeared to be a devoted, loving couple.

We were born when they were nineteen, christened and named after them; John and Mary - that is who we are. Tollcross at that time was a mix of young couples, students, nurses and a mature local community. Drugs were moving into the area, and the flat below them used as a distribution point for amphetamine. One night in Feb 1984, around 11 pm, they were awoken by a disturbance in the flat below. Mary was troubled and fearful as she could not soothe her children and urged John to quieten things down. His statement revealed, he knocked at the door and met with a barrage of abuse from behind the door. Something snapped in him: as he kicked open the door open, a violent fight began, ending with him knocking the three occupants unconscious. He was injured and bleeding badly but had the sense to go to the A & E at the infirmary nearby. That's where he was arrested, and, the statement, no one else in the block made any attempt to help. He was charged with Hamesuckin and remanded in Saughton Prison. It is on record that Mary visited him the following morning and found hanged later that afternoon.

That evening, she abandoned us.

*The police could find no trace of our Mother. The car found abandoned near
Stranraer, but there was no evidence of her onward journey. She had disappeared.
Investigations into the hanging revealed that there had been some doubt about
whether or not it was suicide. Inmates questioned as it's known that prisoners will
give up any information for a reward of cigarettes or extra privileges - they say
there is a code of honour. Still, they are all mercenary and look after number one.
A rumour arose of a cash bag in the downstairs flat had started the in-fighting.
The ring leader had not been in the flat and when he returned, found the money
missing, there was no evidence, so the case was closed. Nothing more was heard of
Mary Lister. Authorities put us into care with foundling names, with me adopted
in late 1984.*

Ten years ago, Mary Lister tried to trace us both through Dublin based solicitors.

*Once again, Jay's thoughts raced ahead of her typing. She played out a scenario in
her mind that she and Ben traced their Mother. She fantasised of all three
embracing and toasting their reunion. The reality check bounced, and she
condensed her whim into a tentative request.*

We could find her together if you wish – I would like that."

Jay started to cry. She became overloaded with emotion never
experienced before typing faster, hitting the letters as if accusing the
keyboard.

*"My adoptive parents blocked the search. It is on record that you were
untraceable—having left the home with no forwarding address.*

*Through her solicitor, Mary Lister made a statement to the Edinburgh police,
who told her version. That account made interesting reading. It transpired that
during her visit to her husband in Saughton, he had told her there was a contract
out on him. He was concerned they would come after Mary and the kids. He had
seen the cash, gathered it up and, before going to A& E, had stashed it in the
spare wheel well of their car parked in the street. He told Mary to take the kids
and leave the city, get as far away as she could. That afternoon she was visited by
a policeman and woman who informed her of his death. By her account, she was
distraught, panicked, packed up what she could and bundled us into the car. She
parked by the meadows and stayed there until it was dark. She had written a
note stating who the twins were, her fears and that you and I should be protected.*

She did not think that she was capable of this. Then some strange quirk of fate occurred.

There had been a hit and run that night, and the area was swarming with police. She drove up Bruntsfield road and stopped at the post office. She left us there with the note. Nurses returning home from a shift found us and informed the police. The news regarding the hit and run took precedence, so the discovery of two abandoned children became buried in a more significant story. Nothing more has been heard of her. A report to the Procurator Fiscal resulted in no charges made. According to the police, there had been no record of money missing, and the child abandonment would be hard to prove after eighteen years. Mary's lawyer inferred that she was in no state of mind at that time to make rational decisions."

Jay stopped typing. Waves of emotion swept through her bringing first happiness, then melancholy. Jay could not begin to think of the torment Mary had gone through. She managed to control the sobbing. As she started typing, the doubt hit her. Would Ben believe any of what had happened?. She persisted in the thought that if her twin could read the report, then questions would flow that she could answer, verify and justify. Jay watched him on the monitor. He was, in her mind, a lost boy; her body shuddered as she considered what his life must have been like with no one around, no one close. She became transfixed on his image; he was staring out of the office window and appeared deep in thought.

A STORY THAT COULD BE TRUE.

Ben felt drained. Ranting at Jamie Farr's image had his mind meandering through many scenarios. The call from the supervisor had spooked him, but he smiled as the thoughts led him to recall that name. Tracy Thorpe.

That was the woman Plant had mentioned. He must have mixed the names up. He remembered that Plant told him she had quizzed him on several things that gave rise to him suspecting she was a journalist. According to Plant, she had picked him up after a gig and had gone to his hotel room, abandoning him after he had worn her out. Ben remembered the comedian's yarn spun, bragging about blowing her mind but not believing a word.

He fixated on Plant and refreshed his image on the screen.

Their time together had been short, six months at the most. Plant was the only person that Ben considered role model material until Plant did the dirty on him. That act of betrayal had been the end of their friendship. He had proved himself to be a traitor to his gender.

Ben thought that he had known Plant reasonably well but never had any idea what his motivation or direction was. Plant did not care about anybody or anything, nor take anything seriously. There was always some ordered progression to his path through life. Ben considered this conduit to nirvana achieved through some non-existent existential route. He worked sporadically as a freelance graphic illustrator to pay bills, but his night time persona as a stand-up comic was what he loved. They had met during a time that Ben now referred to as his Bette Lynch period; his lifestyle was a mess. He had been reading material by American drunks, which led him to decree that the answer to enjoying life was to glut on every form of high available. He believed that the life of a functioning person, who lacked sobriety in any form, was the identity for which he had been striving. Drink, narcotics, gamble, shag, eat, then work. His problem was that he was in a relationship with a girl he loved. He did not know it then but now felt the pain of love lost. A feeling of melancholy came over him as he remembered Dana and how special and magical she had been to him. They had been together for about nine months before Plant had entered their lives.

He winced, remembering the night he now regretted.

They had been to a Plant gig and were drinking in a club afterwards. Plant's alter ego 'The Baron' had been on form that evening. The audience, consisting of women, were social workers from the Edinburgh Homeless Unit on a night out. Plant tailored his material when he discovered this. He believed he possessed an acute perception that could sense a weakness then expose, subtly, through a story or joke. He did this to embarrass the audience into questioning their perceptions and misconceptions. He revelled in the response as the audience realised they were laughing and looking inside themselves. He was the Joseph Heller of joke tellers. It was just a pity that he could not look inside himself.

Plant spun a yarn that night about being dry ridden by a family member, then convincing himself he was gay after a scout leader coerced him into mutual masturbation. Ben marvelled in Plant's ability to relate a story, hands and eyebrows animated, almost conducting each other to great effect and revelling in portraying the fact that he had enjoyed being abused and starved of love as a child. The bad feeling started when Plant had confessed to the audience that he preferred to have sex with homeless women - so he could drop them off anywhere he wanted.

That line caused the audience to react with venom, but that was a mistake. Plant revelled in retort to hecklers, but this time it was vicious. He asked for a show of hands from the ladies as to how many had children. Ben remembered cringing with disbelief when Plant informed them the childless ones in the audience could take the joke and had a comfortable and open outlook on life. They were not uptight, nor did they exude anxiety. This, he preached, was due to a recently discovered medical phenomenon known as clitoruism. He was working the audience now; a few were shouting abuse, but most were listening, jaws agape. He continued to reveal that, during childbirth – natural or otherwise, a chemical exuded from the newborn child agitating the nerve endings within the clitoris. This action affected the Mother's brain, short-circuiting nerves and frazzling the rational thought zone. He concluded by asking if the audience had considered Botox or cosmetic augmentation. If so, they should consider FGM as a device to enhance inner beauty. The Amazons, the ultimate warrior, self-mutilated for efficiency - lessons should be taken from history.

The majority of the audience erupted, not with laughter but with anger and hatred that Ben considered justified. Plant knew he'd gone too far, and his expression betrayed his bravado. He was on the verge of being lynched when the M.C. interjected and pushed him off stage.

Plant, who usually signed off,

"Remember the wisdom of J.P. Donleavy;

When you find a friend
Who is good and true
Fuck him
Before he fucks you."

He was shouting it through the radio mike as he ran offstage. He was shaking when he joined Ben and Dana in the venue bar. He tried to justify himself by stating that the childless were laughing, Ben noticed Dana was not.

Ben zoomed the camera out to gain a full view of the corpse laid out on the gurney. He smiled as the thought that Plant had now well and truly fucked himself.

In hindsight, he knew they drank too much that evening and Ben, taking Plant's lead as a comedian, came up with the line he now regretted. A couple of ladies from the audience, who Plant's ranting had amused, joined them. They were curious to know why his act was misogynistic. He tried to explain that it was not that – it's basis was audience misandry. They stared in disbelief as he tried to convince them that they were getting angry at themselves, and he was the instrument of anger used to whip the tribe into a frenzy. He explained that he was not a misogynist but treated all females in the same fashion that he treated males. The material he performed on stage was a comedy routine, not serious. They were observations that made people think about their perceptions. He respected all opinions regardless of gender or race in the same way and similarly responded to them.

"Listening well is a gift". Plant said.

"The ability to hear what someone says and not filter it through your own biases is instinctive but, there is something in all of us that likes the fact that what we hear - is filtered through the biases of others."

Ben remembered these words and that Plant had ruined the philosophy by asking the two ladies what their speciality was. When they questioned him, he offered the theory that all his previous sexual partners had a unique practised act performed during foreplay or intercourse. Plant followed with the concept that he could see a woman's face in orgasm five seconds after meeting. Dana, who disliked his manner, and hated that he called people by their surname, knew of his exploits and branded him a slut and sexual predator. She likened him to a wasp, stating that there was no reason for them being on this planet as neither of them contributed anything. She had followed up by telling him that he was a throwback from the sixties, the last century male that was so insecure he had to use sex to create a form of family-based on his conquests. Had he not learned from the social diseases that were rampant around the world and, older man as he was, had to give in to reality and accept that he was past it, clutching at straws and paddling against the current. He tried to dismiss this too, citing sex as a mutual act and conceding that perhaps he bragged too much. He was no different from the person he had encountered. Dana, who had a discerning mind that outshone Plant's, would not let it go and kept on at him about his disrespect for anything female. A man that hurt those who loved him.

Ben thought he would defuse the situation by introducing a funny remark.

Unfortunately, the alcohol and the pills popped did not aid his delivery and what he thought was funny was not. He cruelly compared his relationship with Dana to Plant's gig, a one-night stand that had gone wrong. He followed up with the only thing that he thought they had in common: a love for alcohol and lightweight fun; they were pinpricks in each other's lives and should realise that nothing lasts forever.

Dana rose, shook her head, and then walked out. Ben never saw her again. He staggered home with one of the social workers. Ben drank himself into oblivion for the next few nights but did not see Plant until the following week. Plant had laid into him with a few home truths, which kick-started Ben into considering his lifestyle. He was grateful that Plant had helped him through and out of that dark time and, even though he knew he had let him down badly once or twice, he still considered them to be friends. There was always some nagging doubt in his head that Plant was holding something back. They had shared various female acquaintances in different bars over this period. During the comedown from the drugs and booze, the resultant paranoia, albeit diluted, kept reminding him there was something he should know. Once described as being like a duck, Plant was calm on top but, in reality, was paddling like hell below. He drank steadily and frequently, maintaining he was not an alcoholic, merely alcoholic; alcoholics went to meetings.

Ben had an adjective for him now – priapic. Their relationship ended when Plant boasted about Dana not being worthy and Ben better off without her. Plant quantified this by telling him that he'd slept with her the night after she walked out. Ben never saw Plant after that day. Perhaps Plant had gone into a downward spiral; he heard his gigs were cancelled and he, poison. Plant had predicted his early demise due to what he termed 'hotel death' due to the nature of too much food and bar visiting while staying at cheap hotels. He was continually reminded of how lucky he had been in life to get away with the things he had but knew he would die before his luck ran out. He had combined this theory because, historically, the average death age of the males in his family had always been below retirement. He had self-penned an epitaph and frequently referred to himself as `the designer that did not know where to draw the line.'

Ben kept out of their usual haunts but had listened to mutual friends. Deeper, darker stories had emerged about Plant's character regarding alleged rape and physical abuse of previous girlfriends that had marked him down as a tragic character. Plant had used complete honesty as therapy but cleverly filtered out what happened. What he relayed in conversation bore scant resemblance to the truth. The females who had known him considered him creepy, or so Ben heard on numerous occasions, and Dana had mentioned this once or twice. He was a master at attaining the sympathy shag. Plant could smell low self-esteem and utilise his stagecraft to gain trust through clowning, knowing the attention shown for collusion was fundamentally for the sex act.

Ben's mind segued into his being. He knew he too had been considered cold, calculating and impersonal. His inability to maintain relationships was down to the fact that he could not sit down and talk about things that mattered to any female. He hated confrontation or anything that made him think, and his answer was to bury his head if anything made him uncomfortable. All he wanted in his life was lightweight fun and preferred to act cool, aloof and withdrawn.

MINDSIGHT.

Jay Thorpe-Tracy was breaking her rules by surfing during work. She had decided to change her name by deed poll, back to the one given by her birth parents. She believed this was the way forward. Perhaps she could get Ben to embrace the same idea, and they could become the family they once were. It was 06:30; she was on track to get the report finished. All that remained was to explain how she'd found him and the reasoning behind them being in the same building on their birthday. She devised a strategy that would make Ben feel sympathetic towards her with the hope to make him understand that specific actions undertaken to gain all information to ensure it was correct before being presented. She used the spelling and grammar checker, corrected a few errors, and rearranged a few words for reassurance. She sighed with relief that she had got the worst down, it was freewheeling from now on, but she must take care of how to present the next section; her words appeared on the screen,

"Ben, on discovering the details of our history, I resolved that acts must follow words. There is a need to explain my exploits which led us to be here on this date. It is no coincidence; it was engineered and, more than anything, I hope you understand.

If you have read this far, you will know my story: adoption, upbringing, school, army etc. When I pieced it all together, it struck me that I'd channelled all my energies into discovering who I am, but how would it be resolved. I discussed it with my friend, Rory, and we put together a proposal to my C.O. to request three months of compassionate leave. That is up in the next couple of days.

I engineered a situation using inverse logic. I submitted a report explaining that the training that made me the person I am had also reduced my compliance levels through stress and attention to detail. I had psychometric test results to back up my case and granted unpaid leave to put myself into a test-case scenario of self-investigation. It came with the proviso that I undergo counselling and assessment on my return. Whatever the outcome, my career now can go two ways - orbit or down the pan. I'm telling you this as I overheard your speech to the monitor earlier and I have seen the books you have in your flat. You can help me.

It is up to you how you take this next part. I am sorry for the intrusion; I had to uncover every aspect.

I had tracked you before my leave. It is a simple operation; National Insurance number reveals name, place and date of birth. The Inland Revenue will then disclose a place of work and current employer. I used deception to gain your address from the security firm that employs you. I manoeuvred a position within their organisation by selling them the story that there was a potential risk of cadavers' theft from the hospital morgue. They were delighted when I offered to go undercover as their Operation Manager within their security department in the hospital. They gained someone that instilled some discipline, allowing me to observe you. I requested you for the shift on the eve of our birthday to reveal this information.

I met your friend Plant and obtained information about you from him. He is no friend of yours; he is a relic – I did not believe men like that still roamed this planet—a horrible specimen. I'm sorry if this offends, but it is how I see it. I visited your flat when you were on dayshift. That was inexcusable, and I apologise. I became possessed with the need to find out everything about you. It is in me to be this way, and it is my job. It may sound unnerving, but I know your history. I know how and where you have lived. I know where you have travelled to and worked. I don't understand why you returned to Edinburgh. Perhaps you had discovered that one could only travel so far before heading back home. The downside of living on a sphere, I suppose.

I know all about you, but I do not know you; I can only surmise. I want to be a part of your life, and I am your twin – we should have many things to find out about ourselves from each other. What you have read exposes me for who I am and what I would like in my life.

Do you feel the same after reading so far?"

TESTER.

The last hour of any shift was, in Ben's experience, the longest. He had devised a methodology to make him forget about time by concentrating on a puzzle he had never solved. His theory was that some entity linked everyone he had ever known. As he was the common denominator, the connection must be through his name and somehow interconnected. It took many hours of thought to use the idea of a crossword grid to associate the characters in a contiguous manner. He had come up with the idea during a phase working as a slaughterman in the Forest of Dean. He was living in a caravan near a hippy commune.

They intrigued Ben; having moved from city to rural life, they lived a frugal and holistic outlook. Their kids, such as Blue, Indra, Sky, Esme, had rebelled against their way of life and became successful professionals. The 'elders', as they liked to be known, had often reminded Ben that he was living in a sleep but could access the waking being through the teachings of Gurdjieff and his disciples such as Bennet and Ouspensky. That had enthralled him, and the hippies fascinated him even more so. They had never appeared enlightened, and his perception was they were living in a life of striving for something unreachable. He immersed himself in the readings they suggested and became further intrigued by George Gurdjieff's theory of the Enneagram of Personality. As he researched, he came across the ideal that '*New spectacular and symbolic actions are needed to wake up the sleepwalkers and shake the anaesthetised consciousness*'. He explored various symbols, including pentagrams and other occult and philosophical ideas, before coming up with the crossword concept. He considered the crossword puzzle a variation on the Fourth Way enneagram created by Ouspensky to provide hope and lead to a form of enlightenment. He became increasingly startled as the more he tried to complete the grid, it vying for the underlying concept of a need for family.

When he left the area, they presented him with a large poster. He had seen the image many times in the commune; it had pride of place. A man with a large moustache staring directly into the camera as if trying to change the thoughts of those watching. This compelled him and drove him on, knowing it would be impossible to solve. Ben discovered it was a futile exercise due in the early stages; they either had been close to him or had influenced him. Ever aware of his lack of family, he hoped that fate would prove his theory when he started a new grid. He had pre-printed grids with his name already in the centre. Some had his Christian name in the horizontal, with the surname interconnected in the vertical at the letter 'B'. Some had them in the opposing vectors. He then wrote a list of names at the side of the grid that had a good or bad influence on him. Invariably he started with teachers, doctors, carers, social workers, old and new bosses; then sexual partners, friends, foes, people he liked and disliked. He had completed the grid once but felt ashamed. He had cheated by using invented family names to fill in the empty spaces. As he juggled the characters into position, it came upon him that he was involved in the act of wishful thinking with the result that he ripped up the paper into tiny shards then scattered them, like ashes, into waste paper bins. He had betrayed himself, and that, in his mind, was unforgivable. The grid sheet he had written the names on during his rant was in front of him and began his routine. He was happy; one hour of this mental callisthenic would eat up the remaining time. As he wrote more names, he considered his options after work. True, he had arranged to meet up with a few friends for a boozy lunchtime birthday, but this was not until one o'clock; the thought niggled away about the meet with the supervisor, about which he now had a bad feeling.

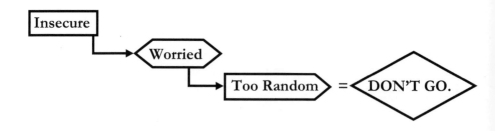

- Trust your first instinct.

He voiced, pencilling the supervisor's name at the side of the grid.

Something did not feel right. In the short period spent with this security company, there had been no communication with any form of management. Ben considered the agenda of the supervisor; was there a promotion? An offer of a different job or a permanent place of work? He was happy in his routine. He turned up, always early, to the location designated by his rota sheet and complied without question to any request made, allowing control of his actions and offering variety. Told on numerous occasions throughout his upbringing, his Oppositional Defiance Disorder would stop him from fulfilling any socially acceptable employment position. He pondered now if this meeting was a signal to move on. He deliberated that he might be getting stale; after all, he was twenty-nine today – thirty next. Maybe it was time for a change, time to become 'normal' – adopt himself! Give up on the things holding him back, forget reading and concentrate on a new form of enlightenment: religion, travel overseas or even join the police force. All the options were there, he just had to take them, and all he had to do was break the habits that put him in this rut. He checked the time, seven forty-five; he looked at the crossword and was pleased it was one-third full. He crumpled it into a ball and threw it at the bin, and much to his surprise, it entered. It was then he knew that, as usual, he would decide whether to turn up for the meeting at the last moment. The noise of the morgue office door opening startled Ben, and he jumped up. It was the first of the day shift technicians. Ben had to clear his throat before greeting her with,

- Morning.
- Hi, morning to you too, came the reply from the blue-haired young woman. You're chipper for a Monday morning.
- I've got a lot on today - onwards and upwards.

Ben felt his face redden. He felt a liking for her but knew she was too nice for him.

- How many more work here?

- Three, Lindsey is always late though. She'll be in about ten past – you can set your watch by her.

Ben looked down at the ground as he caught the end of her smile. This girl was just his type, but he did not know how to react. He stammered,

- I'll get my stuff together, then go. There's nothing to report. I don't understand why anyone would want to steal dead bodies anyway.

The girl nodded but had a look on her face as if she did not understand what he was saying.

- Okay, have a good one.

Ben collected all paperwork and utensils then put them into his bag. As he opened the office door, he looked back at the girl. He was transfixed; her hair, smile, demeanour and the way she walked all conspired to make Ben feel worthless. He never had the chance to meet friendly, real people like her. Clean people: not those sullied with the smell of homes, thoughts of the unloved and the harshness of the unfeeling. He looked down at his boots then back at her. She was humming whilst sorting out the case files; she looked back and smiled at Ben. He looked up to the ceiling, shook his head, and then walked out of the morgue office, the large steel door slamming shut behind him.

Jay watched Ben's exit from the office with trepidation. Would he turn up? There was still half an hour before they meet. It would take him fifteen minutes to walk around from the back entrance to the foyer. No doubt he would freshen up in the toilets at the exit gate; there was a shower there, and that is where she was planning to visit after she had signed all the paperwork for the day shift handover. She printed two copies of the report and stapled them; she placed one in a large white envelope and one in her attaché. It was her last night working with the security firm. None of the others knew, and none had bid her goodbye as their reliefs had taken over their stations. As a Manager, all there was to do was hand over the night report and standing orders to her relief, who was chatting and smiling with his charges.

She left her office then handed over company paperwork whilst exchanging pleasantries for a few minutes before walking out of the control room. She sensed all eyes were on her as she closed the door behind her. Over, work was done, which brought a smile to her face as she strode towards the hospital foyer. Checking her watch, she noted that it was eight twenty-two.

Jay stirred her coffee and watched the tiny ocean of black form a whirlpool. She glimpsed the foyer clock just as the long hand moved to the vertical. It was at nine o'clock. Her intuition told her that Ben was not showing up. Her mind went blank as she looked back into the coffee. A tear fell from her cheek into the cup.

She stopped stirring.

Removing the report from the envelope, she read it, then replaced it, sealed it and wrote her name and address on the front, adding that she had discovered that they were twins and the contents of the envelope explained the whole story. She signed off with "Happy 29th Birthday", followed by a big XX. As soon as she had written those two letters, she regretted it. She drove to Ben's flat in the hope that she got there before he did. She put the envelope through his letterbox, then returned to Rory's flat and took a shower.

The clock on the mantle struck noon when she heard the sound in the hallway. Looking out the large bay window, she noticed a figure hurrying by wearing a large shoulder bag; he was difficult to recognise, but the hair on the back of her neck bristled as she walked to the hallway and picked up the envelope. Attached to it was an envelope addressed to "Jay" containing a handwritten letter. She sat on the bed and read out loud.

I'm returning the package – unopened.
Your address is on it.

I do not know if you will understand why
I cannot read it. It,s not personal; it is self-
preservation.

From reading, I have created a self-
contained life that is my own; I cannot
function with anyone else. On my shift
last night, I read case files that proved to
me that there is no such thing as a happy
family. No domestic bliss; a family home
is not always a comfortable place to be
and, more importantly, proved that there
is no real definition of what I missed out
on remaining un-adopted.

I learned more in one night with the dead
than all my time spent with the living.

If you are my sister, and you reveal that
you were never abandoned and adopted –
how do you think that makes me feel? If
you inform me that I have birth parents
that are alive – how do you think I will
react?

I believe in the Scottish School of
Common Sense, but must be sceptical and
say that you and I could never build a
relationship. We would be starting exactly
twenty-nine years behind each other, and
the only thing we would have in common
is a complete inability to comprehend
unconditional love. I have an
uncomplicated life that suits me, and it has
taken my lifetime to achieve, so now all I
want to do is get through life the best way
I can, without hurting myself or upsetting
others. I hope you understand and do not

try to find me again. I am leaving
Edinburgh today; please tell our employers
that I will not be returning to work.

This poem by William Stafford may help
you understand the way I am.

Jay studied each word, sighed, and then placed the letter on the
marble mantle. Her shoulders slumped as she took in the landscape,
framed in gold on the wall above the fireplace surround. She
recognised the hill as being Tinto and had visited school friends
there. She placed her forearms on the mantle shelf and buried her
head in them.

What had she been thinking?

She read the first lines of the poem,

"If you were exchanged in the cradle and

your real Mother died

without ever telling the story

then no one knows your name,"

Jay screamed,

"I hate male poetry."

Then read the last.

"Who are you really, wanderer?"--
and the answer you have to give
no matter how dark and cold
the world around you is:
"Maybe I'm a king."

Had she truly believed Ben wanted to meet her? He doesn't want to know who he is.

Jay questioned each action, trying desperately to pinpoint the failure. She had taken her eye off the obvious and cursed her naivety. It had stared her out, then slapped her in the face when she read his words.

The flaw lay in her adoption.

Ben was self-made; she, manufactured. Instilled in him was what she had learned; the world does indeed get more significant when you are on your own - or maybe it just felt that way.

When her trance finally broke, she went to the bedroom to pack her case.

Back in the sizeable Georgian room, she felt small, lost and out of place. She read Ben's letter one more time before crumpling it into a tight ball and throwing it on the empty grate.

As she pulled the front door shut, a phrase from the distant past came into her head: eventually, everything, even life, becomes work.

FREEDOM TO FAIL.

Jay threw her valise into the boot of the car and decided to take the scenic route South. It took great effort to force her small mass into the driving seat. Her body trembled and became sore to the touch as she manoeuvred herself into the vehicle, pulled the door shut, strapped on the seatbelt and adjusted the mirrors. These delaying tactics amplified the flow of what felt like an electric plasma flowing through her veins and arteries, all playing to an erratic heartbeat pulsating in her ear. The throbbing gave way to a blinding headache and low volume tinnitus that made her neck muscles arch until the nape was on the headrest. If the wrench from Edinburgh was compelling her to stay, then arrival in York was doing the opposite. She focused on the car's number plate in front and took deep breaths in her mouth and out her nose until the pain and noise abated. Her mind became dulled and enveloped in anguish. Fuzzy logic took over as the sound of the engine forced gear engagement then movement. No going back now, leave and forget. Get back to work; reality would progress her life. Perhaps sit her Majors exam and move up the ranks.

A plan.

That was a plan.

As she drove through many small coastal towns dotted along the South Forth coast, the wretchedness came. She tried to hold it back. A few details caught her eye and lingered in her brain. They came and went just long enough to keep the onslaught at bay. She noticed an old couple out shopping, helping each other by sharing the handle of a shopping bag. He wore a flat cap and she a headscarf. They exuded contentment that could only come with tolerance. Did they had children and if they remained in contact?.

Flat capped men; no one wore flat caps anymore. The romantic illusion of the nostalgic disappeared as she passed a pub where a slumber of older men guarded and smoked in its doorway. Their uniform was of faded training shoes, ill-fitting denim, washed-out hooded jackets and brightly coloured caps carrying random names of machinery manufacturers: Deere, JCB & Lansing.

Was there anything worse than an older man in a baseball cap? The thought loitered and brought a smile. Summer and winter wear at the turn of a peak.

As she thought of the life, love and tolerance of that couple, demons crawled from the back of her mind. She envied their happiness whilst questioning the self-same emotional response that was exclusive to the unfulfilled. They had reminded her of her adoptive parents; perfect on the surface but dig down, just a little, then the lies and scheming become visible. They had created an illusion of life for her, developed her to be a machine that believed that life was black and white, right and wrong, with no tolerance for all points in between. She questioned what her birth parents would be like if they were still alive – they would be together, that is a certainty – they would be in their forties – not old at all. Jay's thought progression transported Ben's image to the fore; she remembered the back of his head, the smiling face at the gateway, tugging his hair; the manic face in close up after the soul-cleansing rant – she smiled then a mist descended that faded the image.

She screamed the words at the top of her voice, spacing every syllable.

- What – have – I – done?

The tears came, surging like an enormous wave. More grief surfed in on every breaker. Aware of not being in control of the car, she struggled to keep to a road that was full of twists and bends eaten up as each spate of grief washed through her. Her face became sticky with dry tears one moment, then cleansed with the ripple of the shadowing salty flood the next. Would it ever end?

Random images flashed as a storyboard depicting the deluge of emotion hovering within Jay's mind. Names and faces appeared then faded. As she drove along the road, she noticed golf courses on either side. She looked at her speed and realised sixty was too fast; she braked in time to avoid sideswiping a group of men dressed in pastel colours led by electric buggies across the road. They were cursing and gesturing at her; she saw their contorted caricatures in slow motion as she passed through them. The car interior had adopted an orange hue as her mind overtook her brain. Instinct regained control of the situation. She found herself driving through a small town, past a castle, then down a track towards a beach. Leaping out of the car, Jay slammed the door then ran up a hill and down to a small beach. Lying prone in the sand, Jay stared at the sky and tried to make sense of it all. Time passed as clouds did. She watched them and speculated where they went, composing a tune and words to describe their transitory path. As she sat up to look around, Jay half recognised the guano covered rock in the distance. There was a lighthouse on an island nearby and a large conical lump of rock behind the mainland. Jay's bearings now became apparent, having recognised the landmarks previously observed from the other side of the Forth. Many years before, the Thorpe-Tracy's had taken a summer let in a small fishing village in the East Neuk of Fife. Fifeshire, she had called it much to the annoyance of the locals. A strange town consisting of city dweller owned holiday homes that swelled the population in the summer then deserted it in winter months. It was home to no one, itinerant holidaymakers or inbred locals. An acronym of Effin Idiots Effin Everywhere her Father used to joke.

A town twinned with itself.

She could not remember the name of the town; it started and finished in the same letter. Jay tried a few permutations out loud but could not recall the name. She did remember that some wag had told her that the big lump opposite the town had been spat out by Edinburgh's volcano then landed all that distance away. It was not called a hill but a Law – whatever that was.

The lighthouse.

She knew that it had inspired RLS to create the map for Treasure Island. Jay laughed at the impossible parallel to recent events. Treasure map indeed, more like a map of doom. Bryce had been right; he had suffered trauma all his career days. He must have experienced and observed some terrible events that had tuned him to that way of life. The tipping point was his father's death, and it was the only experience that had any consequence and aftermath. The website, albeit misdirected, was the perfect shrine to release grief. It was multi-faceted, allowing him to direct angst at an object hated by his father then supported by the thousands who agreed with his perspective. He knew his Father would approve of the sentiment; it was a shame that Bryce never received that honour.

As she sat in the sand, her arms splayed out behind; Jay stared out over the water. Clear thoughts created an inner revelation. Invigorated by the sound and smell of the sea, an easterly wind on her face and the soft sand in her hands, she retraced her path. Bryce, that mad aunt, Ben, adoptive parents, death, Rory ah Rory. She became lost in the thoughts of the physical and emotional smite. His help was, without doubt, the primary factor in uncovering the story of her parents. She should have consulted him on how best to deal with allowing Ben access to the information regarding their parents and, ultimately, the abandonment of twins that she and Ben had become. Perhaps Ben may have wanted to know if things were handled differently. Jay knew she had lost control; she had to get back to the Army, back to work.

She had never understood the concept of existential despair, but now that it had slapped her head. She understood and felt sympathy for both Ben and her birth Mother. Was this unconditional love?

 The image of the bereavement counsellor came to the fore – Jay could handle her. Jay's confidence became stronger – it was all work; this time, she knew that help from others was necessary for the first time. That was the solution to the current problem; resolve all issues.

 She strolled back to the car, her spirits lifted. The journey south would be okay now. She would use the Army for the counselling offered to purge these memories.

Start anew with a spring clean of the psyche—a fresh eye for future solutions. 'Strength comes from weakness,' she repeated under her breath as she climbed into the car.

IRONIC SELF REVELATION.

As she tied up her hair, Jay considered the reflection on show in the full-length mirror. It was good to be back in uniform; she looked smart, powerful and, as she put her redcap on – the confidence of being in control. Over the past few days, there had been a noticeable change in her left eye colouring. At first, she thought it was her mind playing tricks, but now, as she walked up to the mirror for closer examination, it was noticeable that the hue had changed from hazel green to a brownish colour. The phone alarm broke the moment, reminding her of the need to be in the Commanding Officer's office in ten minutes. A shudder of anticipation and fear ran through her, and a tingle in her loins brought on what felt like a mini orgasm.

- You can handle anything. Telling her reflection as she did an about-turn and marched out of her billet. She passed a pile of mail on her desk and sighed.
- More paperwork. Affecting the speech with a raising of eyebrows and an exaggerated tut as she pulled the door closed.

Entering the C.O.'s office, Jay was surprised to hear the Senior Officer greet her by name and offer open arms rather than the customary salute. She smiled back and made the traditional gesture. He replied, relaxing the situation with a tilt of the head. This incongruity overwhelmed Jay. The personal attitude counteracted by the impersonal feeling exuded by the other figure in the room. Jay recognised her by the shock of frizzled hair.

- You've met Captain Brown.

- Please call me Linda.

Jay shook hands and smiled.

Her smiled betrayed her inner thoughts; Jay felt no warmth.

- Captain Brown will be your contact for the counselling process.

She is much like you, our most experienced counsellor and superlative in her field. She's my choice to bring you back into the body of the kirk.

Jay thought this a strange comment but contained a response. Silence was the best option to conform.

- We'd like you to compile a report that portrays events of the last few months. Captain Brown will assess it to decide a plan of action. There are other light duties – internal cases, trifling files that need boxed off. They will be excellent exercises to get you back into the work programme. Meanwhile, I'd like you to go for coffee and get to know each other.

The C.O. saluted and opened the door.

It was Brown who broke the silence as they walked towards the breakout area.

- You can tell me how you feel at your own pace, and there is no hurry. I want to think that you can trust me and tell me anything. If, like me, you want to know all the ins and outs of the processes – I will be as honest as I can with you. We can do this together and learn from each other.

Jay dropped her head, smiled as she looked up and replied.

- Thank you.

Jay's inner defence mechanism was under test. Insincerity was not a normal reaction, but the counsellor opened up too quickly, creating a barrier. Jay knew to play along, realising as long as Army got what they wanted - no more, life would return to normal soon.

Jay completed the report that afternoon. It was a simple task of editing the file sent to Ben by removing any personal feeling and sensitive information. Second-guessing what the counsellor would be searching for, Jay deleted the data that might lead to awkward questioning that may affect Ben, her Mother, Thorpe-Tracy's and Rory. With efficiency and work ethic returning, the thought of giving Rory the report for a once over before submission. She would phone him later, arrange a meet for supper then ask his opinion.

After checking that the Bryce investigation outcome had gone as expected, Jay sifted through the stacks of emails, deleting the superfluous and categorising the actionable. There were a few from D.I. Lambert – they would keep.

Rory's voice exuded genuine excitement on hearing Jay's. He was full of questions, but her mind was focussed now on herself and cut him short; he would have to wait for answers.

They met that evening. Rory was surprised by her appearance; she had lost weight, and her face showed a gauntness that betrayed recent events. His greeting, remarking that she looked terrific, invoked an unexpected reaction. Jay embraced him, held it for more seconds than expected, then pulled him in tighter, holding him for longer. He sensed her trembling as she used all her strength to make him feel as if she would never let go. He realised this was going on for too long and slid both hands down to her waist and squeezed. Jay gasped, laughed, then let go.

-   It's nice to see you again, Rory.
-   Nice to see you too, Jay.

They found a table in a quiet area where they sat facing, holding hands over the table in silence until a waiter arrived. With drinks on order, it was Jay who broke their silence.

-   I've made a terrible error of judgement.
-   Best try to put it behind you. Forget about it all.
-   Easier said than done. It's like it is stuck halfway in my head. I can function normally, and then without warning, it comes to the fore. I have to tell someone what happened. Will you listen to me, please.
-   Of course. Let's wait until the drinks come to give you time to get it into order.

The drinks came, they ordered food, then Jay related the series of events wary of omitting the episode that happened during the drive south. Rory listened, knowing when to ask questions to break her flow. He could sense her anguish, but it was right she was getting it out. The food arrived as she completed the tale with the events of the C.O.'s office. Rory smiled and reassuringly clasped her hand. Her face had lost some of its hangdog expression; the relief was noticeable as Jay smiled, raised her eyebrows and said

- I'm famished, tuck in Rory.

They ate and drank their wine in silence, content and relieved that the other was there. Over coffee, Jay passed the report to Rory; he read it in silence.

- Comparing what you have told me plus what I know from before, you have nailed the salient points. I'm marking superfluous sentences to remove; they are open to interpretation and don't want or need it. That counsellor will have a field day with this. You know she'll get a PhD from this.

Jay's expression turned serious. Rory sensed an error.

- I'm joking with you. It is bread and butter to them – bereavement, grieving, loss, frustration, anger, acceptance and most importantly, getting to the root of it and helping you forget about living in the past.

He smiled again.

- Don't patronise me, Rory - I've been involved with this stuff before.
- I'm not patronising you. I'm helping. Did I ever tell you about my sister?
- No, I never knew you had one.

Jay sat back, took a sip of wine whilst opening her eyes with attentiveness.

Rory's opening line grabbed her attention further.

- My family history may be considered more dysfunctional than yours. They all need conflict, doom or past glories to exist. I have one brother and one sister. My father was Army through and through. Passing out from Sandhurst at the end of the war, he was a Major during the Berlin airlift, Suez crisis, Cyprus set up and all points in between. My Mother was an Army wife and at the mercy of that system for financial support when her husband deployed. Did you know that Officers wives had to negotiate for money to live on when husbands were away? They had to convince C.O.'s that the money was for the family rather than frippery.

Anyway, we were educated apart. Different Army schools all over the country – I cannot remember us all being together too often. My Father retired to the Cowal peninsula and still lives there; he's a gentle old soul that loves his wife and has many pastimes that keep him going. I feel no bond with him nor my Mother. They remind me of a bygone era, a time warp of love and happiness. My sister lives near them now, and I see her when I see them. Like you, we have no bond – no history. Her name is Patricia, although she is known as Missy due to some misplaced class system family ideal. She lived in London in the nineteen-eighties, and I think she trained as a nurse then went to Art School to become an arts and crafts person or whatever they call them – all this funded by my parents. She met this guy, Manny, a self-styled Marxist and fell under his spell. He was active within a group, and his disciples believed they would change the world; I had my doubts that the Isle of Dogs would be the world's revolutionary centre, but hey, ho. He was as sluttish with jobs as he was with women - but she loved him.

All her money went on keeping Manny; he gave her a sense of purpose, and perhaps there was an underlying need for family security in her. They married in Paris at her expense - he left her soon after for one of her closest friends. I've met him a few times, and he is a personable chap – he has an ingenious charm that is infectious. I forgot to mention that he has this thing about keeping close friends with his ex-lovers. I suppose it is like an entourage of disposable women needed to remind him of something. There is one exception: the lady he left my sister for, they had a child, and she refuses to live in his world of past and present lovers. My sister's pain was evident to me when I met her at that time, strangely enough,

I'll never forget the hurt, sorrow and anguish I saw in her eyes, he broke my sister's heart; she took him back a few times but was soon off again. She found solace in Alan, one of the quieter guys within their Marxist enclave; he was a few years younger, but what we would consider a stable, upright guy; he had principles and values that he stuck by. Perhaps too rigidly, but they made each other happy. When I see them, she looks at him as a puppy does to its master to gauge how he reacts to others that don't share his views. They're settled, as I said, near my parents. They have good jobs, she's into the local arts and crafts, and he changes pastimes as often as Manny changed women. My sister never had children; she must be around fifty now – they have dogs from a rescue home. Their world revolves around these stand-in offspring and their precious ways. For example, for reasons unknown, their dogs do not like bagpipes. When the local highland games are on, they must be transported via a converted doggy friendly van to visit friends that tolerate these idiosyncrasies. Anything Missy and her husband like or have opinions against is transposed onto their four-legged friends.

Rory paused; Jay acknowledged the sad look that came upon him, sensing his mood darken. His iron coloured eyes looked smaller as he furrowed his brow. He took a mouthful of wine then continued, punctuating each sentence with a short pause, as if choosing each word with care.

- All this might sound normal, but here comes the money shot: my parents and my sister revere Manny. He is considered part of the family, and his name is associated with a freedom that none of them enjoyed or understood. He has expanded their small world. When in company, including Alan, my sister will bring Manny's name into the conversation as soon as she can. He was invited to their humanist wedding and still visits my sister and her new spouse for weeks on end. He is her metaphysical consolation, as some put it. My point is that she cannot move on from him, even though she now has what she always wanted. Her husband calls him "friend Manny", but I'm sure he'd slit his throat if given the opportunity. It must be hell for him living with that heavy baggage preventing his wife from trekking through life.

Rory leaned forward and looked into Jay's eyes, recoiling for a second as he observed the differing colours, lowering the volume of his voice,

- My point is, if you do not deal with what has happened, you will become stuck in time as my poor sister is, and, like her, you will never be able to enjoy what will be right for you.

Jay nodded.

- I must deal with it. I can, Rory, believe me – I have no hidden agenda. Thank you for being here for me. I cannot believe what I'm becoming. Since we last met, I have had a hard time keeping my emotions in check. I get angry about nothing. Things that used to wash over me are now clinging to my being, like thick syrup. My brain festers at night - just before and after sleep, and what goes on between is utter madness. Ben sent me a letter back with my report – he hadn't opened it. That hurt me, and I don't know why. He tried to justify it all with a poem. A fuckin' poem. What is that about? A security guard shows his feelings with another man's poetry. I've always hated poetry, especially male poets.
- One good thing about the army is that it managed to dispose of a good few of these lost individuals during conflicts. This may sound all wrong to you, Rory, but ever since school, I've thought of male constructed poetry as a feeble route to feminist affinity or even gay and misogynistic code. Conceits, metaphor, simile, and other devices are no different from Polari or any other Lavender linguistic used over the years to convey a hidden message. Ha, I can make myself laugh at the stupidity of those thoughts when I'm with you – but when I'm alone, they gather momentum, snowball then explode into a myriad of others mad ideas that follow a similar pattern. I cannot keep them all in check. I am starting to feel burnt out, as if everything I have done has been for nothing. I have no tolerance for anything, no sense of reason and worst of all, disapprove of everyone and everything. I forget things

too. My memory retention used to be one hundred per cent but now, tormented broken sleep, outrageous thoughts, and the attention span of a hamster are conspiring to remove all my motor and thought skills. It's battle fatigue – without war.

Rory sat back to scan the report once more, highlighting the edits.

- Do you know what they have in store for your rehab Jay?
- No idea, have you?
- The Army is using a variety of techniques, depending on the level of trauma. I don't know where you would sit within their scale, with the deaths and all other events compounding the grief, that it would be in the higher end. They'll know after the first session – it is all on your re-action.

Jay listened whilst perusing the edits.

-I had army counselling a few years ago.

She looked up. Rory was the last person she considered that would need help in any way.

- I'm surprised. Why would you need such a thing? You are the most together, complete person I have met in my time on earth.
- You would never believe me if I told you.
- I'd rather you did not challenge me, Rory, not with my current state of mind. Either you tell me, or you don't.

Rory smiled at her and thought of a frosted rose.

NAVER.

- Okay. You don't know this, but I was married for several years. I was my wife's first lover. She had a lonely childhood, a day pupil to a private school in Aberdeen, you'll understand her situation better than most. She was considered an outcast by the boarders, and the effect that can come with that stigma coupled with a sheltered background made her quite an intense person. Her father was a wee free minister, and her Mother an elder of their Kirk. She was their middle child. As a couple, we enjoyed a lavish lifestyle in the Stockbridge flat you stayed and then, after gaining my WS, I joined up. She never altogether took to that way of life and considered the other wives obtuse; however, she coped with it even after what we endured. Or so I thought.

  I was on a defence case in Sennelager, an AWOL squaddie, I recall an unusual diet, but that's irrelevant; the upshot was I was away for about a month, and when I came back, knew there was something not quite right. Her reactions became calculated, and acted weird when I asked how things had been. The physical side of our relationship was incredible, and she was insatiable. I was confused but put it down to her stuck with a peer group she did not enjoy. I thought she was just glad to see me. We started to experiment with toys then, at her request, pornography. She became obsessed with the idea of group sex. She talked about all sorts of things I'd never thought about; I put it down to one of her fantasies that obsesses her. One night in bed, she told me she had made a movie with two men. I can still see the look of devilment on her face as I watched her waiting for my reaction. I lay there, heart pounding, a numbness came over me, and the tightening of my scrotum became painful.

  I did not know what to think. At one point, I was fearful of throwing up. I asked when, where and who, and the reply was when I was in Germany she visited a house with two guys. I asked if the film was in the house, and she nodded. I will never forget the gasp that came from my body as if the air kicked out of me. She put her face in mine; the invasion was intense and deliberate, and asked if I wanted to watch it. Her face was as I had never seen before. There was no shame, disgust or guilt – she just smiled as if nothing had happened, as if nothing was wrong. What had she become?, her loss of innocence disarmed me.

I recall getting out of bed and dressing to the sound of her laughter, rolling around naked and asking me for more sex, not the usual kind but an act we had never performed before. I thought it was me that was the prude, but I learned to see it for what it is after counselling. I left her then.
As I lay in a hotel room later that night, my thoughts were all over the place. Like all men, I have watched porn, seen group sex etc. It comes to me now that I thought of why I watched that stuff. Did I watch it to see men performing the act, or did I watch it to see the woman getting it? I resolved it was the latter and considered the female as the focal point. Was I looking for joy in her or seeing her as an object to be used. I wondered if the two-dimensional moving images was enjoying what she was going through. Then I thought of my wife being in that situation of her own volition.
Through counselling, I realised my wife's vision of the line between fantasy and reality had become blurred and had mine in many ways. I've never indulged in porn since.
- What happened to your wife?
- She had made her mind that Army life was not for her, and we managed to resolve the situation amicably. It was not easy. She left, we divorced: we kept in touch for a while, but it petered out. Last I heard, she was living with some guy in Cornwall.

Jay put her hand on his.

- If it is any consolation, I enjoyed our night together. You are a kind and considerate man that should have any self-doubt.

She leaned forward and kissed him.

98

- During my therapy sessions, I tried art and writing therapy to help the process along. I tried painting with pastels, but it was useless childlike art. It is frustrating when you have an image in your mind and then put it on paper. The hand and eye conspire to show you how untalented you are. I wrote a short story, though, based on a tale an old Edinburgh lawyer told me. I mixed it up with my issues, some folk I had known from school and events in the news. It was great therapy – helped me a lot just getting out, making it tongue in cheek but expelling the emotional upset. I'll send it to you to read – it will cheer you up as I think you will get the humour. It was about a guy who cloned himself to screw. Nuts.

They sat in warm silence for a few minutes before Jay broke it.

- Thank you for opening up. I'll change the report and hand it in tomorrow. I'm keen to get this started; the sooner it is over, the better. Brown will test my patience, but I'm more skilled in negotiation and interview than she. Can I stay with you tonight?

Rory smiled, paid the bill, and they headed to his townhouse off barracks. They sat up and chatted about nothing for an hour; Jay could feel a sexual tension that she diffused by claiming that lying close and holding each other would help her the next day.

As she lay in the colourless ambience of Rory's bedroom, Jay's mind kept her body from sleep. At times it felt that her body weight was in slumber, but her mind wide awake. As she lay there, wrapped in the arms of Rory, she imagined every possible scenario with Brown. Each consequence triggered another memory which made her mind wander, which elicited another. Plans were formulated, discarded and replaced with devious solutions to situations that never would happen. With her mind in this unhinged state, she tried to alleviate the pain by rubbing her eyes which sparked a visual firework explosion of colourful confetti. Respite came in the way of a deep slumber, but the alarm went off just as she felt subdued. Weary, with a numb mind, Jay dressed and returned to her billet to prepare for the day's events. The report in hand, she headed towards the C.O.'s office for the ten o'clock session. A bright sounding voice broke her step and thoughts.

- Morning Ma'am.

It was Bryce. Jay took her time in recognition as he snapped to attention and saluted.

- Sergeant Bryce, good to see you.

Jay returned the gesture.

- Corporal now Ma'am had to give a stripe up - but small beer for what might have been. All down to you, Ma'am. I need to thank you for seeing the truth and for helping me. I am indebted to you if it means anything; you can call on me – anytime, anyplace for any help. It is all I can offer.
- Thanks, Bryce. I appreciate that. I've come to understand your actions and, believe this or not, understand why you created the website. Just as well we caught it in time. Take care now.

Jay walked on with a spring in her step. Bryce would not offer favours lightly.

An energised Jay entered the C.O.'s office with confidence. Her body language exuded vitality, alive and receptive to the situation as the report placed on the desk.

- A concise chapter of events as I recall them.

Brown spoke first.

- Thank you, Captain. From a practical point, I will read, and we can discuss how we can progress. Do you feel as if you can trust me – if not, we can assign another.

Jay looked deep into Browns eyes, looked down for a second, then over to the C.O.

- I trust you. I believe you can help me.
- Excellent – voiced the C.O, dismissed, get on with it.

BRAINSPOTTING.

As they walked, Brown explained the practicalities; the initial process would take a week and suggested that Jay returned into a routine and immersed herself in work to get back on track.

Jay winced at the clichés; she considered Brown's presence sucked the energy from her, reduced her tolerance levels, and created changes to her mind-set.

Jay sat at her desk, shoulders slumped, surrendering to being alone. This was the lowest point of her life. She checked her emails, tidied them up – something was stopping her reading D.I.Lambert's and as she hovered the cursor over them, closed the programme down. She resolved that it was up to her to make herself better. After a heavy sigh, Jay wrestled up self-determination by opening up the work in progress case files, scrolling until one fired her interest. As she read, her gut feel was that it could be resolved and prove useful to get a quick result. The satisfaction to her would be enormous, and it would show the C.O. she still had the ability.

The case revolved around one of the drivers who had been using the pool cars for private use. Hardly a hanging offence, but new directives had decreed that all fuel cost must have a cost code assigned. The mileage discrepancy flagged it up, and, as usual, a squaddie swayed with greed; it was inherent in them that good Queen Bess should be paying for all their hobbies. Jay considered arranging an informal interview with Private Davinder Singh to get his side of events but thought better of it. It was not routine – she would wait until after the first session with Brown, evaluate that, then talk with Singh. The thought crossed her mind of researching another case in tandem, but common sense prevailed; Jay was proud of her decision. She added to the notes, "It's a start." Then saved the file and decided to have coffee. The following days dragged by, her mind felt as if grass was growing on it. A wave of body nausea highlighted the lack of self-worth. Some existential sense of futility and uselessness plus the routine that she had enjoyed post-Ben Black had become monotonous. Gym visits became shorter; she was swimming less, snacking more, including enjoying a house measure brandy and hot chocolate during the last television programme watched. Jay could not concentrate, noise that helped her pass the time. She became addicted to a vibrator purchased online and relieved herself after work, just before sleep which came in fits. Rory had called and emailed asking her out for food or drink but fobbed him off. She only had two targets, talk to Singh and listen to Brown. She developed a cough and a cold; everything was slow, and she began to question her effectivity as nothing progressed. Jay felt her life was stuck on pause. The word drudgery appeared in her brain, time after time.

The one week that Brown had promised for evaluation had passed - it had been ten days, which created concern. Jay's concentration reduced to seconds; she needed some recognition, an email, text or a missed call and checked her mobile with such regularity that it became an obsession. The lack of communication was creating a distraction and checking army and personal emails with such frequency that she could not remember if there had been any. She was alone, and Brown was her salvation. The laptop was in her eye line all day at work and was beside her at home and in bed. Her phone was on buzz alert for any incoming message or call with a defined tone that highlighted Brown's number. She could not progress work. Any attempt was looped back to the start through lack of concentration broken by the need to hear from Brown.

When the email did arrive, Jay's posture modified in an instant; she had begun to feel dirty and grimy, her toe and fingernails had felt long, her facial hair bristled, and her hair contaminated with god knows what. That email prompted her to react. As soon as it was read and replied to, with the first session accepted with Brown at 09:00 the following day, she arranged an appointment at a local salon; she needed pampering. Invigorated, Jay returned to her flat. She cleaned the place, binning the vibrator, the booze and all the distractions that had comforted her. It felt good, cheerful and hopeful. Her favourite music was playing, and as she worked, Jay danced, discarding the clutter.

She had a sleepless night anticipating the unknown. Torn from the torment, the scenarios she created when awake carried on through the staccato sleep that continued the uncertainty. The alarm woke her just as it seemed she had fallen into a deep, relaxing sleep. A cold shower brought her back to her senses. Wearing a clean, fresh-pressed uniform, Jay was pleased with the reflection that greeted her in the mirror. Presenting herself to Brown ten minutes early, Jay's confidence broke as she sensed her real state of mind was worse than she looked. Jay anticipated failure then threw it out of her mind; losing was an alien concept. The issue to complete the evaluation was for her well-being; no one else could do this for her. Too many clichés stormed her brain but, regaining her concentration, Jay decided to embrace it and question nothing. Brown wasn't her nemesis. Brown was her guide.

As Brown talked, Jay knew that she had to get the ideal of the counsellor's falseness out of her train of thought. It was a well-practised routine that irked Jay, and it lacked sincerity – but Jay had to do it. She could be as false as Brown.

- The first session is an intake one. I need us to discover your issues, if counselling is suitable and what resources the Army will provide. There will be no advice; we'll gauge the problem.

Jay nodded her understanding.

- Shall we go to the counselling room and get comfortable. Are you okay with it recorded?

Jay nodded, her face betraying the anger building due to Brown's patronising; Jay got up, sat back, then pushed herself out of the chair and followed her. A few corridors and doors later, they entered a door marked Counselling Suite. The room was welcoming; a large window overlooked the meadow garden at the rear. The natural light streaming in and clever Feng shui created a space that put Jay at peace. Uncertainty, fear and stress melted from her; relaxed, she suppressed an urge to hug Brown. The furniture and plants placed so that they beckoned her. The colour was a soft pink, but the lighting created different yellow, blue, red, and violet hues. Various artworks hung on the long, high walls depicting smooth, curving and circular forms and light, horizontal lines to enhance peacefulness and tranquillity. Jay sat first in one of the upright movable chairs on offer, Brown on a lounge chair about two metres away.

- Comfortable?
  Jay smiled.
- Thanks, Brown. I wasn't sure about this. I still have some trust issues.

Jay propelled her chair, remaining seated using her heels over the soft flooring towards Brown.

- I have to be honest with you; I didn't think you could handle me, but that feeling is changing.
- That's good to know - thank you for being open. Do you want a drink, or shall we chat?
- I want to talk.
- Would you like to tell me what you would like to get from this experience?

Jay sat back in the chair and stretched her legs out.

- Can I take my shoes off?

Brown nodded. Taking her time, she undid the laces; Jay's mind whirred into overdrive, trying to formulate the opening reply that would set the agenda.

- I need to reduce the anxiety and anger I have been feeling of late. I need to get back to my mind-set before the death of my adoptive parents. I need to regain the composure to fulfil my work potential.

Brown was scribbling on her pad.

- I find the note-taking off-putting. Can we do without it; can you take notes from the recording?
- Sure thing. I'll set up the machine.

Returning to her chair, Brown offered Jay a scenario.

- It would be good for us to have a couple of informal chat sessions, getting to know each other, gaining trust before we begin therapy to suit. I want to try a Brainspotting technique that will move the thoughts and situations that block you from releasing the traumas. I can explain it upfront. How do you feel about that?

Jay smiled and nodded at Brown. She was warming to her.

- I believe your issues are post-traumatic, and there are no physical injuries to deal with, mainly the anxieties of recent events. Talk or exposure therapy will work, but I believe you will get tired or bored with these as results take time. There are plenty of others that we can use, but if I tell you the mechanics of Brainspotting, you will want to try this. I don't want to clutter you with pretentious theories; Stop me if it is getting too much. EMDR came about late 80's. It was popular but had its critics. It involved an eight-step approach to address the past, present, and future aspects of a distressing memory - using eye movement to pinpoint the area of stress. Brainspotting is a "body to body" approach, with the distress activated by us talking; it is located in the body by your eye position; this finds the Brainspot. The difference between the two is, in EMDR, the traumatic memory is the target; in Brainspotting, the Brainspot is the focal point. Everything's aimed at activating, locating, and processing the Brainspot. We then discuss ways of removing this. You've heard of the saying "put it to the back of your brain" well, this is what we are going to doing. We will move the trauma that is making you anxious and angry. It is blocking you from functioning as you did. We will move it from where it is stuck into the recycle bin at the rear of your brain. Then we'll dump it.

Brown pursed her lips into a small smile.

- You know the score Jay, – I do my job, you help me do it, and we will both come out of this with positive careers ahead. Our first two sessions will build a safe and trusting relationship, where, unless you tell me otherwise, you should feel heard, accepted, understood and ready to take it to the next level. How does that sound to you?

The overwhelming desire Jay felt rendered her silent; Brown had turned this around. Jay was smitten. She pictured herself kissing Brown, caressing and nurturing her. She almost called her "mum". Jay stood and walked towards the window. Gathering her emotions, she spoke calmly.

- I look forward to working with you, Brown; I have every confidence in you.
- Thanks, Jay, it means a lot to me. Please call me Linda, I'd like that, and it will make our sessions smoother.
- Okay, Linda.
  They shook hands.
- Now, let's finish this session, but I'd like you to consider a few points for our next. Think about what happens if somebody says something that makes you feel angry. Look at the feelings and try and examine where they come from rather than react to them. If you need to argue, try to direct things towards a solution rather than go over the same issue. An argument should be to resolve problems rather than go over and over the same problems which get you nowhere. Do not assume you know why someone reacts to something - if you make assumptions about others' behaviour, and many times it is not correct, you will start to build these into the way you see others and your relationship with them. This will create negativity; please try to make all communication transparent. If you have time, write the solution down and the issue - the issue by itself is no good as it does not help in any way and will cause an adverse reaction.
- I'll try it. Jay promised.
- It won't be easy, we have covered a lot this session, and it has all been positive. Keep in touch by email or phone with any thoughts you have on going forward.

Jay strolled back to her office, her thoughts forcing her to stop at intervals to contemplate the problem. It was all there for her now; this was going to work. Brown had proven herself and barriers broken. She developed a mantra to repeat. She kept it going in her head until seated at her desk. "It's a matter of time; it-is-all… a matter of time".

PENNYLAND.

Jay was cheerful at her terminal. Clicking open the Singh case, she picked up the telephone.

-   Captain Tracy here from Special Investigation Branch – we need to talk. Are you free now?

Singh tried to put Jay off, but she was adamant that the interview had to take place immediately. Singh conceded and could meet within the hour. Invigorated, Jay stood, put her cap on and marched out towards the carpool. She would make mincemeat of him. On her return, Jay returned to her desk to type her report. An aura of self-worth surrounded her; she was pleased with how things had gone. Singh was no fool; he had tried to wriggle from the charges levelled at him, citing ignorance as his defence. He had tried to charm her with flattery, open his body language and endear himself with small talk.

As Jay reflected, she analysed her strategy. Let him chat, and he'll dig a hole that will make his defence useless. She had the mileage records; there was a consistency that proved he was on the same run every time. She smirked, recalling his face as he realised his guilt. There was no malice in him. It transpired that his family lived near where his barracks, and when an opportunity arose, he would ferry them in the army vehicle around their houses for visits. It had made his parents proud to be driven by their son in uniform, and he gained joy in being able to do it. It was one of the most straightforward cases she had worked. She had offered him options: a fine which would go on his record, if he wanted to contest her decision, he could take it to a tribunal where, if found guilty, he could be dishonourably discharged. There was one final option she kept until last, making him sweat. Her experience had helped her formulate that he was no deliberate crook; his demeanour mirrored his feeling of remorse. In the hour they spent together, he became a self-confident rogue turned virgin squaddie.

The offer of a verbal warning if the fuel repaid was grasped with the desperation of a man given a second chance. As she left, he was still calling her Ma'am and thanking her profusely. This experience had raised Jay's confidence; the session with Brown had been the basis on which to build. Jay typed up the requisite report, populated the database fields and forwarded the report to her C.O. to close it out. As she clicked the tick that sent the file, she sat upright, content that it had been a good day – and it was only 15:00, she picked up her mobile to call Rory. She wanted to see him now that the recovery process was on track. He did not know how lucky he might be tonight, Jay mused with a coy smile.

Rory had been delighted to meet up and suggested the same place, which made Jay tingle. He had not seen her going through the madness of the past fortnight. That had been the lowest part of her life, but now it was past. Rory had not seen her shorter hair, so she decided to dress for him. Make her feel good and him too when they met. Her intuition told her that he liked her a lot and was still holding back for whatever reason. Perhaps it was his ex-wife, or more likely that he did not know how to help her with her issues. She walked the hour back to her flat, which made her feel good too. Once over the threshold, she picked up her mail then played ambient music. There was a letter from Buxton with her parent's solicitors frank. She made tea then sat at the table, staring at the letter. Halfway through the cup, she tore a strip off the envelope and, with trembling fingers, opened the folded sheet. It was good news; the estate had been finalised, paperwork required signing before funds released. The figure staggered Jay, money had never been an issue in her life, but that amount could change her life. She needed advice, and Rory would oblige. Jay showered then dressed for the evening in control of emotions.

Rory sprang upright when she walked into the bar; she approached him with caution then hugged him. She did not want to let him go, and they stood in the embrace for longer than would be expected.

- Drink? He asked.
- I'd like a gin, please, ice'n slice and tonic.

- My drink is over there, nodding at a secluded table.
- I got you a big one. You look well, unique and happy.
- Thanks, Rory, you are a gem, cheers big ears.

They laughed; Jay looked into Rory's eyes as they clinked glassed then took a sip.

- Mmmmmm, I needed that.
- Hard day?
- I made it so. I had my first session with Brown. I was okay, my senses tell me it will succeed, and I'll work through it. My perceptions of her have changed; I had the creepiest feelings towards her. Perhaps there was some professional jealousy on my part that she wasn't as good as me. We are different women, that's all.
- That sounds positive, Jay, and I'm happy for you. Good for you.
- I closed a case today, too, so double whammy for celebration. I need some advice. Again!!! I'll tell you about it later. What news?
- Oh, this and that. My brother came to visit. Did I ever tell you about him?
- You have a brother? – You told me the last time we met about your sister.
- My brother makes my sister look normal; I'll tell you later if you wish. Do you want to eat?
- Let's have a few more Vera's. I'm in the mood.
  Jay caught Rory's eye, then looked down, then up again, meeting his gaze. He smiled back.
- Oh, I have the therapy story I wrote, remember.
- I do. Can I read it now? Is it a lot to take in?
- Naw, it's harmless fun. A bit of mad fiction, I had fun writing it, and it did me good to get the stuff that was clogging me up onto paper to discuss with my counsellor. Mind you, he was a bit shocked.
- You're a dark horse Rory; still-waters, eh?
  Rory passed Jay the script from his inner jacket pocket.
  - Can I read it now?
  - If you wish, I'll get the drinks in.

- Rory, the bill is on me tonight – please let me.
- Okay, if you insist.
Jay opened the folder and began to read.

Jay set the folder on the table as Rory returned with the drinks.

- Rory, where did this come from? – I never would have thought you had this stuff in you.

- Are you hooked?

- I want to know what happens if that's what you mean.

- Ha, I told you before, it was from a story I heard from an old advocate, I set it differently, but the storyline is the same. How far have you got?

- The obsession has been revealed. Will I read on?

- Why not? You can quiz me. The only other person to have read this was the counsellor… and he didn't comment. He was content in the fact that his therapy had been productive. I don't think he read it all. Are you hungry, ready to order food, or do you want to drink and read?

Jay clinked her glass with Rory's as she picked the folder up.

- I'll read it, then we can order.

Jay placed the folder on her lap and took a large sip of the gin, and read on.

- Rory, I dread to think where this is going. Is there a home movie - is there reference and closure with what your wife was involved in?

Rory's smile hid his hurt; Jay picked up on this,

- I'll read it all, then ask the questions.

Rory nodded, his eyes glazed.

Jay looked up from the manuscript,

- Rory, don't tell me you're the lawyer – please.

She smiled, goading him.

He remained silent, maintaining a face that betrayed his feelings.

Jay read on.

- HA, great ending – "Will they ever stop shaggin' in Stockbridge" -
It didn't stop us, did it? Jay teased.

- Do you know I never put the two together until you mentioned it?
That is spooky.

Rory sat back, enjoying the revelation.

Jay put her hand over his.

- That must have taken a great effort to write considering the trauma
caused by her actions.

- It got it out of me, put things into perspective. Made the personal
impersonal. It drained me, though but was great therapy. Can you see
that?

- I can. You went to one of those schools, didn't you? I did too. Not
pleasant, all the stuff that gets bottled up inside. I think that you did
well putting that into a cautionary tale. Obsession taking over life
then breaking you up inside.

- Thanks, Jay. Let's order – what do you fancy?

Jay looked deep into Rory's eyes, pursed her lips, licked them and
smiled.

- Hmmmmmmm, now or later?

They enjoyed their meal then more drinks that created convivial
compatibility. Their conversation stimulated relaxation. Again, Jay
insisted against Rory's protestations to pick up the tab, and they left
in a taxi destined for Rory's flat. During a nightcap, they kissed and
held each other in silence. Passionate lovemaking followed with the
chemistry creating an afterglow of affection. As they lay side by side,
Jay's curiosity drove her to ask,

- Tell me about your bother.

- My brother. Ha. He's a bigger control freak than the nut in my story. Are you sure you want to know about him?

- I do, can't be that bad.

- Jay, I don't know where to start.

Rory ruffled his hair, then Jays. He cupped his face with his hands, rubbed his eyes, looked into Jays then spoke fearfully.

My brother always wanted to join the army, be like our Dad, but he failed the medical. I don't know the reason. He did, however, join the Reserves. He blagged the rank of Major due to the illness of the deserved recipient. That blew his ego; his life was now compared to the Army. Let me tell you, he was hell to be around. His wife suffered him; she had supported him whilst he did a series of dead-end jobs. She was a manager within some big organisation and had a successful career. They had four boys born at unusual intervals; my brother cared for them as a house husband whilst his wife worked. Using Army vehicles on the sly, he started a delivery business that grew with his ego; he helped people – that's what he did, becoming a trusted part of the community. He got taken advantage of, but it never fazed him, money wasn't his motivator, but he did enjoy the fruits of his efforts. His boys grew, the older three were what he's called outside boys – they loved the outdoors, climbing, running, sailing – everything was there for them in the rural area they lived. He had no control over the older boys, he tried to steer them into Army ways, but they rebelled. The more he wanted to control them, the more they fought back. All three were known to the police for drinking, fighting and other high jinks that the adrenalin created. They weren't bad youths, just in the wrong place at that time of their lives. Their Mother adored them and loved that they were real boys. She lived life through them and was devastated when they all left home - as soon as they could. The remaining boy, named – would you believe – My brother cosseted Bertie, who had an unhealthy bond with his Mother breastfeeding until about 5 or 6 years old. Bertie became an inside boy. They put him into private education, but he had to travel to the nearest city, thirty miles. The business grew, and my brother had to take on staff. His wife was becoming stressed at work as her direct reports were all vying for her job and were sticking the knife in, she started to drink to compensate, but he ignored it. He was spending all his time between ferrying Bertie about, his business and the Reserves. His wife had an affair, was pensioned off by her employer then had a breakdown. He ignored all this, hid his head in the sand. Bertie came out of 250 grand's worth of education with failed exam results.

There was no other choice but for him to work in the family business, which had grown substantially. My brother was now a councillor, an elder of the church, and numerous steering committees and the king of his empire. No one could question his decision; if they did, the stock answer was, "That's how it's done in the Military" He stripped Bertie of confidence, telling him that he could never work for anyone other than his father. In time he would inherit the business. Poor Bertie, he'd failed the written part of the driving test, which meant he'd never drive in his father's eyes. Poor guy had it instilled in him, old sergeant major style that he would never do anything. My brother stopped talking to me when I got my commission; I had taken what was dear to him, our own father's pride in one of his sons following his footsteps. Of course, it was all in my brother's head; my father never talked to me about it, his army life was in the past, and he had no intentions of sharing experiences with anyone. It had been a means to an end for him. My brother exacted revenge in his way. He scammed my parents out of thousands of pounds, making them part of the business then asking them for loans to pay taxes, upgrades to equipment etc. He took money pretending that his eldest son had a child, needed money for his fledgeling business, etc. All sounds unbelievable.

Rory turned his head to face Jay; she was asleep; he placed his lips on her forehead,

 - Goodnight, lover.

With a relaxed smile, Jay sighed in a loving tone.

When Rory awoke, Jay was gone. A note on the table thanked him for being so kind and asked if they could meet again that evening. She had things to discuss.

The first email Jay opened was from Rory informing her that he had been called away on a case and would not be returning for a fortnight. This news threw her mind out of kilter. It was the first hurdle at her first step. Panic came over her as she believed that Rory had let her down. She needed him. Jay stepped out of the office to walk around the barracks; a light rain stung her eyes which brought clarity. Rory had not gone; she could email her plan to him and get his advice that way. Pleased with this revelation, she marched back to her desk to evaluate what required Rory's input. Jay created a list of possibles, definites and probables to be achieved in tandem with the counselling that would make the new Jay freed from the past. Jay composed the reply requesting his thoughts and ideas.

- Change name by deed poll to Mary Lister.
- Contact her birth Mother through the Dublin lawer.
- Invest inheritance.
- Sit Major's examination.
- Find Ben, try a different approach.

Jay nodded in self-approval. She had to keep the positives going, it was going to be along two weeks without Rory, but his return would be something to anticipate. The dark side took over her thoughts; it was also going to be a long two weeks without human interaction, there was no one else to confide in, only Brown, and that was work. It struck Jay that she had to keep the two separate, running parallel with no cross over. Six days until the next session, she would have to find something to delve into to make the time pass. Jay opened the cold case list; there would be something juicy there to keep her occupied. As Jay trawled through the unfinished cases and cross-referenced the dates with the competed items, she realised a pattern of non-events dating back to when she left for Edinburgh. Once the case was resolved, the standard procedure would be that the junior officers would activate the `close' tick within the software; this would generate the sign off process that required an `approval' tick by those further up the ranks. This would never have occurred pre-Edinburgh as Jay was always on top of her sub-ordinates to ensure there was no backlog; she had taken ownership of this procedure to ensure the smooth running, both a blessing and a curse. The benefit was that she could lose herself in these cases to initiate close, but the curse was she would have to take the bollocking that came with her superiors receiving bucket loads of approval requests. She satisfied her with the adage that one can always take a bollocking, her then set to clear this administrative backlog.

Mind-numbing work for the ambitious, but the repetition, along with the concentration required, would be ideal for her to get a routine going. She was amazed that this was not picked up, but… this was something she could highlight after her therapy to make the department more efficient. The days passed quickly, with Jay working the weekend to eat up time. Nights alone, either visiting the movies or cooking elaborate meals for one. She often thought of Rory, his family's stories, his wife, and the half story she had heard about his brother. His advice about writing therapy motivated Jay to keep a journal of the day's events along with her thoughts and struggles. She had no family tales to tell; her life in Buxton took on the memory of a sham; it was too contrived, did it happen at all? Perhaps she should add some of that to the list for Rory to consider. Should she confront the mad aunt about the truth? Did the mad aunt exist, or had it all been a dream. These thoughts haunted Jay propelling her to create two columns in her journal, one entitled "cheerful" the other "tearful". When doubts journeyed into her head, she pencilled them in and wrote her thoughts on how best to deal with them. Jay took heart in this exercise, it made her happy, and the productivity made her feel as if she was contributing to her recovery. By the evening before the next session with Brown, Rory still had not replied to her email, and it was eating away at her, increasing self-doubt. It was the first thing she wrote in the tearful column each morning. She had reverted into the anxious email, phone and text checker but had managed to keep the emotions in check by convincing herself that he was a busy man, had a pressure job and would not have time to think of her predicament. The antithesis was that she cursed him for not being efficient; <u>she</u> made a point of answering communication as soon as <u>she</u> knew the query's answer.

But he wasn't her.

After four nights, everything was hurting; she looked at others and speculated if they were the same. Dread crept over her as she thought of others co-existing with the sadness of being alone. Something in the back of Jay's mind reminded her of a saying that she had heard but could not recollect from where. Walk slowly and drink water - that made no sense. Dismissing that thought, Jay focussed on one thing; she was alone, alone with no family or friends. She stayed awake at night with the thoughts darting in and out. References; relevant and irrelevant, attached and unattached kept her from sleep. She considered her symptoms then made the mistake of attempting self-diagnosis – one answer repeated itself -lack of strength, both mental and physical. Everything around became doubtful; she got out of bed and looked around her flat. Things appeared tidily arranged, so she moved the furniture about until everything placed diagonally opposite its original position. She put on her uniform, then sat and stared at her reflection.

Was the livery a disguise or an aspiration? Dressing in this regalia had made it an instrument of ritual. An imitation of greater hopes that she might become more like her image. Magical, incantatory. The earliest theory of art itself, mimesis, a replica of reality, or was it 'a reality'. Jay tried to stand up, but the room began to spin. She sat again and stared at her reflection. The feeling of putting the uniform on and perfecting her make-up made her stronger. She felt like a new person going out to face the world, head-on with refreshed persona. The words of a Scottish author who championed the value of role models flew into her brain. She had heard it back at school, but the understanding lost until now. "A man lives by believing something." Her form master had told her that we could become more than what we are or become a different type of person by believing in something. Or we can find ourselves out of place, wearing a suit that doesn't fit—pretending to be someone we're not. Then he had touched her breast. Jay had forgotten that experience, but now that and many more were attacking her, aerial bombs of the mind. Jay had felt calm, but she stood up and shouted at her reflection at full pitch.
 - What would Jesus do?

She slapped her face.

- Snap out of it. You are neither disconnected nor insubstantial. You – are – in - control.

Jay undressed, returned to bed, masturbated then fell asleep.

117

SNOWCLONES ARE AS THEY ARE.

Jay awoke a few seconds before the alarm clock buzzed. She was ready for the next session with Brown. The first thing was to check her email, nothing from Rory and one from Brown. Jay opened it fearing the worst, and she did not want this rescheduled or cancelled. Relief came as the opening words suggested they meet in the counselling room rather than Brown's office. Jay sighed, relieved that the day had started in her favour. Jay dressed in a freshly cleaned uniform, with no make-up and hair combed to sit naturally. For no reason, she decided to wear two sets of underwear, a throwback to school-days. Inners and outers, as she put the second pair on, the thought of a learning day entered her mind. Today she would be a sponge; she would let Brown drive the conversation without any questioning.

Brown was staring out the window when Jay entered the counselling suite.

- Morning, Jay.

- Morning Brow…Linda. Oops, Brown sounds rude. Sorry, I'm twittering, not had anyone to talk to for a while.

- I like this pink.

- Me too.

- There is a reason for it; I only found out recently the Dutch pioneered the snoezelen room, which catered for all sensory therapies. All too theoretical for me.

- Okay.

- How have you been Jay, anything been holding you back, any positives from last time. Take a seat if you want.

- I felt good after the last session. Energised. I closed a case, got myself back into work mode and started keeping a journal of thoughts and actions. Don't ask me to show it to you as I am not ready for that. I've identified a few things I'd like to do in my personal life. I'm in the process of making these happen.

Jay sat on the chair next to where Brown stood and looked up to her.

- It's like learning who you are from the outside in - then the inside out. It scares me.

- It's good you see it that way, that's a positive. Today is going to tire us both out. Do you feel comfortable in yourself to tell me the traumas you've endured?

- Can we have a coffee first?

- Sure.

They sat in a content silence whilst sipping their coffees. Jay finished hers, returned her cup to the tray and waited for the counsellor to follow suit. Jay took this time to gather her thoughts. When Brown had her back to Jay as she returned her cup, Jay spoke.

- Five events come to mind. Finding out I had a twin brother. The death of my adoptive parents. The story of my birth parents. My birth Mother tried to make contact but was rebuffed by my adoptive parents, then rejected my twin when I tried to make contact. A few other issues, an aunt I made contact with and a form master. Perhaps the biggest problem is the guilt of having an idyllic childhood whilst my twin had the opposite; it seems my adoptive parents rejected him. That all sounds heavy to me.

- Why heavy?

- Because in the big picture, these are personal issues, I've enjoyed a privileged life and worse of all, I've never been exposed to the wrong side of anything.

- We are on our way if you recognise that. Do you want to try the Brainspotting process? It can be painful.

Jay moved to stand then sat back down.

- That's why we are here.

- Okay, Jay, that's the spirit. I'd like you to turn and face the empty wall. Move to what you feel is a safe distance away.

Jay moved her chair towards the end wall to about three metres away.

Brown moved her chair alongside and raised the height, so she looked down at Jay's face. She spoke in a low tone,

- I'd like you to imagine a straight line running from one end of the wall to the other at eye line. It can be as thick or as thin as you like, any colour you want, just as long as it is straight. Do you have it in your mind's eye?

- I do, I have a squash court service line, but I have it in yellow – the full length.

- Perfect, Jay. Let's relax here; take a few deep breaths. Would you like to listen to some music, or do you feel okay in silence?

- I'm okay like this; I feel we are doing this together.

- I'm pleased with that, and I know we are good at working together. I'd like you to follow the line from one end to the other, and it doesn't matter which. Just do it slowly. Can you try that for me?

Jay followed the line moving her head through an arc to maintain a consistent speed.

- That's ideal. Now here comes the hard bit. I'd like you to follow the line in the same fashion but think of the traumas you mentioned before, in any order you want.

As Jay's head moved, Brown watched her eyes, fascinated by the different hues of each. After 20 seconds, Jay's eyes started to roll, and her eyelids flickered. The counsellor spoke quietly.

- Jay, stop there for a moment.

Jay's hand moved to rub just beneath her chest.

- I have a pain here, just like a stitch. It is worse; it's a shooting pain that is throbbing.

- Stay there, Jay, keep your eyes on the spot on the line. We've found the first Brainspot. Is the pain unbearable, or can you continue holding that thought?

Jay nodded and forced words through gritted teeth.

- You keep it going.

- Concentrate on that pain. You know how you have had period pains and pushed them away with your mind, try to do that now with that pain. Shout at me if you want to relieve it. Shout out what you were thinking at that time. We have to get it out, get the pain away.

Jay screamed.

- Fuckin' twin, I have a fuckin twin, I have a fuckin twin.

She kept shouting until all her breath had gone. She took a large swallow of air then kept her breath in. Jay held her breath until the pain in her lung was beyond the pain in her body; then, with a loud grunt, she let the air and pain out.

As Jay gasped for breath, she shouted once more.

- It's gone, it's gone.

Brown had both hands on Jay's shoulders during this period. Jay remained focussed on the wall.

- You did well there. Has all the pain gone?

Jay nodded.

Brown removed her hands.

- Let's have a rest. Take deep breaths and make sure the discomfort has gone.

Brown moved to face Jay, keeping out of her stare.

- The pain you felt was that of the trauma. Your body was holding that. The unconscious mind stores the pain in your body; it could be anywhere. Now that we have one out of the way, you know what to expect. If it's any consolation, the first pain is often the worst, but I can't guarantee that. Do you want to carry on?

Jay nodded.

- Okay, keep moving along the line at a slow speed, don't anticipate. Just think of what you have gone through recently.

Jay continued her journey with Brown holding both her hands. Brown saw the eye flicker then felt the pain rise in Jay as she straightened her legs out of the chair.

- It's in my kneecap. She screamed.

- You fuckin liar Brown, this is fuckin agony.

Jay moved her leg in and out with both she and Brown rubbing the knee.

- Thorpe-Tracy, Thorpe-Tracy, Thorpe-Tracy.

Jay continued this mantra whilst rubbing her knee in violent spasms. She stopped as fast as she had started.

- That was quick.

Brown smiled.

- You did great there; we may have to revisit that. You want to keep it going.

- One more just now. Jay stated, feeling in control.

The next session exhausted both parties. Jay's mind had focussed on her Mother, and the pain had manifested itself as a cramp on each calf muscle. It took frantic rubbing by Brown as the pain ebbed and flowed. Thirty minutes passed before Jay's sobbing lowered from a violent heaving to a gentle murmuring. After the pain dissipated, Brown carried Jay across to the day bed where she lay alongside her. Two hours later, they awoke. The experience had drained them; Jay's mouth was dry, as she swung her legs over the day bed to get a drink, she fell flat. Brown jumped to pick her up.

- I think we went too far for this first session Jay.

Jay burst into laughter that sounded both excited and relieved.

- I think that it was best to push me. I can't explain how alive I feel, even if my legs don't work.

Brown hugged her; Jay kept her hands at her side. In an awkward tone, she asked.

- Can you get me a drink, please?

- Sure, sure.

Jay sipped at the bottle of water.

- How do you feel? Brown asked.

- Strange. I feel energy released in a gentle flow. My blood has a sense of tingling in my veins. I can feel a slight shaking, like a chill and, although I cannot just now, I feel a desire to stretch.

- It's your body's natural response to unfreezing. The trauma held from the past now expelled. You'll experience a lasting mental relief upon realizing the stuff that was knotting you up.
Jay nodded. Stood up then stretched her arms. She touched her toes several times, then looked at Brown.
- Thank you, Linda. That was quite an experience to share with a stranger.
- That's okay. We'll call it a day there. I suggest you go home and relax in a hot bath. Try not to think of what you did today but what the result was. We might uncover more next session. Meet again next week?
- Anything I should do until then?
- Just keep yourself busy; don't dwell on trivial matters. Try to take up a new hobby, even if it's just for a week. The secret is to keep occupied and to keep moving forward. Together we'll get these knots to the back of your mind.
As Jay left the office and stepped outside, she took in a lung full of fresh air. It tasted clean; she felt energised as she took her bearings. Where was Rory when she wanted his body?

Jay strolled a couple of miles to her flat, her mind devoid of negativity. The shaking chill gone, it still felt that her skeleton was shaking inside her flesh. She looked up at the sky and asked herself out loud why she hadn't noticed the hue's depth. Everything appeared new and clean. The usual hour walk had stretched to two, with Jay stopping now and then to take in her surroundings. Once back at her flat, she lit candles in the bathroom, then lay in hot scented water. Relaxed, she did not feel the need for sleep. Jay drifted in and out of differing mind scenarios as she lay in the security of the warmth. She gained hope from Brown's experience, and, as she climbed out of the bath, she spoke to her reflection.

-    A few more sessions, and I'll be right as rain.

She smiled then blew a kiss.

Jay felt a weight gone; the depression was lifting at a slow pace. She glanced at the laptop screen and noticed the small yellow envelope icon. Sipping a glass of red as she opened it, the warmth returned - a reply from Rory. He apologised for not replying sooner, but… the words faded from her view. At the end of the mail, he offered the advice she hoped. Why change your name? – it will only remind you of the unknown. Jay composed herself and re-read. She smiled at the politeness of his recommendations. He would initiate the process to contact her Mother; he suggested an army advisor for finances and hoped they could meet on his return. Jay closed the laptop then lay on top of her bed. Jay sensed her mind had become detached from her body; she imagined her torso had melted flat into the mattress with only her head intact to hold her brain. Jay woke with a start as the alarm buzzed; her legs ached as they did after a 20-mile yomp. She straightened and stretched a few times, then took a cold shower. As she left her flat for the office, Jay felt a newfound vigour.
 - It will be alright.
Jay's workload increased then diminished over the following week. Gone were self-doubts. She had taken up ambling of an evening. Walking with no particular destination, thoughts came and went, but none lingered. Rory had emailed a couple of times to remind her of their meet-up, but she would not reply - she would wait until the day. She enjoyed living from moment to moment, not in the frantic self-prophetic way of the last two months – it was a refreshing change.

Her attitude towards others had mellowed too; there were more smiles, gentle banter with the juniors, which created a morale rise. The backlog of work cleared; this meant that a big juicy case would be next on her agenda. Feedback from the C.O. had been positive, so it was with pleasured anticipation that Jay entered the counselling suite for her next session.

Another Brainspotting session with Brown had taken its toll on Jay. They had followed the same pattern as the previous session, but, perhaps being too ambitious and keen to rid her id of the trauma, Jay had unconsciously brought forward three events from her youth that had lain dormant. Brown re-assured her that this was not unusual. Jay's issue had been that if these events had never affected her before, why would they expose themselves now; Brown had an answer, but this irked Jay as Brown, in her mind, had an answer for everything. Jay left the suite with a wave of anger that matched the previous week's joy. She wanted to put off meeting Rory but pushed herself to think that perhaps he could help kick start something. Jay drank two large glasses of wine before leaving her flat. The alcohol had fuelled the anger to make Jay uncomfortable company. Rory greeted her with a kiss and offered her a gift-wrapped package and card as they made their way to sit.

- Happy Valentine.
- I forgot, why didn't you tell me. I feel bad now.
- Relax, Jay. It's nothing; it's a token.
- Why do this? Why let me make a fool of myself?
- Jay, you're overreacting.

In one step, Jay rose then headed to the restrooms.
Rory ordered gins.
Ten minutes later, Jay re-appeared.

- I'm so sorry. I had a bad day, and the last person I should take it out on is you.
- It's okay. Sit down and relax – I got gin – is that ok?
Jay nodded.
- I am sorry; I'm like a spoiled brat.
She opened the gift to find a bottle of her favourite perfume.
- How did you know?
- Edinburgh – remember.

Jay leaned across the table and kissed Rory and, at the same time, cupped her hand over his groin.

- Mmmmmmmmmm. I missed you.
- I missed you too. How was counselling today?
- It did what it was supposed to. Let's not talk about it.
- How was your trip?
- It was what it was. Let's not talk about it.

They both laughed and sipped their gin.

After eating and consuming a bottle of red, they sat content with coffees and brandy.

- I'm not going to change my name.
- Wise move, Jay; it has too many issues attached to it. You are Jay to all who know you - only a handful know the story; best keep it that way.
- Thanks, Rory. I needed to hear that. I have the paperwork for you from the Irish solicitor that represented my Mother. Can you kick all that off for me? Organise contact if she wishes. I'll ask Brown next session what to expect or do or if I'm ready to do it.
- Okay, Jay, I'll get that organised – leave it all with me. Did you contact the finance guy?
- I did, but it is a large sum of money. Obscene almost. I don't need it. He wants me to put it in long term investments. He's putting a proposal forward, and we just have to wait.
- Jay, we need to discuss you trying to find Ben. It's not a good move just now. I think you need time, get this counselling malarky out of the way, then get a couple of meaty cases behind you to get on top of life. Get the confidence in your own being back before risking all the excellent work done…just in case it does not pan out how you hope it might. It may be traumatic meeting your Mother, but…she wants to do that – we know that.

Jay leaned over once more to plant a kiss on Rory's forehead.

- You are right. I'll say no more about it
- One thing I should add. Start the exam process that'll give you something to strive for – help keep your mind on track.

They finished their drinks.

Rory asked

- Your place or mine?
- Let's get a hotel, my treat. Let's go somewhere special.

SUI GENERIS.

Ben Black struggled to fight the sleep that pained him. With his head rested on the window of the bus and through half-opened eyes, his brain painted surreal art with the white, red and amber lights of moving traffic. It was his sixth overnight bus journey in as many weeks; he was hopeful that this would be the last for a while. Money draining away stopped his thoughts from moving on. The trip to Ireland was, in hindsight, a mistake. Ben believed at the time that getting as far away as possible would be the practical solution to being tracked down by the Tracy woman. He had taken the first bus that had left Edinburgh. Running from the Newtown flat, up Dundas Street to the bus station, he had been in a state of panic, too scared to look round to see if she was following. As he entered the terminus, a bus was pulling out, and he managed to jump on as the door was closing. The driver looked nonplussed as Ben asked where it was going: Glasgow.

Perfect for an onward journey.

The first bus out was to Stranraer to link up with the ferry to Belfast. It all fitted in, too well perhaps, but Ben took the opportunity to follow fate. He had visited Belfast before, staying for a few months off Malone Road. Ben stood on the deck, arms on the railings looking out into the distance as the ferry pulled out of the harbour. He reminded himself of his previous experience of the place he had dubbed "scumbag city" with no thought of looking back. When on holiday in Tenerife, he had met a girl from Belfast; she had invited him for a weekend that turned into much longer than anticipated. Ben, being a visual thinker, replayed her image. She had perfect teeth and an even more admirable figure. She had been a tigress in bed. Treating his manhood as a puppy would a slipper; this experience had kept him there. Her biggest turn-on was to hump his leg whilst treating him to the visual pleasure of her toying with him. He smiled as he thought about their sex; he likened it to a capsized yachtsman in a storm clutching onto any mast, spar or sail available to prevent him from being thrown off. She had been a wild woman. He teased her about having been trained by the republicans as a type of Feldhure, a basic pleasure model for general issue usage. Ben knew how lucky he had been that she had not understood. She was uneducated and described as "thick as shit in the neck of a bottle", her temper had matched her passion. Her family lived in one of the sink estates, a hotbed of republican activity. Ben couldn't remember the name other than it began with an A. She took him there once to meet her sisters in a pub known as "The Sitting Duck"; due to the frequent addition of bullet holes to the stone and glass. It was there he witnessed the venom she possessed; one of the sisters had referred to their drink dependent parents as "alchomom and alchopop". It had taken a few minutes for the sentiment to set in, but the effect was immediate. Her face had changed from a smiling delight into a set jawed monster. The expletives lubricated with the spit they were delivered with, and the mood changed to that of hate between all sisters. Ben had never witnessed such a poisonous hatred. As they left the bar, minutes after the barman had told them to, she was still screaming at the top of her voice, defending her parents to the end. Over the short time they had together, Ben felt her wrath on many occasions. The last being the reason he had packed his bag and left without telling her. He had sworn as he boarded the first ferry out, albeit to the Isle of Man, that he would never return to this nation of hate. It was tribal, inherent and innate. There could never be peace in that province; hatred was everywhere, even amongst themselves.

He laughed at the irony of having one telephone directory for the whole country.

It was a place no one could hide.

Ben smiled at landfall. Disembarking the ferry, he fashioned a plan based on the memory of a friend who had announced that he was to travel through Ireland, visiting every town that had a name in a song. Ben noticed a bus with Carrickfergus as the destination. Within the hour, he was on his way out of Dodge.

The next few weeks brought serenity to Ben. He visited Dublin, saw the floozy in the Jacuzzi, the tart with the cart and the hag with the bag. Lisdoonvarna, Spencil Hill, Tralee, Killaloe, ending the voyage in Galway Bay. One week on the coast of Galway had been enough, nice enough to see, and the weather was fine but…sleazy. Even by

Ben's standards, the place had an underbelly that beggared belief. He had stayed in a backpacker's hostel, but the availability of every drug known made the place a haven for crusties, conmen and crooks. What had annoyed Ben most was that he had to repeat every sentence as none of the assembled bunch of itinerants understood his accent. An overdosed boy of sixteen found under a bunk in the hostel led Ben to pack his bag and leave. He decided to journey by bus to Rosslare to get the ferry to England. There were too many options open to Ben as he made his way across the terminal at Pembroke dock. He booked into a travel hotel to decide on a diverted adventure in the morning.

The journey to Hereford had taken longer in Ben's mind than in real-time due to his fellow passengers' truculent air that created an ambience of separation. He needed a beer, a long, ice-cold lager to both satisfy his thirst and to make time to think of his next move. The town clock had struck the last of six when he stepped toward the paint flaked door of the first pub he saw. He had to negotiate his way through five or six shaven-headed males smoking in the doorway. Their instinct was to close ranks to make it as difficult as possible for Ben to get through this unnecessary guard. Unintentionally, he nudged the smallest member of the group then apologised in an instant by raising both hands. The little man glared but remained silent. As Ben opened the inner frosted glass door, he heard their growls but could not make out the words. Ben walked to the far end of the bar, where a free space beckoned. Ben noticed a local cider on draft, and once presented, held it up, looked at the cloudy swirl, then finished it in four gulps. The barman smiled as he watched Ben; he took his empty glass but then gave him a discouraging look as Ben requested "something similar" As Ben sipped the second pint, the atmosphere in the pub became apparent to him. He became aware of his surroundings; instinct brought his thoughts to life.

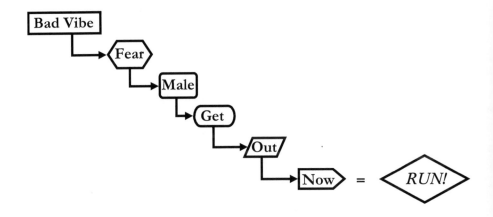

Ben finished his drink, then took small steps towards the toilet. As he entered, he noticed one of the shaven heads at the urinal. He attempted small talk with no response. This added to his fear; as he washed his hands, he saw the worry in his eyes reflected from the mirror. His loneliness came to the fore. He knew no one here; he had only a bank card as identification; his money was running low and shivered at the realisation that he was alone in the world. He'd been awake in this nightmare many times before. He enjoyed his own company, but this was a feeling of anxiety. For the first time in his life, Ben needed a friend. One thing he was sure of, he had to get out of this mad place. Staring at his reflection, Ben realised he was a series of temporary and isolated lives, with no aim or direction. He could not recall the last person he had talked at any length; he needed to speak, not to be listened to but to talk to another human being. He needed companionship to survive. Staring into his own eyes, Ben muttered,

- You should have met up with Jay, given her a chance. You made a BIG mistake.

Taking deep breaths, Ben settled his mind as he prepared to open the lavatory door. He slung his backpack over his left shoulder, leaving the right arm free in case a punch or push was needed. He walked through the bar with determination, taking a bearing on the light filtering through the frosted exit. He scoped the angry group near the door on his left-hand side at the bar and instinct directed him to the right of them, leaving about two metres between them. Ben was focussed on the exit, his pace quickening and did not see the smallest group member reversing out of the huddle. The little man lifted his right foot behind so that his heel clipped Ben's shin. Ben stumbled, dropped his pack and spun to face the man, having to look down to meet his eye. Ben tried to diffuse the situation by apologising.

- Sorry mate, my fault... I never saw you there.

- I'm not your mate. The man growled, anger oozing.

Ben stepped back.

- Sorry.
- You saying I'm too small to see.

Ben stammered,

- It's my fault; let it go.

Ben smiled, dropped his guard and looked over to the group trying to appeal to a sense of reason. They remained motionless and stared back at him. Ben looked into the small man's eyes. He saw nothing but hatred. He shouted at Ben,

- I didn't do tours of the shitholes of the world to be insulted by some poxy jock.

- C'mon. Ben implored. Let's forget it, just let me walk out of here. No hard feelings.

Ben reached over to shake hands, but the gesture ignored, then he rubbed the man's head. Ben had not used this gesture for many years. It was a muscle memory instinct stemming from an orphanage upbringing.

- Don't touch my fuckin' head – no one touches my fuckin' head.

The barman shouted,

- ENOUGH!

Ben's eyes were distracted as he moved his head towards the barman; the squaddie let fly with a left hook followed by a right uppercut. Simultaneously he spat in Ben's eyes then butted him. Ben felt the first blow, saw a white flash, then fell like a folding chair.

LOCK-IN.

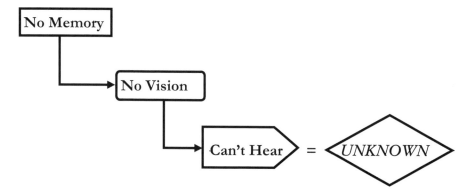

Panic overwhelmed Ben. His first thought was of being interred into a bespoke coffin with no body movement. His head held in three axes of constraint, but he could feel nothing holding him. He used a childhood technique borne in the homes for comforting when alone; his brain would feel parts of his body. He scanned his body first, left arm from shoulder to wrist, down each finger, then repeated the action for the right arm, then neck to shoulders, torso to the waist, groin, buttocks and then down each leg and all toes. Every square centimetre of his surface area felt as if it was there. Panic set in again as Ben's mind flashed that amputees still feel their missing limbs, he felt himself laugh as the next thought was an old joke about a patient telling a doctor that he could not feel his legs, the doctor's retort was `that's because we cut your hands off`. Ben repeated his scan action for his neck and the inside of his skull. One area blocked the process of this brain feel, but he knew it was a futile exercise. Up to then, all actions had assured him that his body was intact. He tried to shout, but his mouth would not move, he could feel the anxiety in words, but the frustration of not getting them out compounded his vexation. He persisted, trying to move limbs and digits but to no avail. He could feel his body but not move any part of it. Ben, through desperation, attempted to flap his ears, knowing it was useless. What could he do? Ben remembered Plant telling a joke about his exercise regime. Every morning, unless hung-over, he would go through the routine of "up/down-up/down" twenty times, then, with that rakish smile, tell whoever that was listening that he would then proceed to the other eyelid. In desperation, Ben tried moving eyelids and eyebrows but had no way of knowing if the movement had transferred to his face. The darkness that surrounded and enveloped him had locked in all direction, speech, touch and sight. All Ben had were thoughts. He tried to sniff but found he could not inhale, no nodes of recognition, his brain told him this meant nothing. The smell could be cleansed and filtered to render situations odourless. A final attempt to understand came as Ben cut off all thoughts to concentrate on listening. His first conclusion was that it was his heartbeat, then he realised it was the pulse of blood throbbing behind his ear. Focussing on this rhythm, Ben heard a faint electronic beep before the thump of blood. He could pinpoint the beat and, in doing so, predict the consistency of the sequence. Ben used his concentration to separate the beep and the thump to attune himself to electronic pulse. Hope, he had hope.

Aware now of being hospitalised and connected to life support, the reason for him being there was a blank. He had no short term memory. His thought process stuck in the present and racked his thoughts for methods to revive memories, fooling his brain into believing he had closed his eyes, but the view was a myriad of what appeared to be multi-coloured neon cylindrical balloons. The more he tried to recall the past, the more intricate the patterns became. Vibrant colours that moved and merged as tiny life forms do when viewed microscopically. Ben made a deliberate effort to cease this brain activity and concentrate on the rhythm of the beep. It remained constant; he deliberated if he managed to stress or agitate himself would the frequency increase. Ideally, he would thrash about in the hope that this would transmit externally. Ben tried to envisage being a fish caught on a line and threshing itself free, but it had to be full body. Movie scenes appeared from nowhere, then the recollection of wanting to be part of the Blade Runner scene when Fliss is in her death throes. Ben placed himself in the scene just as Dekker shoots her; Ben imagined embracing her as she lay screaming and fitting; he envisaged making love to her in her last few seconds. This would be her final experience. He lived this fantasy for as long as his concentration could last, then stopped. He felt out of breath, but the beep was still at its constant rate. It was beginning to grate

1,2,3 – beep

1,2,3 – beep

1,2,3, - beep

Ben could work out time from this. He felt a non-existent shiver
thrilling his every nerve that came with the knowledge that he was
kept alive artificially. He ceased trying to control thoughts and let the
mad movie of neon shapes entertain him.

Time ceased to exist. If each beep was one second, then he could
pass time counting, a futile future unmeasured. All he could do was
try to manage the predicament by it. It was the silence of deafness to
a backbeat. Was he alone with thoughts or not alone because of his
ideas? The face of a Belgian philosopher flashed into Ben's mind.
Trying as hard as he could, the name did not come. His ideals
championed living in the sensory world. True happiness was living as
a fragment of nature. Ben considered his predicament then set his
mind to link both situations to create a coping mechanism.
Understanding that his cerebral processes now operated beneath his
consciousness level, he could disentangle himself and live as a
secondary aspect of his true identity; his mind locked into primary
nature; alone again but inside himself.

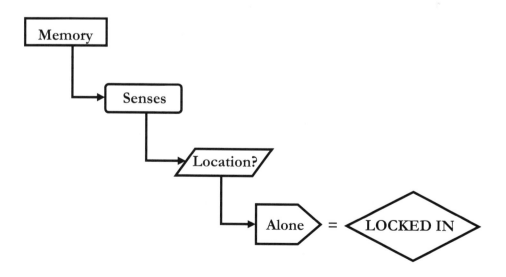

Ben's mind meandered through history, having come to terms with no point living in the now. All he had was his past - due to the uncertainty of his future. Words flashed through his mind in scrabble form coming in as a horizontal and vertical movement. This brought new words and meanings – homophones abounded. Patience was rewarded as Ben managed to hold an array of words to form a matrix that now defined him. Much like a cheap Xmas cracker toy, letters where are pushed around a square frame but with one piece missing to let the word or picture appear.

THE OUTSIDER WHO BECAME AN INSIDER.

He clung to this mantra, his new doctrine; it was his and his alone. He owned it; no one had made this transition before. Nothing he had read had considered that phenomena—a life raft on an ocean of nothingness. Analogue sound waves began to accompany the monotonous beep. There was no way of knowing if this was a new sensation or if it had been around all this time, and he had not tuned in to it. Sympathetic resonance perhaps, then he recognised the words. Ben...Ben...Ben...

- It's Nurse; I have to take your blood pressure, give you an injection, then turn you over. Can you hear me? No, of course, you can't, but I have to ask. Please, Ben, please wake up.

He felt the tourniquet tighten, then the prick in his arm. The strange sensations of the nurse's voice and the pain shook him; he tried to talk but still nothing.

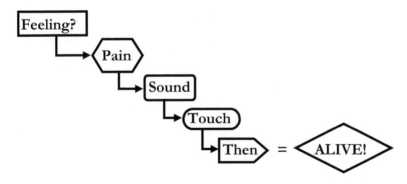

Ben recognised the voice as female. It was a strange sound as it synchronised with the beep before throb of the neck pulse. This cacophony and movement stirred a change of perspective within Ben's thoughts. The previous lack of physical sensations awoke a sexual desire in his mind. A female voice shouting his name to a biological rhythm, controlled by his and her orgasmic thrusts, the intensity raised and lowered by the momentum and acceleration. The monotone, iambic pentameter beep reminded Ben of his first serious sexual relationship.

He had pursued Antje Schulter; she hooked him by introducing him to Mann and Hesse's works and other post-war Germans' writings. Antje was like no other girl he had met. At eighteen, Ben had enjoyed many physical encounters but now his first cerebral love. The desire created within drove him to despair, and when Antje did succumb to his attentions, he found that the sex act did not provide the satisfaction to fulfil the desire. Reminded by the beep's coldness once again, Ben saw Antje's face as he remembered her when they made love. She appeared to be going through the motions of sex without enjoying the journey. There were no moans of anticipation when he mounted her, no visual or physical reciprocated sexual desire. He would watch her try desperately to reach her orgasm, and it would create wonderment in him and, just as it appeared she was approaching her nadir, she would stop. Ben would be shaking with the onset of his climax, then would hear, in Germanic tones, "Nein – No more – It won't work" then push him off. She would then masturbate him or put him in her mouth until he ejaculated, but she always appeared to Ben to lack interest in this act. It was as if she was going through the motions of an epilogue of requirement. Sometimes she would be trying so hard to achieve satisfaction that she would get distracted, hear a noise in the distance, then get up and leave the room. With time her pleasure came, but she insisted on Ben reaching his before she did. She then achieved her orgasm by having him lie on top of her whilst she manoeuvred him into a position that worked for her. She would tell him that he was the wrong shape for her and that his body size was not according to her requirements. He had never experienced different aspects of sex before, so he stayed with her until this novelty wore off. He loved her and the education he had gained, but in the end, the real lesson was that they were two different people with one common interest. They loved their days together, reading, discussing and philosophising.

Antje pursued Ben with the same vigour he had on realising that he had lost interest in her; this resulted in Ben moving home several times before Antje finally got the message. The intensity of the memory of sexual desire stirred Ben. He doubted that he had ever felt physically satisfied. The sexual delusion was now a thing of the past if he did not escape this skull prison.

Ben had learned that the complete sex act, in his opinion, the full play of many acts, was a trick of the mind. He had always maintained that pornography had ruined any pure love that he may have hoped to attain. He advocated the theory that when a person ejaculated on the face of another, any equality was destroyed. Yet, cheap porno loops and amateur home movies used this device to conclude. A bodiless appendage spurting into or onto another human's first point of recognition. It was now a given that this was part of the fore, and after play, the bulk of Ben's sexual partners had come to expect; the placement of seed externally rather than internally. Masturbation had its place as a therapeutic device, he mused. Ben could discipline his emotions, knowing that he had none but could never discipline his sexual desires.

He would have to now.

He laughed at the thought of him masturbating whilst in his catatonic state, or even if he could communicate by Morse or semaphore by moving his dick. A Plant story about a prodigal son returning to the family home after many years brought joy. His Mother had maintained his bedroom as a shrine, and as he entered, he noticed all his old belongings. He had lain on his bed and put on the old fashioned cushioned headphones attached to a tape deck on a nearby bedside table. As he lay there, eyes closed, listening to Supertramp – waiting for the scream - a comfort enveloped him that manifested itself in superfast masturbation. When relieved and wondering what to do with the tell-tale residue, he turned to see a sandwich and a hot drink on the foot of the bed which his Mother had brought in.

Ashamed, he left through the window, never to return home

Thoughts flew and were either dismissed or explored. In Ben's mind, he had achieved a form of nirvana that allowed him to visit any location. He talked aloud to himself, but he could also converse with anyone he brought into his mind's eye. He thought, then analysed as he descended into himself. He trained himself to forget that anyone he talked to could reply only with what he said they would say and think what he thought they would. Family and place came to the fore time after time; this became a barrier that proved the most significant challenge to keeping his brain efficiency at its peak.

Reliving and creating scenarios became the method for Ben to understand his predicament, thus making a defence against it. Hermetically sealed, he could go where he had never before travelled in the depths of his mind.

The thought of belonging became an obsession. A part was missing because of this. He belonged nowhere and to no one. He had yearned for this in his youth. A family to take him into their home and let him be part of it – unconditionally. Not having a father had made him delve into thoughts about who he was and what had made him who he was. When he stripped it bare philosophically, he had no reference point to milestone the journey through life. The lack of alternatives allowed by family made his journey route one only. There was no history, no family storytelling, nothing unique that he could add to or present as his own. Ben could not recall the originator of the philosophy, a nihilistic pessimist who described a father's tendency to sMother their son. This person had been content that his father had "the decency to die" after he had sired him. Ben had lived with the fact that he would never know his father nor find out anything about him. He had come to terms with that but never explored how his father would have felt if he had been the son's orphan. A history or a place to belong was important to Ben, he knew he would never have it, and the consequence was that nothing would ever be his. Nothing would ever belong to him in life. Not one thing throughout his short life had the consistency of familiarity. There was nowhere for him to return to as a man that he had enjoyed as a boy. Ben thought about the question. "Where do you come from?" He had always wanted to reply with "nowhere", but that had sounded as corny as "All over" or "everywhere" Ben's crazed self-interrogation continued.

His Mother and father had reproduced themselves to create him and his twin if he believed that crazy woman. Fighting his will, Ben brought the thought of Jay to the fore. Her report – and his refusal to read it. Ben should have read it; perhaps he should have met her and found a voice of love that would help remove the self-discrimination he felt. It may have changed her too.

Still... too late.

Now Ben had no legacy to pass on. No one to try to get to know him, no pedigree to breed. No bloodline. No one knew or cared where he was; he had no communication method, no identity, no one to think of him. He had been dead to the world for many years. A bank knew him as a number, as did the I.R. and the N.I. He was a non-person in a world that did not care. Optimistically, he could now consider himself a prophet, hidden away with a mind detached from a body. All he had was the ability to think without distraction. Was this nirvana!? He could think freely without any feeling – emotional or physical. He would create a virility of the mind that he never possessed - Ha, no sixth sense, just a single one that could transport him anywhere. Finally, a place of his own and a purpose, albeit fantasy.

DE BONO MORTIS.

Rory had written to the law firm involved with Mary Lister's previous
approach and was surprised to learn, given that over ten years had
passed, that they still represented her. He had travelled to Ireland to
meet with their head partner, Stephen Hall, to discuss the best
method to progress; he had kept this from Jay, his strategy being to
provide her details in a report format. She could work her schedule
from that. At Rory's request, Mary Lister had to be informed about
access to her history. As Rory compiled the documentation, he
became aware of how similar the two persons that had never met
were. Bloody minded with a sense of isolation, topped off with a
survival instinct. These traits were foremost in his thoughts as he
condensed the history into salient points that Jay would have to
explore. Rory's anxiety grew as the report did - would Jay think he
had overstepped the mark by presenting too much information, or
would she see it at face value with the help of a friend.
The meeting with the lawyer had taken place in their plush offices
overlooking the Liffey. As they made small talk, they connected
through mutual acquaintances. Stephen Hall had been one of the
Ireland rugby team front row in the 1990s. He was a huge man with a
smile to match. He put Rory at ease as soon as they met.
They discussed the case history. Initial contact with the law firm had
been to trace her twins; the boy was untraceable, lost in the system.
The girl had been easier to track down, but her adoptive parents had
placed a block on contact until she reached eighteen, but Mary had
second thoughts about the consequences and had not pursued it,
hoping that the girl would track her. Mary also was aware of the
effects of abandoning her children, plus the possibility of her past
actions. Under her lawyer's instruction, she decided to take the risk
and faced the Edinburgh police for questioning.
 Stephen informed Rory that Mary tended to consume wine at an
alarming rate. According to the lawyer, their business was conducted
over lunch, during which Mary would conclude her affairs before the
entrée then enjoy gin martinis as an aperitif, wine with each course
topped off with brandy or calvados if available. She loved the social

aspect of her business and revelled in picking up the tab. The lawyer warned Rory not to cross her; she had a ruthless streak that had left male associates near to tears. Rory shared a confidence that there was no doubting that Jay was Mary's daughter.

Over coffee, Stephen informed Rory that Mary had suggested she sit in, but she would understand if Rory did not want this. Mary was in an adjoining office, awaiting his decision. Rory stated that he had to think of best interests; Stephen's counterpoint was that the report would have a better chance of accuracy if it came directly from source and any questions ratified there and then. Rory agreed; Stephen left and returned with Jay's Mother. There was no denying they were Mother and daughter. Rory's embarrassment told on his face, and the heat from the blush stung his eyes. His thoughts flickered between maintaining a professional stance and having sex with an associate's client's daughter. He had an urge to embrace Mary. She was Jay aged to perfection. Her confidence enhanced her attractiveness. Stephen introduced her as May Taylor; they shook hands then sat. He poured a glass of water, dabbed some on his brow then drank the contents. She thanked him for conceding to her request, took off her jacket, sat then began to talk.

Rory scribbled in his notebook as she asked him to confirm he had read the police report from the past. He nodded; she talked slowly in a measured manner with a polite but determined tone.

She had settled in a small fishing village in County Down under her maiden name of Taylor, shortening her Christian name to May. She took a cash in hand job as a seamstress in the local aircraft seating factory. Cash was king; her landlord never questioned her history and, as long as she paid her rent on time, never bothered her. She adapted quickly and quietly; most of the girls on the machines were catholic, so she adopted this side of the sectarian situation that was prevalent in those times. She worked hard, maintaining a low profile. She looked at her lawyer for approval as she informed Rory that the money from her dead husband had been stashed in a double bottom kist she used to store linen. Revealing that she initially removed two thousand pounds for expenses and laundering it into Bank of Ulster notes, she had never looked at the cache for the first four years. Girls came and went in the factory; her friends married, had children then moved away. Over time May had become the chargehand, battling with Unions, bullying, and the pseudo terrorists' underlying threat - they were the most dangerous. A word from the wrong person could result in nasty things happening.

May got up and walked to the window. She looked back at Rory

- Do you know my daughter?

Rory looked at Stephen.

-I'm here as a friend. I'm a lawyer in the Army, but you'll know all this. I've helped Jay over the past few months; she's on a quest to understand certain things. I don't know the whole story, only what I have helped find. All I want to do is help. To answer your question, I know Jay and consider her a friend.

-What is she like?

- She's like you in many ways.

- Thanks. To be honest, I did not trust you, but you have a way about you that I feel I can. I'll crack on.

May opencd up about her past. She was proud that she had coped with her new environment by staying objective; she made friends quickly and believed she endeared herself through old fashioned values. She had made a good friend in the factory manager; an Englishman brought in to streamline production. Mutual respect had grown to make them a formidable team that adopted lean manufacturing techniques to make the product output profitable. It had an adverse effect as the parent company put the business on the market to sell as a going concern. The factory manager engineered a management buyout, but the investment did not include the upholstery section as the demand for fabric seats replaced by faux leather. With her friend's help, May negotiated the machinery's purchase then started up on her own, supplying the main factory that manufactured the frames with the covers, developing a unique form of fixing using hook and eye fixings. She used the cash as her share of the investment, passing off a deceased rich relative on the mainland as her benefactor. She talked with pride as she explained that the business thrived as the market grew, her innovative method was picked up by competitors and began to expand. Her vision had propelled her to look at other markets, which stopped her from relying on one or two vendees. May concluded her story by stating that she moved from her rented place to a new build bungalow overlooking the mountains of Mourne.

- Tell me, Rory, is that enough.

- Thanks May, I'll write it up for her. What do you want to happen?
- Can you give me her email address, and I'll make the first contact. I know this is not a legal thing, but would you advise against me getting in touch and offering to meet her in a Spa hotel or something, a neutral place.

She paused; the emotion was apparent in her voice.

- All I want to do is meet my daughter.

Stephen spoke first.

-I'm sure Rory will make sure that happens.

Rory glanced at Stephen, then caught May's eye.

- I'll do what I can. I'll suggest you meet...

- At my expense. May interrupted.

- Okay, I'll conclude that you will make contact by email with text and phone being available too. Can I say that it will all be on Jay's terms...?

- Please stress that Jay can pull out at any time; there's no time limit, no rules and no pressure. She can bring a friend too if she needs it.

- Will do May, anything else?

- Nothing, it's up to her now.

Stephen stood and beamed a large smile.

- Anyone fancy a drink.

Rory gathered his paperwork.

- Not for me, I've to catch my plane.

May moved to the window.

- I'm going that way; I'll give you a lift to the airport.

- It's okay, I'll get a cab.

-I'm going that way, Rory. Indulge me, please.

Rory looked at Stephen; he was gazing at his shoes, shaking his head.

Rory paused for a second then replied,

- That's very kind. Thank you, May.

Stephen walked them to the doorway.

- They'll be no charge for this young Hall. May voiced in an authoritative tone.

- No, May. Stephen replied.

He shook the hand of both May and Rory as they left the building.

- I'm in that car park over there. A parking meter here earns more an hour than all the shyster lawyers in Dublin combined.

Rory smiled.

- I believe you too!

May was a maniac behind the wheel. Rory's muscles tightened at every corner; he closed his eyes several times as she negotiated her way through city traffic. There were soon on the dual carriageway towards the airport.

May broke the silence.

- You can't give way to any of the feckers in that city. Trust me; if you do, they'll feck you over quicker than a knacker. Do you fancy a drink, Rory, just me and you?

Rory had never encountered a woman like May before. It felt that what May wanted, May got. He had to be diplomatic; the thought appealed to him, though. He was attracted; there was something about her, a presence that frightened and put him at ease. It felt dangerous, and this added to the attraction. He had the urge to be what he considered terrible, spontaneous, uncaring and selfish. Deep down, he knew that it just was not him, he had to remain and be true to himself. May was about his age or older, although her body looked younger; hardness in her face gave her a worn look. Rory played on his naivety.

- I'd like to have a drink May, but if I don't get back to the barracks for a meeting, I could be posted AWOL. I don't want that.

As he spoke, he knew the next sentence would come back to haunt him, but it was the only way.

- Another time perhaps, I'd enjoy that.

- Okay, you're off the hook this time, but I'll hold you to that.

Rory smiled, his face betraying his inner thoughts. The rest of the journey was in silence. As May pulled up to the drop off point, she took hold of Rory's face and turned it toward her.

- Do your best; it's a big thing for me to meet Jay. Just let me know of any resource you need.

Rory nodded.

- I will, May, and thank you once again for the lift.

As he got out of the car and looked back inside to say his farewell, May gave him a thin-lipped smile.

- Don't forget either, we have unfinished business.

She pulled the door then sped off.

Rory let out a sigh of relief as he walked to the departure gate.

On the plane, Rory ordered a brandy and coffee. He was happy with the day's work. Contact made with the other party agreeing to the request. The report would contain a history to read with intrigue to triggered Jay's investigative nature. He would give her the hard copy at their weekly dinner. Rory's fondness feelings were growing, May had confused him, but he was back on track. Jay had taken over his daydreaming thoughts; her well-being had become his – he would do almost anything she asked, but he still had the hurt from his wife to contend with. He had blanked out the tragedy that encouraged her actions, but forgiveness was in him. The hurdle with Jay was her way with things. They met, ate, chatted, laughed then made love, but she always appeared distant. He needed to talk to her about his feelings, but some instilled Presbyterian ideal made this challenging. He conditioned himself to wait until her issues were resolved.

With all the details in place, Rory emailed Jay to reveal the trip and suggesting they meet at the usual time and place to outline the way forward. Jay's speed of response brought forth a chuckle that was the same day as the end of her sessions with Brown; there could be a double celebration if all were to plan. A throbbing thrill replaced the chuckle sensation. Anticipating good company, a happy Jay, meant a passionate end to the evening. Rory was smitten, he was more than twenty years older, but as their relationship had grown, that variance had never appeared to be an issue. His thoughts raced. Some may assume him to be her father, then the depression of the tragedy came; he had to tell her; he would tell her.

THE INADEQUACIES OF SELF REALISATION.

The notion that the counselling process was concluding created mixed emotions. That solitary thought had prevented Jay from completing or starting any work the day before the final session. She gazed at everything, her mind taking longer to take things in; nothing followed a consistent path. She exhausted every method she knew to focus her mindset; meditation, communication, a walk with short bursts of speed. Nothing could harmonise body, mind and soul. As she sat at her desk, she became aware of her leg moving as if she was stomping on an imaginary bass drum pedal. It played on her mind, making a conscious effort to stop this involuntary movement created further angst. It would start up when she had forgotten about it; a vicious circle needed breaking. Jay made the excuse of visiting the archive department to get out of the office. The neon's false light outshining the natural light, the air conditioning whirring then cutting out, plus the low-level buzz of human communication were all eating away at her. Jay could feel sweat forming under her arms; she rubbed the tips of the fingers of her left hand from left to right across her forehead; they felt greasy and sticky.

-   Icky.

Then suppressed the urge to stand up and shout at top volume.

Shaking her head as she felt she was doing too often, Jay rose, flattened out the uniform skirt, then marched out of the building, saluting a superior Officer as she went. In the fresh air, Jay arched her back as both hands held her haunches. The next move was to bend forward with hands remaining in the same place. She inhaled deeply then exhaled slowly.

- Best for me to get home.

Jay kicked off her shoes and pulled off her tights, discarding them as she walked. She removed her uniform shirt then flopped on the settee, lifting two heavy legs to fill the rest of it. She stared into space, then spoke to fresh air.

-   Jay, get a grip on reality. Think about it; it's a good thing to worry – means that you're not complacent.

She fumbled for the remote control, flicked the television into life, then channel surfed until there was a soft-spoken voice to listen to; three hours later, Jay awoke. Exhausted, she swung her legs over onto the floor and stood up. She had to sit down again as dizziness brought a white light to her head. As Jay sat with head in hands, she started to sob. It was all getting too much. The loneliness was eating away; she talked with Brown and Rory that was the extent of her communication circle. Both wanted to help, and her bond was strengthening between both, she wanted friends, she wanted to be able to phone or call on someone to share thoughts, ideas and, more recently, laughs. At twenty-nine, the thought of death entered Jay's whirlpool of ideas. Why had she never built relationships before, why had she never been allowed to feel good about herself, had an argument then made up, thrown back her head and laughed at the futility of it all.

-   Jesus - I'm so fucked up,

The sobbing ceased, and she stopped feeling sorry. Jay slapped her face, then decided to get it all out tomorrow. The final session would be the chance to spill emotions. Brown's pen would be red hot.

Jay decided a hot bath surrounded by candles would do the trick. She poured a large glass of cold white then lay in the pampering bubbles. Once again, she fell asleep, she woke in cold water. Confused and dazed, Jay made her way to the shower cubicle and stood under the running water until revived.

- I can't go on like this.

Shuffling towards her bedroom, she fell on to the bed and manoeuvred the duvet to cover her. Her body was weary; she felt it meld into the mattress. Her next sensation was the alarm flashing six-thirty. An unknown force sparked Jay into action; sleep had invigorated her. In the shower, Jay realised she was singing and increased the volume; she broke off and shouted with a mouthful of water,

- It's going to be a good day.

Jay's spirits lifted further by a text message from Brown with the greeting

'Today's the day we put it all away.'

Jay beamed; Linda had proven her wrong, they had become more than acquaintances, a connection made, they mirrored each other with smiles and body language and more recently had begun to embrace, laughing as they said "No air-kissing" when they met. Jay had her first girlfriend, and that made Jay happy. The happy thoughts left as Jay considered the final session. Brown had prepared her by talking about it at the end of the past three sessions. She stressed that even discussing the last meeting would be a sensitive issue, as the concept of endings is associated with loss – which was what the brainspotting had identified. Brown had held Jay's hand as she explained the word 'ending' and how it should conjure up images of an open door, new opportunities, adventure, or the satisfying completion of something. Brown had succeeded in convincing Jay that the negative connotations of the word did not apply to her. This doubt would be in someone attending counselling because they were vulnerable as they had experienced loss or been traumatised by past separations. Jay did not fit into this category as it was not affecting life/work balance. Jay agreed that she was not scared, sad, or daunted by the ending of counselling, but, given the intensity of the relationship that had developed between them, she was experiencing discomfort at the thought; even if at the same time she felt proud that she was able to face the world independently. Brown had picked up on the change of Jay's eye colour. Over the sessions, she had noted the colour darken and mentioned that she did not understand the reason. She would research then add findings to the final report.

There was a spring in Jay's step as she entered the counselling room. She touched the nameplate on the door, smiled at Brown, then performed their customary greeting before taking her usual seat.

Brown handed Jay a coffee,

- Ending a counselling relationship, especially if it has been positive, can be a tricky thing. Ending a therapeutic counselling relationship can be more complicated than cutting ties with a lover or significant other; for both the one receiving therapy and the therapist. What we have to do today is end this meaningful and intimate relationship in a way that reflects its importance in your life.

Jay did not respond. She sipped her coffee until finished, put the cup down and clasped Brown's hand as she said,

- I don't want an end to our friendship, just to the therapy. Can that make it easier?

- It could be. I'd like you to tell me if you feel you have learned something and improved yourself and your situation during counselling. We can discuss the importance of recognising the positive impact and expressing appreciation or otherwise how you felt it went. We can discuss what you have gained from your sessions to serve as a reinforcement to continue acting on lessons learned and, who knows, may also reveal areas where there is still potential for growth and change.

- Each session with you has been dynamic. I left the first few feeling vulnerable to the world outside of the counselling room. We explored some challenging topics, but I found that your timing of the session end was sensitive to my needs. I found it refreshing that you left time for a summary at the end of a session. It confirmed and gave me confidence that I am understood. It demonstrated empathy and understanding, and it allowed me to clarify issues. It was validation - that's what it was – validation.

Brown stood and walked toward the window; she turned to look at Jay then paused for a second.

- Jay, my problem was that I know you were independent and self-reliant, and I think we both recognize that it's a good time to end the therapeutic relationship. You may feel you achieved what you came for in terms of insight and understanding, and I know I provided as much guidance as possible. Our sessions created a safe place to discuss your thoughts, feelings and issues and allowed you to gain a new perspective and learn new ways of addressing your world and the people in it. After counselling ends, you will continue to face the world without this safe place to fall back on. I could encourage ways to meet new situations in your life, but we both know that we would be wasting time.

- I understand that, but I'd like to know that the door was open for the future

- Ha, you could do my job. I was just about to use those words. Leaving the door open for the future, not for counselling but for where life will lead, is a crucial way to end your experience on a positive note. Let's stop for coffee, take a break. It's all getting a bit too serious.

Jay walked to the coffee maker; her demeanour took Brown by surprise. Brown watched as she appeared to labour over making the coffee. From the rear, it looked as if Jay was acting clumsy. Jay smiled at Brown as she walked towards her with a cup and saucer.

- Here. Just as you like it.

As she approached, Jay appeared to trip, and the cup tilted towards the counsellor's outstretched hand. Brown, expecting to get showered in hot coffee, tried to rise off her seat, but the shock prevented her; she wailed, closed her eyes and contorted her face waiting for the pain. When nothing came, she looked up in astonishment to see Jay with the handle of the cup dangling on a teaspoon; Jay's smile beamed as she laughed out loud.

- Ha, got you there. Bet you never expected that.

Brown took a second to get the joke, albeit a cruel one. Jay watched Browns face change from anger to joy as the relief turned to laughter. Jay brought the two coffees she had prepared over and sat next to her friend.

- Bet you do that to someone else. Just don't do it at the start of a counselling session.

151

They sipped their coffee in silence, content in their world.

Jay spoke first.

- I've understood a lot more about myself from these sessions. I had never considered my way of doing things, treating people as I do, seeing things my way, and the façade and barriers created could have stemmed from abandonment. I never equated it to me being me.

Jay stood and paced the room. She placed both hands on a window ledge then pushed her nose against the glass. After a few moments, she cleared her throat and, in a cheerful tone, declared,

- I am a person first and a soldier second. It has taken me a long, long time to realise that, and that is what I thank you for most. The insecurity and doubts I have suffered over the past few months have dissolved now. If not for these sessions, I would not separate the difference between emotional and physical abandonment. The intensity of the feelings I had of unmet needs was taking its toll. Everything I attempted to do or say gave me the sense that it was just not quite right.

Jay turned from the window and walked towards Brown.

- I need to hug you.

Brown stood and let Jay embrace her; she returned the gesture, quelling the instinct of patting her on the back. Jay pulled away, walked back toward the window; without looking at Brown, she took a deep breath and, this time in a tearful, soft tone, said

- I know if we do not continue as friends after this. I will feel as if the connection is lost and my emotional needs not met. I will consider myself abandoned. Deep down, I'm afraid of being alone and believe that's my destiny. My unfulfilled relationships have been rife with insecurity.

Jay paused, returned to her seat and, whilst looking at the floor, asked,

- Do you think I'm fearful of actual abandonment through a mad self-fulfilling prophecy?

Brown remained silent.

Jay continued.

- The confidence I have from our sessions has come from the knowledge that my insecurity and self-doubt were symptoms of deeper-seated issues – and we have identified and resolved them, but I don't believe they stem from my childhood. I was dependent upon my adoptive parents to provide a safe environment, and they did. I never felt the world was an unsafe place, that nobody should be trusted or that I did not deserve love or care.

Brown wiped a tear, trying to hide it from Jay and interrupted.

- I did.
- Pardon?
- I felt like that growing up.
- Do you want to tell me?
- I do, and I don't.

Brown's head dropped, her shoulders fell, and she slumped forwards in her chair.

- My childhood was one of fear. My parents lived the pretence of being together in public, but home life was hell in reality. I never knew what they were hiding from me, but I was aware something was not right. They fought when drunk. I'm not talking about family arguments; I'm talking about the screaming of insults that no child should hear. Crockery was the weapon of choice but always aimed away. I laugh now, but at times it was like a Greek restaurant on the night of the

Athens Derby. I had no appropriate supervision; my meals were either tinned or microwaved, the gas, electric and phone were cut off many times, and when the power became a prepaid meter, the money would go on booze or to the bookies rather than heat. That emotional abandonment caused me to hide part of myself to be accepted, to not be rejected. I learned the opposite of you. I was led to believe that making mistakes was okay, that it was not okay to show feelings by being told that they were not true. Alcoholics thrive on the facts that not everyone is allowed needs, that theirs are more important, and the most hurtful of all is that any accomplishments or successes discounted and dismissed.

Brown stood and asked Jay to hug her. They stood in the embrace until the tears dried from their cheeks. Jay spoke first.

- Do you want to tell me more?
- I want to get it out. Will you listen, please.
- You know, I will.

Brown sat back in the chair; she lifted her head to stare at the ceiling, lowered it gradually, looking into Jay's eyes, she continued.

- Functioning alcoholics and gamblers have no expectations in life, so I had none; they held me responsible for this and their actions and feelings. I felt disapproval for my entire being rather than my behaviour.

The lack of emotional and physical protection from my parents turned my fears inward. I lived in constant dread of being left uncared for, which led to a cumulative fear of abandonment. No physical or emotional protection from them created a toxic shame within me; my mantra became "I don't matter. I have no value", where theirs was an oft-repeated ditty that made them laugh together. "Drink bought with gambling money tastes best". There were no boundaries between my parents and myself; they could not see me as a separate being from themselves. They gained a twisted form of self-esteem from my behaviour in their moments of clarity. Worst of all, they would or could not take any responsibility for their feelings, actions or thoughts and instead, they expected that from me. I know from my training and experience that emotional and physical abandonment with distorted boundaries does not indicate that the child is bad. The entire perception is false beliefs and values of the adult who hurt them. You and I are lucky, Jay, in that we have identified it and worked through it. If we had not, the pain could last a lifetime, and if the wounds remained unclosed, the feelings of shame would be overwhelming. The pain of abandonment is challenging to heal.

Jay took hold of Brown's hands,

- Come; let's have some lunch – my treat. It's my turn to thank you now!

They walked in step towards the commissary, but Jay took the initiative to walk them out of the barracks to the first pub they encountered.

- Ever been here before? Brown asked.
- Nope, you?
- Never. Neutral territory, the best place for an in-depth moan.

They sat and ordered soft drinks. Jay continued.

- In many ways, my childhood was worse. I was a prize, a piece that made my parents respectable. I don't know if they could have children, but it would not surprise me that they would consider a ready-made an easier option, takes out risk, that was my Mother. Paraded around friends and neighbours for every exam passed, every trophy won and every prize given. I was a success to them, and that made them happy. I doubt they considered my feelings; they made me who I was from nothing—an orphan who had been given the greatest start in life imaginable and how lucky I was to have been adopted, more so by them. I wonder if they ever grieved of their inability to conceive. I've learned that adoption is not a substitute for having a child; adoption is one of many ways to make a family. I capitulated; I was never defiant or uncooperative, angry. I never tested or manipulated. They never knew my behaviours were coping mechanisms and not personality traits. In our sessions, you mentioned that abandoned children walk through the world looking for their lost twin or someone they resemble. Did you call it the Ghost Kingdom, a place where adoptees go to imagine life if not adopted?

They could give me anything, but now I understand the one thing they omitted was the thing I craved most. A loving childhood. They never praised me for my efforts but extolled my virtues in front of others as if I was not there. I've been thinking a lot about that over the past few months. I've worked it out, I don't need it any more, but it was good to know what I missed

Jay stared into Browns eyes.

- What we missed should be foreign to us, perhaps they are, but we know they are. If I tried the same Q & A with a person brought up in what we would consider a typical family, they could not answer; they would take those as fundamentals.
- I cannot argue with that logic. However, the reason you and I are so driven and in the Army is that we have known this sub-consciously and have raged against our parents' machinery issues. We know we matter; we know we are not worthless, lonely or sad. We may appear to be, but it takes a special event or a series in your case to feel the betrayal and validate the fear. Neither of us has enjoyed a healthy romantic relationship, as we know it may become dysfunctional or fall apart altogether because you and I would prevent ourselves from becoming fully available for fear that they will leave. Even our relationship revolves around fear. So, now tell me if you agree with my questions.

Jay laughed.

- Only if you tell me you found the coffee cup gag amusing.
- I did, you know I did. It was the shock and perhaps my fear of crockery in flight that spooked me. First question; do you feel support?
- Without a doubt.
- Do you find people and relationships exhausting?
- I did but no longer.
- Do you feel invisible?
- Not anymore.
- Do you feel unlovable?
- No. Things are working nicely between Rory and me.
- Can you trust others?
- I don't know about that.
- Are your needs met, are you insecure and need approval from others?
- Great question, but I know that department is now in order.

The waiter interrupted their flow; they took time out to order two courses and two spritzers. After the first bitter sip, Jay made a face then asked.

- Do many of us struggle with abandonment issues?
- More and more, according to my trade journals. Many now realise these feelings as natural but based on false realities. There are other common feelings you and I have not discussed.
- Tell me.

Brown took a sip of her drink and made a similar facial expression.

- There is anxiety, the fear of living life alone and the expectation that one will always be alone. The feeling that they wear a mask, and if someone gets too close, the truth will be revealed. There is depression, loneliness, and of course, defeat. We never mention that.
- Did you ever get dumped by a boyfriend at school or later? I never. Jay admitted.

- I never had a boyfriend at school, I was too embarrassed. I've had a few failed relationships, but I ended them. I put myself through therapy when I did my training. Self-therapy is not all bad. My parents needed each other to survive. Although their relationship was destructive, it created an emotional bond between them. Fear and loathing are as intense as love or hate. It is still glue. Their investment in booze and gambling was far higher than in me or each other. In the end, my father fell down the stairs. He didn't last too long and resulted in my Mother locking herself away to drink herself to death. It's not nice to a see parent in the hospital with fluids oozing out of their skin with all the organs destroyed by alcohol. An improbable image - that will stay with me forever. You will learn to forgive one day, Jay. That is not easy, but if you can, you will become a better person. It's a vital part of life. Especially for those abandoned as children, we must learn to love ourselves and that child who no one loved. We must heal from our wounds, but never forget the scars - they're a part of who we are, but they do not have to define us. It's one of the first things you learn as a counsellor. I think that's enough now. Here's the dishy waiter with our food.
- I've got to hand it to you, Brown. You are exceptional at what you do.

They ate in silence, both aware each had opened up more than ever.

GOD'S AWAY.

Jay was running late; the shower had proven a difficult place to leave after the emotion of the day. She sent Rory a text, "Late; desire large vera", and smiled as the sent box confirmed delivery; there would be a fresh drink waiting alongside Rory, he would be smiling, nothing fazed him. Her brain wandered - she thought about squeezing him and holding him close. Their relationship had been like that text, almost like old telegrams. Their initial dialogue had been emotionless; communique. If she had not seduced him, it would still be that way; in the past few months, affection had grown. She looked forward to seeing him; their time together made her happy, he made her smile, and she had not had much to raise her spirits since before her birthday. Still, that was over six months ago – onwards and upwards, she muttered as she dressed. Thirty minutes later, Jay embraced Rory, put her cheek next to his,
- Rory, I'm delighted I know you.
Rory blushed, offered Jay her gin, waited for her to sit then toasted in an emotional tone.
- Cheers big ears, queers and ginger beers.
- What? Where did that come from?
Jay smiled at his charm. He blushed again.

- I don't know. I'm flustered and do not know how to respond to your kind words. I must have heard that somewhere in my distant past. How have you been?
- I'm fine. It was the last counselling session today; I'm glad that is over - Brown gets right into it. I couldn't do that, and she lives every moment. She must be one individual that has been drained by the traumas of others. I wonder if she can switch off.
- Forget about her; it's over now. Cheers here's to us, wha's like us etc.
Jay clinked his glass and caught his eye.
- Enough of these toasts, it's great to see you, and I'm happy to be here. That's all that matters.

- Okay, Jay.

They sat in silence whilst sipping their drinks. Jay spoke first,

- How did the Dublin trip go?

- All to plan, Jay. I've put it in a report for you. Read it at your leisure.

Rory passed the folder. Reluctant to take it, she left it on the table and asked,

- Did you meet my Mother?

- I did. I met the solicitors, and she was there. She requested my approval to sit in and relate her story; I couldn't say no.

Rory looked at Jay; he could see her brain ticking over. Trying to anticipate her thoughts, he added,

- They are up to speed on everything. One thing; they know nothing about the past six months.

- Thank you, Rory.

- You don't have to keep thanking me; it's my job. It is all up to you now and how you want to progress it.

- Do you want to know about her?

- No, I'll find out in due course. I'm going to the bar, same again? – shall I get some menus?

Rory watched as she stood up and walked away. It was evident that she was thinking about the scenario, possibly playing it out in her head. He watched as she laughed with the barman and kept the smile as she walked back to the table.

She looked into his eyes.

- Special is monkfish Thermidor, Mmmmm I'm having that. I fancy an excellent Chablis too, how about you?

- Sounds ideal, Jay.

- Let's finish these, have another, then order then.

- Fine by me. Jay, I need to tell you something before you make your plan to meet your Mother. It's quite severe, and I need to say to you tonight as I'm off tomorrow to Hereford on a case. Now or later?

- Better tell me now, Rory, it's not a good idea for us to be together tonight. Mother Nature has conspired against us.

Rory blushed again.

- Ooh, I understand.

He took a large gulp of gin then realised that it was too much. Taking time to compose his speech, he took her hand.

- I told you the story of my wife?
- You did, and I read your therapy yarn, remember?
- Of course. I need to quantify her actions; there's more to it than I told you.
- Fire away, Rory, I'm all ears. Big ears. It seemed to me that she was bored when you were away, and perhaps her strict upbringing led her to experiment with her sexuality.
Rory did not react.
- We had twins, much like you and Ben.
Jay leaned over and clasped Rory's hand.
- Oh, I am sorry, Rory. I shouldn't have mocked. Tell me, please.

- My wife blamed herself. I blamed myself. We blamed each other.

The nightmare of twenty-odd years still clings. We were visiting my parents and decided to take a picnic on the beaches near Fingal's Cave. As we walked along the coast, looking for a sheltered spot, the twins began to find the constraints boring, so they went up on the dunes. My wife and I found a place then called them down; we put all out stuff in a pile on the beach where they began to enjoy burying each other's feet in the sand. It did not take long before they were bored again, so they stripped off and ran into the sea. I told them not to go too far. They had swum in the ocean before; both were good swimmers, healthy, sporty kids. At first, they were jumping over the waves and paddling, it was quite a windy day, and the waves in the distance were big. It looked safe, but I warned them not to go too far. I think they found a little area to swim in near some rocks and wanted to go onto them to look for limpets and crabs. My wife had been waving at them and shouting, but they couldn't hear her, so she got concerned and walked towards them. She headed out to where they played, and as she swam towards them, I heard shouting; I knew then it was not good. She was getting closer to them, I saw my girl doing the front crawl, trying to get back, and she was very close to my wife - I thought they were fine, but when I saw my boy was going out, I became worried. When I saw my wife had got to the girl, I realised they were in trouble. Everything in my head became louder, and it appeared there was spray coming off the sea. I could sense panic. I ran towards them and waded in, shouting at them to swim with their legs, lie on their backs, take big deep breaths – anything I could think might help. I was screaming at them to breathe – keep breathing.

I got to the boy just in time to pluck him from the water; I must have had a hold of him about three times. He was grabbing me around the neck. He said he couldn't swim anymore. I was exhausted too. I kept thinking I just don't want to let go of him. I managed to stand up just as a wall of white water hit me; I hoped it might take us back to shore, but a freak wave followed, and I lost my grip. I couldn't hold on to him. There was a lot of seaweed on the rocks, which made everything slippery and difficult to cling onto, but somehow I managed to gain my footing. As I turned to look for my wife, I saw her washed up on the rocks laid flat. I got to her as she came round, her face was screwed up, and there was blood dripping from her arms and legs. She was screaming, 'I couldn't save her, I couldn't save her – she just slipped from me.'

As I carried her back, the water became eerily calm; it was as if the sea had come to take them, then once it had, returned to normal. In my arms, she kept repeating, "they've gone, they've gone." It was a blur after that. I remember the ambulance being there and our going in it. We were united in shock.

I've relived that moment many times in my life. I lived the minutes before when I should have stopped them and the minutes I had a hold of him.

Jay remained silent. Rory took a long drink.

- I had to tell you, Jay. I had to ask you to give this reunion a chance. It may not work, but you have to try; otherwise, the regret will eat away.

- I will, Rory. I will, not just for me but for you too. Can I come home with you? Can we go now and get some takeaway? I want to be alone with you tonight, can we? Can we comfort each other?

Jay took Rory's hand, picked up the folder and led him out the door. On entering Rory's home, Jay pulled him towards her and held him.

- Tell me all about it, Rory. It will help me.

- I'm hungry, let's eat at the table, and I'll share more. It is all very sad.

Jay set plates, cutlery, and glasses out, poured two healthy wine measures, and then offered Rory the serving spoons. He spoke as he chose his food.

- We had no counselling. We tried to help each other; the bodies had been recovered two days after the…accident – I still don't know what to call it. The newspapers had the story and hounded us day and night.

It was a terrible time. Everything became a blur until about a month after the funeral. I think that is we realised that things would never be the same.

Homelife became hell.

Every night I was subjected to torrents of abuse, it became so that all I could do was listen to what I considered the deserved onslaught - it was vicious. I used to watch her face contort and animate. Eventually, sympathy for her plight took a back seat to cynicism; my irreverence became a consistent thrill and inspiration to maintain my silence. I could not offer advice to anyone; the twins' death took me to a form of nirvana when it came to acceptance. A belief that circumstances and events were what they were, not interpreted. There was no coincidence, destiny, karma, nor fate. If life's followed by oblivion, then I knew our marriage was heading that way. The rage continued daily. She told all that was wrong with me – as she saw it: emotional and aesthetic detritus, a disavowment of all my faults. I used to watch her face and mouth as she fumed, spittle used to wash out words I never heard. I became a voyeur to my faults, watching her scream at me whilst looking somewhere to my right then, without looking at me, turn and set her gaze somewhere to my left. She looked like a profile puppet expressing the point with pleading jazz hands. I remember words like "weak man" and once noticing a single unshaved hair under her nostril before retreating into my autism. I can recall watching in wonder at her being and considered a naturally aspirated engine that expended more energy than provided by the air and fuel contained within. She was running on thyroxine, supercharged by the fact of being in the right - that is all she ever wanted to be.

I've learned that one of the secrets of life is to learn to cope with and understand tragedy in all forms. When I watched the hurt within her unfold, I understood. She had loved me but now did not like me; some part of me that no longer existed had awakened her liking of me but was now lost or forgotten. She reminded us both of that. If you were to ask me the root of the problem, I would say that it was when my wife was told she would never give birth again. I don't know the details, but something happened during the section. Deep down inside, intuition had regurgitated the knowledge that she would never be a Mother again. I don't think any parent could ever get over that. I'd had a vasectomy at her request after the pregnancy was announced as she declared then that she wanted no more than two.

Demons called many times to remind me of my inferiority. I was now getting the reaction that would happen to all men at some time. The sense of unhappiness was upon us both. It was fear and habit that kept us together. I knew she was right, and I was wrong, and that was that. We were both catching up with ordinary human emotions at the same time, knowing that the only way to hurt each other was to hurt ourselves. Perhaps the mutual dislike could now end. She played on what she called "the most intimate of human difficulties" She must have read or heard that somewhere. She became aggressive and maintained her stance by spouting about "the embodiment of female orthodoxy". All this was new to me, and I had no idea what she was trying to say. I remembered why I had fallen in love with her; it was her relentless search for knowledge and something new. For the briefest time, I loved her again until she decreed, in an almighty shriek, that it was an idiot that had written: "marriage must be permanent even when disturbed by masculine lunacy". I was lost, realizing then I would never be allowed to forget this incident. My wife had become a fully paid-up member of the SCUM Manifesto, with the mental act of cutting preferred to the physical. Over the following month, I became subjected to emotional, verbal and physical abuse but could not work out which was worst. She became aggressive during sex as if trying to punish me with her body; she became verbal, real dirty stuff, with words I would have never dreamt of her saying. She became insatiable, talked of doing things at risky locations. It was as if she wanted to get caught and reprimanded for having sex. You'll never believe what happened. Some vindictive neighbour posted photographs to me of what was happening when I was off on Army business. There was nothing sordid as such, but they showed a succession of single male visitors. When I tell you I did not know what to do, that would be an understatement. I deliberated long and hard. Should I confront her? And if I did, what would it achieve. Our lives were in pieces; work was keeping me alive; she had nothing. She had no one to talk to; her days must have been blurs. She was drinking but, like most, hidden. When I was home, the odd glass of wine was no doubt supplemented by the odd vodka in a tea or coffee cup. I decided to let it run its course and was content to do so as long as she didn't get hurt. Ha, I mean didn't get herself in trouble. She did, though, not through adultery but shoplifting. I had to call in a few favours to keep that quiet. The police called me; she had gone into the local supermarket, put four bottles of wine in one of their carrier bags, then walked to the in-store café where she paid for lunch and a soft drink. It was all on CCTV. She just got up and walked out of the store, bold as brass. I could tell she was drunk, but she hid it so well, no one else could. I managed to smooth it all over by explaining the tragedy, and a warning was issued; she was banned from the store. She never apologized nor thanked me; as we walked out of the police station, she gave me a look I shall always remember. It was one of pure devilment. The same look after telling me about the movie. All she wanted to do was hurt me. Plain and simple, and she succeeded. I watched that movie. It was amateur. She was staring into the camera whenever she could - that unnerved me as if she was watching my reaction to her actions. The camera was shaking and handed about; male faces were not seen, only hers. There was no look of enjoyment in her; it was a look of helplessness, a look that said to me – Look what YOU did. I still see that look now sometimes when it all comes back to haunt.

Rory stopped to eat. His eyes darted between his plate, his glass and Jay's face, which appeared close to tears.

- Did you not respond at all, Rory? Was communication never two way?

Rory sighed,

- It was pointless. Experience had proven that it was a fruitless trying to interject, knowing if I had tried to speak, my sentence would have been cut off, with a single word taken out of context then repeated to silence me. The wind from my sails was gone; I had given up. My saving grace was that I could be away from her due to my workload. The army had offered compassionate leave, but I needed to get back to work, or, I shouldn't say, this but away from her.

- What about your families?

- Typical Scots buried their head in the sand. They could or would not face the fact that it had happened. It was never discussed.

My parent's accepted sympathy from others, but my wife's wee free Father was the worst. He claimed it was God's will – that had an adverse effect, with God getting the blame for everything. She cut her folks off. I had to force her to consider her actions as she spread the stress around. I can laugh now, but she used to leave answerphone messages at her parent's house every hour – on the hour. She would sing the Wait's ditty

God's Away, God's away
God's away on Business. Business.
God's Away, God's Away
God's Away on Business. Business.

Then hang up. It was nuts. Her Mother phoned me a couple of times; poor woman was stuck between the stoicism of her husband, her troubled daughter and the grief of losing her only grandchildren.

Jay stood, walked around the table and hugged Rory.

- It's over. Are you okay with leaving it at that?

Rory stuffed two spoonfuls of food into his mouth and nodded. Jay returned to her seat, and they finished their meal in silence.

- Shall we watch a movie, snuggle up on the sofa, then empty our brains.

- Great idea, you set it up, and I'll finish up in here. Shall I bring your wine through?

- I've had enough, Rory. I just want to be close to you.

By the time Rory had cleared the rubbish, Jay had set the mood. Rory sat next to her; she moved her head to his shoulder.

Rory was first to talk; he stroked the back of her neck with the tops of his fingers.

- It's my birthday next week. Did you know I'll be the same age as your Mother? I'm worried that I'm going to lose you.

Jay turned to kiss Rory.

- You won't lose me. Let me get the Mother thing over, then you and I can enjoy more time together. You okay with that?

- Thanks, Jay. It looks like I'm out of town for a while with a new case. Some squaddie went to town on a civvie, not looking good for either party. Plenty witnesses both army and local, all with inconsistent stories and varying agendas. Right up my street!

SIDESHED.

Jay's email box was full. A pop up instructed her to delete or archive those unwanted or unread. The thought caught her unaware.

- That'll waste an hour.

Jay had never worked that way. Time had always been precious, not to be wasted; the counselling sessions had worked in an unsure manner.

As she scrolled through the unread, she was surprised to see the ones from D.I. Lambert ranged from six months to two weeks. A cold sweat came over her; the old Jay would never let that happen. She grouped them by name then opened each one in chronological order.

Lambert had been methodical; Ben's bank transactions highlighted his travels. The ten or so emails detailed movements from Stranraer through Ireland and the last being South Wales. Jay's cold sweat turned to a hot flush at the thought of Ben. Her daydreams took her back to his letter. Where was he? Maybe still in South Wales. The idea of Mary Lister, Ben and Jay together made her gag. It was too much; she would not try to push things again, lesson learned. She archived Lambert's messages, deleted what seemed to be hundreds of emails that all appeared to be point scoring or tittle-tattle from fellow Officers. As she freed up space, a plethora of new emails flooded in. One from Rory, thanking her for last night; that brought a smile. She was falling for him; he was a nice, gentle person that had endured more than most. Stilled shocked at the story, strange he had never mentioned their age. She never asked questions. Smart interrogation techniques had proven that those who want to tell would do so without prompting, with any interruption making for an adverse reaction. As she replied, she considered his strength to cope with such tragedies, plus the burden of his wife's reaction - then that porno thing. She shook her head and puffed out a breath of non-understanding. No one would ever know how that person felt, what baggage she must carry. This was new territory for Jay. She was considering the feelings of others and how they coped with what life throws at them. Jay was confused with these thoughts. She thanked him for sharing his past and how much it had helped her about meeting her Mother. She finished by suggesting to meet on their return and discuss what had happened. Jay put an `x' after her name. She had never done that before. She considered removing it before sending, but she hoped he would pick it up. There were the usual other emails regarding work cases, meetings to attend, and documentation requests for delegation. The final new email shook Jay. It was from Mtaylor@airfurn.org and carried one word in the subject box; "Hope."

Jay felt a throb; a tightening pain forced her to move and clench her thighs together.

She took a few moments before opening the message. Rory's report had been concise; it outlined the information Jay wanted. She felt no urge to investigate further but read that her Mother was to contact her and now knew the name. A gasp of thrilled emotion came as Jay read her Mother's words. She wiped a tear and tried to control them, overcome by an inward sob. The message read,

"Jay, it would make me the happiest ever if you and I could meet.

If you agree, we could meet on neutral ground, a health spa perhaps – it would please me if you would consider being my guest and bring a friend. Gleneagles or Dunblane?

Anywhere and anytime you suggest, just let me know.

With fondness and love, M."

Jay stared at the screen, reading the words over again. She liked the way it read and how long it had taken to write. Had May had cried too? , it appeared both impersonal and personal. Was the final M for May, Mary or Mother…? Jay printed two copies and placed them side by side on her desk. She cursed as she read them over.

`The old Jay would have responded by now! `

She composed her reply.

The first letters flowed, but she stopped as she saw they were "Mu".

She deleted them.

"May, Let's meet next weekend; how about Chewton Glen in the New Forest- I've heard it is popular and quiet. I'll bring a friend.

J".

Regret followed the millisecond after clicking send. Without thinking, Jay called Brown's extension.

THE INADEQUACIES OF SELF-DOUBT.

As Jay waited for the driver, she reflected on her friendship with Brown. It had taken some persuasion but managed to coerce Brown into providing moral support to meet with her Mother. She had used the follow-up card, playing on Brown's ambition, planting seeds to fire her interest in a subject in which she had no experience. Jay and Brown had discussed expunging the dregs of trauma; Brown had encouraged her by revealing snippets of her life and background. Hopes and fears traded as were half-truths and half-lies. Brown had dropped her guard to expose the weakness that Jay predicted. Jay, empowered by the counselling's success, had reverted to an alpha-female with the addition of cunning and subtlety. Brown's failing was she had never worked in the field; all her cases had been textbook.

Rory had organised everything. In some ways, Jay had resented his involvement but learned to trust others' judgment and ability. One positive from the counselling was she realised her elitist attitude was and had always been misplaced.

The driver appeared; Jay was pleased it was not a limo or some other flashy form of transport; - it was a people carrier. The driver took her case, placed it in the boot, and then asked if she was comfortable before driving to Brown's address. Jay was curious to see how her friend lived; she instructed the driver to wait whilst walking to the front door, citing Brown as 'notoriously late'.

The first sensation to hit Jay after being invited in was the heat, it stung at her eyes, and she had to rub her closed eyelids with her fingers to lubricate them. The next was the smell, hard to define, but became evident as unemptied cat litter; Jay sighted at least four cats, their evidence everywhere: scratching posts, food bowls, clumps of hair on the wooden floor. Brown had never mentioned a love of pets. In Jay's experience, lovers of four-legged friends believed their animals smarter than humans and could do no wrong. Jay could never live like this; the place had a dirty atmosphere, grime hung in the air; she became transported back to her childhood, farmers and landowners had kept similar homes. A homeliness of acceptance of all creatures, each adding their smell to the living areas. She was glad to do an about-turn to leave when Brown announced her readiness. Jay cringed as Brown turned to lock the door and shout in, "Bye babies, home soon". The driver took her case, placed it with Jays, made sure they were both comfortable then drove towards the dual carriageway.

- It's about five hours to the South coast, anything you need before we go?
- We're fine," they replied in unison.
- Just let me know when you want to stop for a bio break or drinks or food.

Jay mouthed the words Bio break to Brown whilst raising a comic eyebrow. Brown stifled a giggle as Jay replied,

- Okay.

They looked at each other, smiled then gazed out of their windows. The distance of one seat between gave the illusion of separation, and both moved a fraction inwards whilst maintaining their outside view adopting the same body position. Jay broke the silence.

- The nerves are starting.

Linda moved her head towards Jay, then placed her palm on Jay's.

- We'll get through it…we'll be fine.

Jay began to cry.

- Thanks, Linda. I mean it.
- Get the tears out, Jay. More will come. Remember what we said in the last session; you've got through it. It's normal; never fear abandonment.
- It's a nice day for a long drive. Jay stated.

Brown nodded in.

Brown whispered.

- Remember the last day of counselling. We talked about forgiveness.
- I do.
- This will be a big test -meeting your Mother.
- I don't feel the need to forgive her for anything. She acted out of self-preservation, protecting her children.
- That's true, but I would suggest you prepare yourself for emotion never felt before. It will sweep over you. You know, since the Ben incident, you have been angry, oppositional, and living in your world.
- That's it in a nutshell.
- And you're out of it now.
- True.
- Well, this new experience will test you.
- Have you dealt with a situation like this before?
- Got to be honest and say no, but I did some research when I knew this would happen. I found out some interesting stuff; scenarios not considered at our sessions.
- In layman's terms?
- It's theoretical; it's a traumatic event for both Mother and child when an infant becomes separated. Familiar sights, sounds, and sensations disappear; this results in the infant believes it to be dangerous.
- Why?
- I read that the only part of the brain developed at birth is the brain stem; this regulates the sympathetic nervous system, which controls the fight, flight or freeze response. The opposite parasympathetic system ability to self-soothe isn't available at that age, so the infant needs the Mother to act as the soothing agent. Events up to three years old are implicit memories; they become embodied because they occur before language develops.

Brown looked at Jay, then added,

- Does that make any sense?

- Some. You are saying that the Mother's presence compensates for this because the brain and nervous systems are not fully developed. How can anyone know this if there is no language to prove its existence?
- I don't know; all I can do is surmise. You never had your birthMother help you, your adoptive Mother aided somehow, but I have no way of knowing how. It may be deep-rooted, but this emotion could come to the fore when you meet May. Do you know when her birthday is?
- No.
- That might be a good opening question. Find out about her before opening up. I think it will come as a shock when you meet someone you resemble for the first time. In some of the case studies, reunions are quite daunting. I understand that the healing process occurs with the repetition of a story and allows the experience to become integrated into their system. It's reported that adoptees tell their story then repeat it, so their account will be known and retold with ease. Some test limits, trying to discover if they will be abandoned again. Others acquiesce, sometimes to the point of withdrawal and forced to develop a false self.
- That's heavy stuff, Linda. I'm just going to get there, meet her and see what happens. Fancy a coffee. Driver, a bio break, please.

The driver's immediate response indicated he had been listening.

- Next service station is ten minutes away, is that okay?
- Sure. Replied Jay.
- Keep one thing in mind; part of knowing who you are is knowing where you came from, and you, confident as you appear, are still striving to find connection and acceptance.
- Linda, enough now. I've taken it in; it's good advice. Can we let it happen then analyse it later?

GHOST KINGDOM.

As the car approached the greeting area of the hotel, Jay's legs began
to shake.

- Look at this; I'm like a virgin on a first date.
- Ha, can you remember that?
- Funnily enough, I can; but for all the wrong reasons.
- Me too!

Their shared laughter carried on until they arrived at the reception
area. As they announced their arrival, Brown noticed a lady approach.
Intuition forced her to step back and watch as the stranger
introduced herself. Their body language fascinated Brown. She stared
slacked jawed as the two ladies mirrored their actions; they attempted
to shake hands, stopped, tried an embrace, stopped again, and then
simultaneously offered the other outstretched hands.

- Jay.
- May.

They laughed.

- One syllable makes it easy, and this is…

Brown stepped closer,

- Linda! - I've ruined the rhyme!

All three laughed. May, still clasping Jay's hands, said,

- I have you in a suite; your luggage is there by now. Let's do
  the sign-in formalities later. Drinkies?.

Brown stood back,

- You two go. I'll get things organised.

Jay interjected,

- Please, Linda, come for a drink. We can all do with one,
  especially after that drive.
- If you are sure.
- We are.

As they walked arm in arm towards the lounge, May chatted in a
cheerful manner creating small talk, and the others kept it going; May
interrupted Brown with,

- What'll it be then - Fizz, wine, cocktails or is it too early for that. Do you think this is one of these places that frown upon dark drink consumed before six?
- I fancy a kir royal. Offered Jay.
- Ooooh, I've never had one of them before. Laughed May putting on a strange Brummie accent, following up with,
- I'll tell you later.

The three ladies sat overlooking the grounds; May took the initiative by summoning a waitress and offering Jay to make the order.

- And keep them coming, please. May added, and without taking a breath, inquired
- How was your journey?"
- It was okay, apart from the nosey driver. How was yours; how did you get here from Dublin?
- I flew into Heathrow then got the same chauffeur service to drive me here. My driver never said a word, I tried to get him to chat, but he clammed up. Still, we are here now.

The waitress brought drinks, and May ordered another round. It was Brown who made the first comment.

- No more for me, I'll have the one then go to freshen up; I think pampering is in order. I'll leave you to chat.
- Fair enough.

May replied, handing out the drinks.

- A toast to fate and all forces that brought us together.

They tapped glasses; May emptied her glass in one mouthful whilst the other two sipped from theirs. Jay caught Linda's eye then raised an eyebrow.

- Where's the next? May waved at the waitress who was cleaning a table on the opposite side of the room.
- Come on, girlie, don't keep us waiting. I think I'll get us a bottle of fizz, take the waiting out of the equation.

As May walked over to talk to the waitress, Jay put her hand to cover her lips and whispered to Brown,

- She's a bit full-on.

Brown watched May talk to the waitress, hands waving and pointing over.

176

- Nervous superfluous energy. She is out of her comfort zone; she does not know how to cope. It's best if I leave, it will help her focus. I'll go now, so she does not have to react. Tell her I've gone for a swim and a sauna and a bit of pampering.
- Okay, text me and let me know what you are doing. I'll keep you in the picture too.

Brown stood then walked away, waving to May as she hurried back to Jay. She was out of earshot when May asked.

- Where's she off too?
- It's four o'clock May; she doesn't drink early. She's gone for a swim and a sauna and will meet us for supper. It's not about her – is it?
- No, Jay, you're right. It's about you and me – or is it you and I?

May paused.

- The girlie's coming with fizz. We can relax and chat and find some common ground. You don't know how much it means to me that you came. I didn't think you would. I was waiting for the call to say you had pulled out at the last minute.
- Why would you think that?

To be blunt, because of my belief that I abandoned you, and you will do the same to me for revenge?

- Oh, May, I'm not that type of person. I've had a bad few months, and meeting you has brought a glimmer of hope.

May sat next to Jay and put her arms around her. Jay's cheek became wet with the tears May was trying to hold back. The stifled sobs jerked through Jay as May tightened her hold. For the five minutes or so that May held on, Jay's mind fanned out images of her childhood, her adoptive parents, her horse, Ben Black's face through the CCTV. The spreading memories brought images and emotions long forgotten. Jay's fascination with this eidetic memory became uncontrollable, but she did not want it to stop. She clung to her Mother, pulling her in closer - the harder she pulled, the more intense the images. Tears never came to Jay, and the experience brought on a calm, cheerful and warm sensation clasped in her Mother's arms. It was as if May was comforting her, but in reality, it was the other way. May pulled back and kissed Jay on the forehead then on her cheek.

- I had no choice to leave you two. I was young, very young and believed we were all in danger. I was lost and had no one to help. What could I do? I knew you would be safe if no one ever found out who you were, and no one did. All I could do was hide away and dream that we would meet again. Now we have, I feel that it will all go wrong again. There has not been one day I've not cried with regret at what life forced me to do. I've missed you growing up.

The waitress brought and poured the champagne. May was quick to drink her glass then finish; she tilted the bottle at Jay. Jay smiled as she shook her head.

May sat back, then looking directly into Jay's eyes and holding back a sob began to unburden.

- I need forgiveness: I admit to wrongdoing. I sincerely apologise and ask for forgiveness. I do this without making excuses or justifying my behaviour or actions. I cannot force you - you must forgive me on your terms. I acknowledge it was all my fault; I made mistakes and learned from the experience. It made me treat others with compassion and. I have tried to forgive myself. Sometimes, I felt resentment for leaving my children, but I never directed anger elsewhere, only at me. Perhaps you don't need to know this, but emotion bred when I was alone, and I was alone a lot. I lived with shame, self-loathing, guilt; anxiety kept me awake, wondering what happened to you. I fought against the curse of low self-esteem that was a constant threat, I was aware that I could be considered depressed, so I had to lock it away with no help from others. I like to drink in company; it makes me feel part of something. I know I take too much, but it keeps the rage away and the internalising that brings the black cloud. If I drank alone, it would be worse, so I cannot do that.

May emptied her glass then talked as she refilled,

- I'm an open book, Jay. Thoughts can be read through my eyes. I have come to forgive myself for past mistakes. That alone began the process of self-acceptance and self-love. The fear of devastation has left, but I still feel a yearning, an obsession and a longing to meet my children and to know they have done well. I blamed your father for everything; if he had not been so protective, then we would all be together. I've lived with anger, and the thought of retaliation at those who I felt let me down. Once that I believed I had forgiven myself, then all those bad feelings lifted. Life began to distract me, and I learned to love myself again. It took a long, long time to work out that love had become defined by fear and anxiety rather than safety and security. These were the emotions that created negative patterns, and I learned to choke them.

May had finished her drink again; this time, Jay offered the refill. Jay looked at her Mother and smiled.

- I have no ill-feeling towards you; I'm sure many would have made the same decision, especially in that situation. You don't need me to forgive you because I do not blame you for anything.

May's face lit as she sat upright, her smile was enough for Jay to see hurt lifted. Tears flowed without sobs from May; Jay sensed pride in her actions, and the emotional release created goosebumps followed by an overwhelming need to cry. Quelling the sob, Jay made her tone cheerful,

- You were entitled to feel anger and hurt. It's great you don't think that way anymore, and you've let it go. I know from recent experience that when we forgive, we release ourselves, not the other person. We are still responsible for the choices made, and nothing can change the facts, but we do have an opportunity to change what those choices mean to us. Maybe now we have met, we can reframe our stories. We can tell them from each other's point of view, tell the story from the third person rather than the first. That will bring us together and create some emotional distance from the events.
- You're a clever one. May said.
- May, tell me when your birthday is. What should I call you? May Mary...Mum
- 30th March. I'm fifty next birthday. Call me what you feel.
- What was my Father like?
- He was my best friend. We went through a lot together. I don't know how much you have found out, but we had a hard upbringing in Quarriers. It was better than a lot of places, but the social stigma was the worst. Your father

always looked out for me; we were the only family we needed.
I have photos, would you like to see.
- I would.
May reached into her bag and pulled out a plastic folding wallet.

- They used to call this a grannies boaster!
She opened the wallet, and twenty or so faded Polaroids,
Instamatic snaps and photo booth images cascaded down, all
housed in small clear plastic envelopes.

- That's John and me as we grew up, there's one of him and
  the twins towards the end. He was so proud when you were
  born. He cried and used to say over and over that he would
  make sure none of what happened to us would ever happen
  to you. You look a lot like him; I can't see me in you, but you
  have his eyes, and the way you carry yourself - is much the
  way he did.
Jay viewed each photograph; she scrutinised every detail and asked
questions about each one. May watched in silence, transfixed on her
daughters face as a Mother watching in wonder at a child. Jay
scanned every square millimetre of each photograph; May emulated
every facial gesture, raised eyebrow, a furrowed brow, smile and
unhappiness in Jay's eye. She answered Jay with as much information
that she could remember. She drank the remnants of the bottle and
ordered another. Her words began to slur as Jay removed the
photograph of her father holding his twin children in front of a
gleaming red car.

- He looks like a contented man. Jay observed.
- We were young! The car was our luxury; we never went out
  or did the things others our age did. We were a happy unit; it
  was us against the world. We both worked in the hospital;
  you had to work in those days to get what you wanted. No
  one owed us anything, an ethic ground into us in the homes.
  We never fought with each other... honest, we never did. We
  fought others to get what we wanted, and we knew how to do
  it.
Jay's phone vibrated, announcing a text message from Brown.

"Will eat in the room. Don't reply if all ok. Hope it is – she's genuine!"

- Who's that?

- It'd Linda; she's eating in her room.

- She has a lovely way about her. Very thoughtful. Do you do the same job in the Army?

- No, May, she's my counsellor. We've become friends. She has helped me in many ways.

- Do you have a busy social life?

- Quite the opposite.

- Do you have a boyfriend?

- I'd like to think so. Do you?

- I've had a perfect friend over the years that helped me in many ways too. It's good to have someone to trust. We've grown together, but he only knows what I've told him. He knows nothing of John or you two.

- Sometimes, that is the best way. I have plenty to tell you, as no doubt you have but…

- I know Jay. Plenty of time. Are you hungry? Any idea of the time? I never wear a watch.

May finished her glass then poured another. She topped up Jay's as she looked at her phone.

- It's six-thirty, and I'm getting peckish. Shall we shower and change and meet later?

- How about we eat now and have an early night. It's starting to catch up with me.

May emptied the glass again.

- I'll get menus.

- She returned with menus and another bottle.

- No more for me, May, as you said, it's a lot to take in, meeting and chatting.

- Ah, come on. A few more will loosen the tongues.

- That's true, but perhaps we should keep some back for tomorrow. We have two nights.

- Easier said than done. I'm too excited. What do you fancy eating? Where? Restaurant or here?

- I'm happy here; it's informal and relaxed.

- I fancy a steak and a bottle of Amarone.

- May, don't want to spoil things but do you think you should.

- That's what I'm having. What do you fancy?

- Dover sole.

- You want white with that?

- I'm okay with the fizz.

May drained her glass again then called the waitress.

- Us again!

The waitress tried hard to contain her opinion by remaining curt yet polite.

- Can I take your order, please?

- Fillet steak for me; blue with salad and potatoes, Jay?

- Dover sole, please, just salad – no dressing.

- Okay, anything else.

- A bottle of Amarone.

- And some water, please. Jay added, smiling at the waitress. The waitress smiled back at Jay, then gave her a look that made Jay feel that she was sorry for her.

Jay's cheeks flushed with an embarrassment never felt before. The greatest quantity of alcohol she had taken before meeting May had been in Rory's company, but that had been limited to a few gins, then a couple of glasses of wine. It had never been a race as was now unfolding with May. Jay had lost count of the number of drinks May had consumed, and now she was topping up with a rich red that Jay knew from experience, not enjoyed in large quantities. Worse still was that May was beginning to slur and her voice raised. Her body language had become animated; she was kissing and demanding "more hugs". She repeated sentences and jokes then laughed at high volume, all new territory to Jay; her distress was becoming apparent as she tried to calm May down. She had made a point of drinking the champagne's remainder whilst convincing May to drink water. May was becoming restless; she could not concentrate on what she needed to say, her sentences were becoming erratic, and her persistence to ask when the food would arrive was beginning to irk Jay.

- Tell me about your home May.

- I've had a bungalow built; my business is doing well.

She tapped her nose,

- Keep it to yourself, though. I hope you'll come and visit.

- I will May, all in good time. Let's take it slowly, slowly.

- Catchee monkey. May offered at a high pitch.

May's high shrill laugh cut through Jay's nerves making her head shrink down into her shoulders and cringe.

As she looked up, a waiter had arrived with their food.

- Steak?

- That's for me! May squealed.

- You brought the wine too?

- That's coming, Madam. The Sole for you?

Jay nodded.

- Anything else I can bring?

- Some mushtard. May slurred.

- Right away, Madam.

- Remember the wine, young man.

Jay picked up her fish knife and, just before she made the first cut looked at May and said,

- You sure you need that wine May, we've had a lot.

- I want it, Jay.

- Okay, let's enjoy our food.

May became restless, looking over at the bar area. The wine arrived, presented by a smart sommelier.

- Amarone Madam.

He made a show of opening the bottle whilst relaying the wine's provenance, then pulling the cork in such a dramatic fashion that brought a giggle to May.

- Look at him, Jay, isn't he lovely. That's my kind of man, one that can open a bottle in style.

Jay's eyes remained fixed on her food.

- Who will taste?

May raised a finger. Jay surmised either she understood her condition, or it was that she could not talk. She sniffed the wine in a well-practised manner, took a sip then nodded.

- It's my red of choice, some consider it too rich, but it works for me. Will you have some, Jay?

- Not at the moment.

Jay took a sip of water; looking over the glass, she saw May gulping the remains of the taster down, waiting for the sommelier to refill her glass. When he was satisfied, he left without speaking. Jay watched him walk away; he caught the waitress's eye and shook his head. Jay looked down at her plate; this was a situation she had to get under control; the problem was that she did not know how. They continued to make small talk whilst eating. May remained composed, but the tell-tale signs revealed the obvious. By the time May had cleaned the remnants of her plate, the wine had also gone. Jay had tried to help, but the red on top of the dryness of champagne proved difficult. Jay's facial expression, brought on by the thoughts of how to get her Mother away from the bar, made May question.

- What's going on in your brain, Jay? Are you plotting?

Jay scoped the waiter making his way to their table. Coffee would be the start.

- I don't eat dessert May, I'd like coffee.

- I don't eat them either, I'll have coffee too!

Jay sighed with relief. She had considered leaving the table if May had ordered another bottle. As the waiter cleared the table, he made small talk. He asked in a polite tone,

- Can I get the dessert menu.

- No, thanks.

- Black coffee for me, Jay?

Jay smiled, the joy of relief reflected in her eyes.

- Black for me too.

- And two large Calvadothes. May added, much to Jay's embarrassment.

- Not for me, May, I've had more than enough.

- Well, I'm having one, or two maybe.

- I can't stop you, but I'm going upstairs after coffee.

- No, Jay, that's not fair. Please stay here with me.

- No, May, I'm turning in after coffee.

- Okay, I'll just have the one large one with my coffee, then we'll go.

The waiter wrote the order then left the two ladies.

May remained silent until the coffee and calvados arrived.

- I told you I had no off button, Jay. I enjoy drinking in company, and I can't help it. It's my thing.

- May, you do what you want to. The thing is, I don't drink like that, and I don't get it.

- I don't do it often, only with those whose company I enjoy.

Jay decided to let it go. There was no point creating a stir about something that was nothing to do with her. May was her own woman. What right had Jay to question her Mother's life choices?

- You know who would enjoy a good time?

- No May, who?

May held the brandy glass to her lips and tilted it upwards, making sure she slurped the last drop out. She washed it down with the last of her coffee.

- Your lawyer pal Rory. He's up for it. I saw it in his eyes. I'm on a promise with him.

Jay looked her Mother in the eye, shook her head then stood to walk away.

- You've gone too far, May.

As Jay walked toward the foyer, she heard a crash, looked back to see May sprawled on the floor. As Jay made towards her, she tried to get up but fell sideways into a large bench chair. Jay picked her up and marched her out of the lounge, stopping only to offer an apologetic gesture to the waitress who was cleaning up. Jay took the keys from May's bag, determined the suite number then manoeuvred her into the lift. As they stood facing each other, May tried to put her arms around Jay's neck but clasped fresh air.

- I'm shorry, Jay. I've ruined it. I tried sho hard. Maybe too hard.

- Forget about it, May. Let's get you to bed.

- You're a good girl, Jay. You make me proud.

187

Jay supported May along the corridor to her room. The key-card clicked and flashed, and Jay pushed the door open with May's body. The suite was enormous, and as they walked through, Jay noticed empty wine and gin bottles from the minibar on the dayroom table. She managed to get May to the bed area then lay her flat, lifting her legs onto the mattress. She pulled May's shoes off then threw them towards her suitcase. May began to hiccup.

- I'm going to be shick. The room's spinning round and round.

Jay sat on the easy chair next to the bed. This was hard work. She had never felt responsible for anyone else but herself, and now she had a drunken Mother. Jay watched her Mother hiccup and splutter. She rose from the chair to move May onto her side.

- You're a good girl, Jay. I don't deserve you. I need the toilet; I need to go to the bathroom.

Jay picked May up in a fireman's lift and headed towards the bathroom. She stood her at the doorway and pushed her towards the lavatory. May managed to feel her way along the wall then turned to sit. Jay closed the door then sent a text message to her friend.

"In May's room. She's drunk, will stay here. Nightmare"

The reply came quicker that Jay expected.

"You need help?"

How many times had Brown coped with this scenario in her youth? Was it normal? She replied to the text,

"Should manage. Sleep well, see you in the morn."

"You too. Holler if you need help."

May emerged from the bathroom, makeup smeared, eyes bloodshot telling the tale of the extent of her sickness.

- That was not good. I shouldn't have had that coffee!

- Jay smiled, perfect May. The dog that bit you was caffeine flavoured. Let's get you between the sheets. I'll stay with you, just in case.

- Sorry, Jay, I feel so ashamed.

- Forget about it. It was all too much for us; we have different ways of coping. You just coped too hard!

- I know. I cannot help myself.

May shuffled to her bedroom. Jay waited to allow time for her to undress.

- You in bed?

- I am now.

- Okay, I'll sleep next to you on top of the sheets. It'll be just like my schooldays.

- I'd like that.

Jay lay next to May and stroked her forehead.

- What are we going to do with you, May?

Within minutes May was snoring. Jay lay on her back, eyes wide open. She felt both lost and at home. There was contentment within that made her tearful. She wanted to leave May's side and be on her own, but something prevented her from doing this, and she could not work out why.

The room phone woke them. May answered and handed the handset to Jay.

- Jay, it's Linda, I've been ringing your mobile, but you must have it on silent.

- What time is it?

May was making coffee; she gestured a cup to lip sign; Jay nodded.

- It's just after nine. Rory has been trying to get a hold of you; he's persistent, if nothing else.

- Have you eaten breakfast?

- I have. Call me later.

Jay replaced the receiver then took the coffee from May.

- May, can you order us breakfast in the room, please. I don't feel like eating downstairs.

- I'm sorry, Jay, did I embarrass you?

- Short answer is yes.

- What do you want to eat?

- I would like two bacon rolls and fresh coffee, please.

- I'll have the same. May replied as she dialled room service.

Jay checked her phone. There were ten missed calls from Rory, three voicemails and numerous texts urging her to get in touch.

- I'm going for a shower, Jay. Sorry again for last night; food should be here in twenty minutes. Can you listen out?

- Okay.

Jay smiled at the thought that maintaining her distance from May increased her angst; she would let her sweat on it for a while. She dialled Rory.

- Jay, good that you have called. I've got serious business for you. I need you here for this investigation.

- I'm on a two-day pass, Rory.

- I know, but you need to be here for this. I have requested your presence from your C.O., and it's agreed. He knows the full story.

- What is the story?

- There's a young man in a coma, got on the wrong side of a squaddie just back from a tour in the badlands. Details are sketchy, but you will unravel it.

- Why me, Rory?

- Because the young man is Ben Black. He has a debit card for I.D. That's all we know.

A knock on the door broke Jay's trance.

- I'll get back to you, Rory.

- Okay.

Jay let room service in, signed the chit then sat alone to eat a roll. She poured two more coffees and waited. May appeared dressed; her appearance belied her state the previous evening.

- Sit down, May.

- Okay, love, are you going to tell me you're leaving because of my behaviour.

- No, May. Eat your roll.

They ate in silence, and Jay poured more coffee.

- May. I think they've found my twin.

May remained silent. Jay added

- It could be, not sure. He is in Hereford after an incident.

- Shall we go there now? I'll get the car firm to pick us up.

- I'm going to my room, shower and change. You pack your stuff and do what you have to; I'll meet you at the reception in an hour. Will you make sure Linda is not left here?

- I'll get it organised.

Jay phoned her friend and arranged to meet.

In her room, Jay opened her suitcase and took out her uniform. She showered, then dressed. She phoned Rory to get details of the hospital and organise her billet. He had sent case files by email to familiarise herself on the journey, as expected Brown visited Jay.

- What should I do, Linda?

- You have to go, Jay. I don't know about taking May, and it could be too much for her.

- I can't leave her now; there is some strange bond I can't shake. I need her.

- What will you do? Rooms are paid for two nights. Will you stay, or will I get May to get you a car home.

- I think I'll stay, get pampered. Get the smell of the army off me. Do you think she'll mind?

- She's in apologetic mode just now. She'll do anything I ask. Let me pack, and I'll see you in the foyer. Rory has sent case files by fax to the reception. Can you pick them up for me, please?

- Sure, one thing. Watch out for May, the trauma of meeting you both may be too much for her, especially if she cannot get redemption from Ben. If it gets too much, call me, and I'll get there to help.

- I will.

May was waiting. Brown retrieved the papers from the office and joined her to wait for Jay.

- How are you feeling, May?

- Rough. I drank too much, far too quickly. I don't understand why I got so excitable; maybe I was overwhelmed by it all. I'm off it now for a while. I suppose it could have been worse.

- Jay understands. It's a big step for you both. She has worked hard to understand her emotional responses. You caught her at a good time. If you ever need to talk about anything, please call me. It's my job.

- I will. Here's Jay now – look at her.

Jay was in uniform, and she marched towards them, they stood to greet her. Brown handed Jay the documentation.

- Linda is staying for the second night, okay with you, May.

- Sure. The car will be here to take her home when she wants. It's all organised.

May wiped a bead of sweat from her forehead.

- A car is coming for us in a half-hour. I've booked hotel rooms in Hereford, settled the bill here and left something as a way of apology for the staff I annoyed last night too.

- Thanks, May. Nice meeting you.

- Nice meeting you too, Linda, I hope to see you again.

- Any help you need or advice, please phone.

- Okay. Jay said.

- Let's get outside May. I hate goodbyes.

May put on dark glasses, the glare of the sun conspired with the hangover to dull all senses. It would be a long drive for both.

TELL IT LIKE IT IS.

The car arrived early, which pleased May.

- Thank Jesus. I'm melting away to nothing here. I hope he has air conditioning. Jay, I'm going to sleep – you okay with that?
- Sure, May, I have to catch up on these case files. I'll be up to speed by the time we get there.

As May flirted with the driver, Jay shook her head, unsure whether to laugh or be embarrassed. May had her hooked; her personality was nothing like her adoptive Mother's. What you saw with May was what you got. Jay had never encountered strength coupled with such naïve charm; May had both in abundance. Jay was learning fast about what she had never been exposed to before the epiphany came to as she helped May with the seatbelt she had managed to tangle around her legs.

Humanity is the trait most liked by others. If you marry it with humility, then the world will love you.

May sat back.

- Driver, how long will our journey take?
- About three hours Ma'am.
- Fine. Get the air-conditioning on and leave me to sleep. Jay, wake me when we get there. No stopping now, driver. Don't spare the horses.

Within seconds May was snoring. Jay gave her a gentle nudge that reduced the volume; a second nudge brought silence. She opened the documents then read from the beginning, taking notes from the text. The testimony from the witnesses conflicted; Rory had picked up on that; Jay would talk to each of them again using the opposite tack from Rory. On numerous occasions, Jay had to take a break from reading, sit back in her seat then rub her eyes. A fine line existed between the professional and emotional approach. The victim was her twin, but she had to find the truth. Perhaps Ben instigated the fracas, or maybe he was in the wrong place at the wrong time.

The Army should be wary of how those returning from conflict are unleashed on society. It was no coincidence that the prison population was over ten per cent ex-military. Brown and Jay had discussed that the army allowed time in training personnel to be killers but not to de-train. They agreed that three or four months within a resettlement process would help. They knew the army expended money on people who've suffered physical injuries but were unwilling to outlay on mental health. This lack of vision was storing up problems for further down the line. Jay had met many returning squaddies over the years and had an in-depth understanding of their plight. They could never tell you the details – friends dying and all the rest – unless they knew you had done it. They believed no one would ever understand. One ex-corporal had come close to explaining it to Jay. He had opened up and told her that he could be sitting in a pub just staring at everyone, thinking they were threats, even his family. He was looking at people who were scared of him, primed to attack them. He had stopped sleeping, turning to drink and drugs to nullify him. Soldiers do not see Doctors because they are Soldiers; they never admit there is anything wrong.

Jay opened the page at the squaddie's history. She knew what it would be before she read it. He was from one of the Line Infantry Regiments, joined up in his late teens. Jay had met many from the same environs, considered as lacking stability and opportunity. Once in the Army, these youths were deprived of the broader life skills necessary to achieve productive lives. No life and employment skills develop, resulting in family stresses, which makes them feel inadequate – they lose the comradeship built up in the army. The biggest issue being that they would be retaining trauma that might not manifest itself for years as combat tempo for Infantry was high, with rapid turnaround between deployments. One of the first statistics Jay had ingrained in her memory was that more veterans who participated in the Falkland's war killed themselves than were killed during the operation. Brown had surprised Jay with her take on the matter, especially Post Traumatic Stress Disorder. The conversation was still exact in Jay's mind; it was the moment that Brown gained her trust.

'It's a label; defined by the Manual of Mental Disorders – the psychiatrists' Bible. Some disease detectives convinced that it is not a problem – only a tiny number of ex-military suffer from it; that is either deception or conspiracy.'

Jay sat back just as May broke wind in her sleep. Her snoring started then stopped when she turned her body around. She broke wind again; Jay gasped in shock. She had never heard her adoptive Mother nor another female do this.

The driver laughed.

- Ha, she's a right sort. Are you arresting her?

Jay ignored the comment, then phoned Linda.

- Hi Jay, all okay?
- Yeah, but you would not believe May. It's like owning a puppy. Anyway, I'm reading the case files; I have a question on PTSD.
- Fire away.
- Remember you mentioned that the numbers of personnel suffering were relatively low? Why is that?
- Jay, don't get me started on that. It's a pet hate. The short answer is that very few are assessed. Those that are, through lack of communication, don't tick all the boxes. These soldiers are trying to deal with pain, but it doesn't match the symptoms of PTSD as laid out in the manuals. The establishment is locked into the conventional view, defined by the N.I.H.
- I understand. Is there any reason for that - is the trauma locked in?
- You ready for this. It's predicated on the amygdala, the part of the reptilian brain. That is where an event is stored as an emotional memory - then held in a neurological pattern. If a

patient hears a car backfire as an explosion, they will flip into an aggressive mood. The important thing about the amygdala, unlike the rational brain, is that it has no sense of time. The rational brain cannot hang on to the emotions that go with memories, but the amygdala cannot let go. Our treatment is hypnosis; it allows them to run the memory forwards and backwards in a relaxed state. It teaches the amygdala to let go – not to hang on to that pattern. The Rewind treatment or trauma-focused cognitive behaviour therapy helps, similar to Brainspotting. Non-intrusive. Does that help?

- I'm trying to get an understanding of an infantry soldier who recently returned from combat and about to be pensioned off.
- Be careful, Jay; these guys are time bombs; convinced no one understands or listens to them. Try to understand his mental health is the key; identify dysfunctional behaviour, but handle him sensitively - he will see this as providing practical help
- Good knowledge. Thanks and see you soon.

Jay had worked that technique with the ex-corporal. He was on remand for a violent offence and confided that when in prison, he felt better in a place that was 'full of mugs'. He was crying out for direction but glad to be back in an institution. He had nothing to lose – prison appealed to him because he got three meals a day and a roof over his head, plus the bonus of not having to kill. He had seen scarier people and situations in conflict than in prison. His other option was medication, turned into a shell of a man – none wanted that.

The case appeared to be straight forward. Witness statements confirmed that Ben had pushed the squaddie's head then, a possibility of muscle memory reaction from the trained soldier resulted in him reacting in self-defence. That was Rory's conclusion. The facts from the case file supported this, and it was logical. Why then did Rory state that all was not as seemed? Jay called Rory.

- Hi Jay, where are you.
- En route should be there within the hour. We are coming directly to the hospital. Where will you be?

- I'm at the barracks. I'll see you later.
- Rory, the case appears to be straightforward. Why do you think otherwise?
- You know I cannot say anything. I suggest you interview the witnesses and the accused. It is too clean and neat. Smoke and mirrors.
- Okay, see you when I see you.

May grunted, belched, then awoke.

- Who were you speaking to?
- Rory.
- I was just dreaming of him. Are we to meet him?

Jay remained silent.

- What's wrong, Jay?
- You are May.

May widened her eyes and looked deep into Jay's.

- We are on my territory now, May. My rules. I can get you in to see Ben, no one else can, and you know why. I want you to understand one thing - I can get this fixed - it's what I do. If you're going to be part of it, you must agree to two things if you let me down, you are out. Understand?

May nodded.

- First, you do as I say; you do not question or argue. I am open to suggestions for the good of Ben. Nothing else. Got it?
- I understand, Jay. What is the other?
- You keep your hands off Rory. Do not flirt or embarrass me. He is my friend; he is also the defence lawyer for Ben's assailant. If you compromise that, you will regret it.

Once again, May nodded.

The driver broke the silence.

- We are here, ladies.
- May, you go ahead to the hotel and check us in and get the
bags sorted, then come over here. Okay.
- Okay.

Jay left the taxi and walked through the hospital entrance without
looking back. She shook her head, uttering the single word -
"Families".

LISTER.

-   Ben, it's me – Jay, your twin. I know you can hear me
    and that you have no way to let the doctors
    understand what you are suffering. I'm here with our
    Mother; she's coming in later to talk to you. I met her
    for the first time yesterday. She's nice. Big heart.
    Different.

Ben was confused; he could feel a hand in his, their fingers
entwined. He sensed it was Jay but could not comprehend
why she was there. Ben's uncertainty morphed into assurance.

-   She's had you moved from the NHS into private care;
    she's paying for the best – that's what May does, she
    buys the best of everything…We've stirred a hornet's
    nest at the last hospital as they misdiagnosed you,
    that's why no one tried to communicate. Doctors
    deemed you a hopeless case, considering your
    consciousness as extinct. We've been here one day
    and got a result. The NHS Doctors treated you using
    the Glasgow Coma Scale based on eye, verbal and
    motor responses. Their grading was wrong. Our
    Mother had you transferred then chased them up to
    get brain imaging scans done, and this has shown you
    brain is still functioning almost normally. You're
    hooked up to a brain monitor now so we can view all
    your brain activity on a screen. I hope you understand
    what I'm saying; the images show that you may.

A male voice interrupted Jay.

Ben tried to scream, but there was nothing to hear,

- **Tell me more!!!**

The monitor translated the frustration into a flurry of brain wave movement.

- Look at the monitor Captain; he's trying to communicate. Can you imagine what it's like to be lying in a hospital bed, in a coma, dead to what is happening around you? He is experiencing it. He hears and is trying in vain to communicate. He's lucky to have the correct diagnosis; anyone who gets the stamp of 'unconscious' on their records never gets rid of it. Those who suffer severe traumatic brain injury are in a coma of three weeks or longer; some die, others regain health. But some remain trapped in an intermediate stage, somewhere between death and recovery: they go on living without ever coming back. It's quite common; so-called persistent vegetative state diagnosed patients are often misdiagnosed.

- How much longer do you think he will remain like this?
- He's been in this state four weeks without progress in communicating; we don't know how long he has been able to hear or feel. We know he feels pain as the monitor displays the reaction to the needle injected. I have organised visits from physiotherapists and speech and language therapists, determined to optimise his recovery.

A nurse entered the light, airy room.

- Afternoon, I'm here to bathe and shave the patient.
- Call him Ben, please nurse, talk to him, tell him what you intend doing.
- Yes, Doctor.

- Hi Ben, I'm Nurse Vincent. I'm going to give you a blanket bath, brush your teeth then shave you. Make you nice and clean. I'll move you around after I've finished.

Ben's tried to respond but knew it was futile; he could see the room and the nurse in his mind's eye; he could feel her hands moving him and the gentle caress of a brush on his gums. His world became that of white linen billowing sheets, the stimulation played tricks, he saw himself on the bed, with Jay and the Doctor talking and the nurse tending to him. He planned to thank her when she finished but became caught up in the sensory joy. Ben's vivid dream evaporated with a shriek from Jay,

- Look, Doctor, his eyes are opened.
- That's quite common. I'm sure Nurse Vincent has seen that happen many times?
- Yes, Doctor, it's scary at first. One day he'll blink. I'll put eye drops in to lubricate. It shows he's strong and determined to fight his condition. They are a lovely shade of brown.

Jay interrupted,

- Ben's eyes are green! I saw them on his HR file. It may not be Ben.

The doctor looked at his notes, flicked through the pages, then put his hand on Jay's shoulder,

- Captain, we have his ID. That is Ben Black, perhaps not the one you expected?

Strange. My eyes changed colour too when I went through emotional trauma. I noticed it, as did my counsellor.

- Are you twins? The Doctor asked.
- Yes.

- Then it is possible. It's a documented phenomenon; it happens to identical twins, not fraternal. Do you know the difference?
- No.
- It's nothing to worry about; it's genetic, you could share the same DNA but unlikely. Interesting to me. Captain, can we talk outside, please.

As they left the room, May appeared.

- Feckin' lawyers. I've put mine on standby to sue the NHS for the misdiagnosis. He is trying to fob me off. One thing I don't need now is an arrogant shyster.
- Calm down, May. The Doctor wants to talk.

- It's okay. Your lawyer is right; it could be a costly battle for you. First, I need to make you aware of a few things concerning Ben. The misdiagnosis does not detract from the fact that he is still paralysed and dependent on care. The NHS called it wrong, but in terms of the improvements he can expect to make in the future, this is incidental. It has no bearing on his prospects concerning his function. That's not to say that people who suffer severe brain injury don't make miraculous recoveries – some do, but the miracles are small and insignificant to the outside observer. It's important to realise that the medical world's measure of improvement and progress is different from that of the general public. It would be nice to think that giving him a different diagnosis gave him his life back. Nurses in our unit are attentive and expert. They will turn him regularly, ensure he is comfortable, wipe away saliva when he dribbles, and administer eye drops when his eyes appear red. I'd like you to keep in mind that when Doctors talk of improvements and progress, they refer to what others consider minute, insignificant changes. Neurologically it will be progress. I'm warning you that there may be a crucial decision to be made—one of life and death.

May stared at Jay in silence. They held each other's hand. Jay made no response; they stared deep into each other as hurt souls, lost for words.

May took the initiative,

- Okay, Doctor, we understand. I'm going to spend some time with my son. Are you off, Jay?
- I have to interview the man who put him there.

May gazed at her clean-shaven son. She sat in silence for one hour, holding his right hand in both of hers. Tears came then dried. She tried to speak but could not. The first words were going to make this the most traumatic experience she had known since leaving her children.

- John, that's the name I gave you. I named you after your Father, and he named your sister Mary after me. We had no parents or family. All we had was each other. Two Marys and two Johns. I've left my fear in the past; I can't control my present-day relationships unless I maintain a healthy perspective about life. Would you forgive me? If your father had not died, and I did not have to leave, none of this would have happened.

Ben crystallised his thought process.

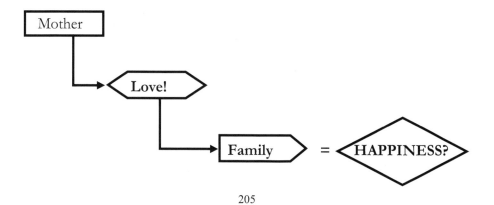

Anxiety set into Ben. His Mother was alive, and his father dead.

Too much to take in when he could not ask for an explanation. He screamed, hoping the monitor would reveal his state. May picked up on the activity,

- Please don't get upset; I'm trying to help. I'm lost, my beautiful boy. I smile and am loud too, but that is a front that hides an ocean of tears. I am tormented, torn and trapped. My soul screams at me, reminding me of the terrible thing of leaving you and your sister. I had to. We would have suffered at the hands of evil people that I believe, murdered your father. I've aged watching families, Mothers with their children, seeing them laugh…and cry together. I've frightened myself with the rage that encased me for those I would never forgive. I ruined me; I destroyed you, and I ruined your sister. I would do anything to be able to heal you; time will, I hope. I doubt time will ever cure me. Would you forgive me? Can you show me on the monitor if you do? Can you please.

Ben's scream came from the heart. Of course he forgave her. She was his Mother; she had come to rescue him. She was perfect in his eyes. He had no resentment, no ideas of revenge. Suffering or pain had always been a part of his life; forgiveness was not his path to freedom; he had embraced negative emotions and patterns. He had been free to live the way he wanted, happy and healthy – until now. Maybe there was an excuse for her actions; time would tell. He had never felt bitterness nor anger; he bore no grudge. Ben enjoyed living for the moment, albeit without a connection to others. Wabi-sabi; Ben contemplated the concept. Perfection with a flaw. The main reasons his relationships with the opposite sex had failed. He always looked for that fault and now realised the stupidity in it being physical rather than a character trait. He had judged on his idea of the ideal somatic female. Ankles too fat, legs too chunky, bottom to breast size ratio wrong, waistless, no muscle definition, bad teeth, lank hair, misshapen nose, facial hair, fat arms… Ben was ashamed as the list kept growing. How could he have been that shallow? He had reacted to the flaw without seeing perfection. The time spent listening to his Mother declaring her fault had shamed him. He had wasted years believing he was righteous in being negative; he should have looked for the person's good. Antje had shown him the good, as did Dana, but his lack of empathy and understanding had blinded him to reality. He felt humiliated. May's voice soothed him.

- I'm not going to bleat on about my regret anymore; it will not help either of us. Shall I tell you a joke, sing you a song? I'd like to just sit with you, hold your hand, watch the monitor, see your thoughts. I wonder what you are thinking. Are you thinking of me?

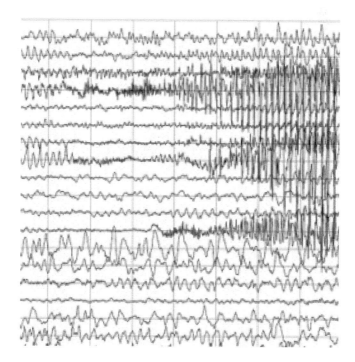

- I hope that means you are. Can you feel the love from me?

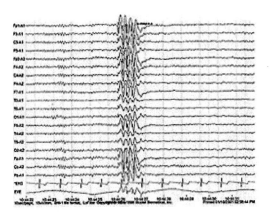

- I can feel it from you.

- Jay has told me what she knows about you. She wrote a report, but you never read it. She told me you sent her a poem, but she did not keep it.

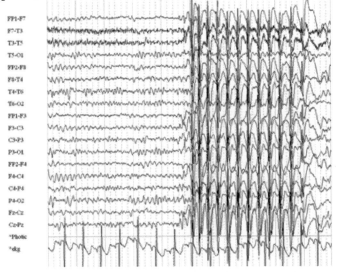

Has that upset you? I don't mean to. She wanted to meet you but knows now that she did it the wrong way. You can forgive her too, can you not?

Ben took control of his thoughts. He tried to empty his brain, house- keep his thoughts to focus on one thing. He questioned May and Jay's motives. It was one thing to get the family together but another to treat him as a commodity. The euphoria from hearing May's first words melted to a state of anxiety. He felt a depth of inferiority and discomfort never encountered in all the humiliation endured. He would choose to communicate with them when he wanted to, not them taking his situation for granted. He was a captive audience with a non-verbal response.

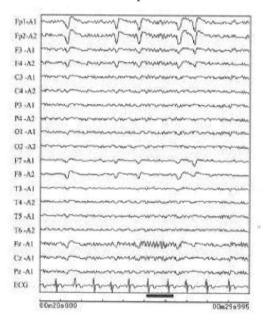

- Ben, don't go quiet on me; I'll worry, please don't be upset; I've only just found you. Don't abandon me now. We only want the best for you.

Ben's anxiety turned into unearned melancholia. He had to step his thought process back, perhaps even reconsider the value of it.

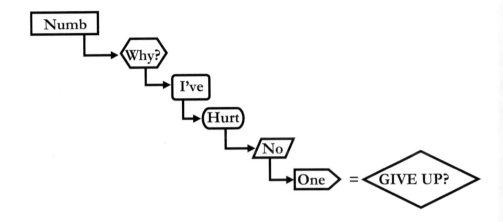

He had to play smart, knowing all his predicament probabilities were internalised. May was pleading for forgiveness; was this for her ends? To heal herself? He must work on the odds in terms of things HE wanted to happen rather than things HE feared were going to. Turn his worries into wants. This was no free-floating anxiety; no concern replacing another. The tension was driving Ben, but he remained calm and accepted it as inseparable from ambition – he would use this to navigate thoughts rather than the flow chart. This self-renewing aspect appealed, stuck in a personal disaster, the implanted fear sparked the cure, the remedy would be to absent himself from it. Shut down his brain.

Ben knew all about existential anxiety, the inescapable kind. He had studied it in-depth and realised that his mortality was not a long shot. That had been his and Plant's shared philosophy; neither had experienced existential agony for a loved one as they had been incapable. That, Ben formulated, freed the mental space to seek out pleasures rather than unfixable problems. Ben thought of how lucky he was to be alive, even in this locked-in state. Ben's spirit rose; he had a good feeling about himself. Whichever idiot had decreed, "Everybody dies, but not everybody lives." had no clue, Ben felt a thrill, a joy of relief. The mystery he had searched for all his life had dissipated, the worry ended. It was clear; Ben understood that he should make things sufficient to live by as they are as useful to experience. There was no big idea worth dying for to find small pleasures worth living for. Even if his body died, his consciousness continues. There was no philosophy required for Ben to understand that he was living the holy grail; mind and brain function differed. Ben became fulfilled and realised that death was not the end of personality.

Ben's euphoria brought back his short term memory; he remembered the situation that had placed him here. He had forgiven Mary and could now forgive the crazy man that put him here. Ben understood the gut-wrenching, heart-pounding, adrenaline-pumped anxiety that man must have endured along with his the heightened sense of alertness, increased physical strength and speed. Ben's accelerated thoughts might have helped avert disaster, but that was the anxiety of doing the job. Ben remembered feeling the same physical responses but had no awareness of what was to occur. At the time, it was crippling and overwhelmed his state of mind and body; perhaps that's why he reacted by rubbing his head. Their shared anxiety was a warning signal that danger was present, but neither could process the data, so reverted to the attack and recoil of the fear and neurosis; both had become anxious about anxiety. The answer appeared obvious to Ben which prompted him to search in the opposite direction, not to the manifestations of fear but its source. Was it simplicity, not complexity? Anxiety, Ben surmised, was composed of thought; nothing else, the principle force that drives our mental life, the energy that can create anything. The power of consciousness makes thought real to us. That is from where all human experience comes. He had learned that every occasion coming to him was through thought; the same for every human being, everyone he had ever known but not understood; always has been, always will be. Philosophy could not solve the answer to anxiety or stress. He had been wrong all his life, and he had wasted precious time looking for something that was not there. He should have picked this up in the homes, be aware of it. The revelation stirred movement within Ben's body. He felt as if he was travelling, walking? He could not work it out; the sounds became muffled, and the beep gone. He screamed the names of his Mother and sister, tried to open his eyes, but nothing worked. Ben used recent thoughts to calm his anxious state.

211

If it were not for all the crap he had read, he would not be here. The words that rang true now in his head concerned the concept that nothing straight was fashioned from crooked wood that man is. There were no philosophical problems, just puzzles caused by linguistic confusion. All these great thinkers quoted lines to be smarter than they were; ha, Ben quipped as he saw it for what it is, head wanking; the next thing to saying a good thing yourself is to quote one. The easiest thing for an academic to do is to appear philosophical by making ambiguous comments; Ben had known many creatives and saw them now for what they were; the more there was on show, the less there was to see. Cod philosophers, the lot of them, none of what they said was insightful. It was devoid of depth. It was a masquerade; inept, incompetent, deficient. It was reflective of useless speculation that appealed to those that Ben despised. Traditional and immoral, it had pigeon-holed and held him back. If an academic did not believe it, then it was deemed to be superstition. Ben's anger was rising. It was this group of fanatics he had held in high esteem for most of his life that he now blamed for his predicament. Suppose he could meet up with those who misdiagnosed him with oppositional defiance disorder. In that case, he could now challenge them to judge their actions with their values honed from these nonsensical theories. He would ask them to think, suppose - then imagine. Ben was exhausted; he felt he had never slept. For the first time in a month, the exhaustion overtook him, and his brain lapsed into sleep mode; Ben took the initiative then shut his mind down.

May squeezed Ben's hand then slapped it, trying to gain a response. She began to panic, staring at the monitor for any sign of activity, but it appeared to her that he had ceased thought. May raced into the corridor, shouting for a doctor or nurse. In her haste, she collided with a porter moving a patient. The impact sent her headfirst into the wall and knocked her unconscious. Porters and nurses rushed to her aid and after assessment she was moved to the room adjacent to Ben's and sedated for observation.

She awoke the following day to see Jay staring down at her.

- You don't make things easy, do you, May?

- What happened; why am I here…how's Ben? His monitor stopped.
- Do you remember what happened? You're lucky, you took a hell of a bang to your head. If you had injured yourself like that anywhere else, god knows what would have happened.

Jay leaned over and kissed May's bandaged forehead.

- What am I going to do with you? I must say there is never a dull moment when you are around. Are you always like this?

May smiled then stuck her tongue out,

- Feck you too, Jay. How did you get on with the interview?
- Squaddies, ha – give them enough rope. I have to write my report. I'll do it here – don't interrupt, and I might read it to you. There's some information I can't submit. Okay?
- Fine by me.

ACTS.

Lance Corporal Mathew Pearson, known to his friends as "one-punch" chewed gum, his eyes drilled deep into Jay's. Expressionless, she stared him down whilst picking through his service record.

- You've done this before, Pearson. One-Punch eh? Is that because you can only take one?

The soldier made loud, deliberate chewing noises.

- Nothing to say, Ma'am. My brief told me everything is in witness statements.

- True, that's what your lawyer would say, but I'm Military Police. We don't listen to what they say. We find the truth. Do you want to tell me the truth?

- Don't remember too much about it now; it was over a month ago. Some civvy Jock pushed my head for no reason, I reacted.

- Overreacted, perhaps?

- Don't think so, Ma'am. He was bigger than me; I feared for my safety.

- C'mon, you were with your oppos; there were at least four of you. What's some civvy going to do to you guys? Was he winding you up, staring at you? Did you feel threatened?

- No one threatens me. Did you read where I've been? You've never been in the field; you have no idea.

- Okay, Lance Corporal, calm it. You don't question me; I ask you, got it?

- Yes, Ma'am. Sorry, Ma'am.

- When does your time end?

- Next month.

- You know how lucky your timing is; if you were in civvy street, you'd be well and truly stuffed now.

- Maybe, but I acted in self-defence.

Jay stood and walked toward the door. He had a smart answer to everything. She would have to change her strategy. She thought back to the advice Brown had offered. Jay modulated the tone of her voice,

- Do you know how many of you guys are in civvy nick?

- Don't care.

- Where are you from?

- Rye.

- You know Lydd?

- I trained there.

- Will you go back?

- Nothing there for me, Ma'am.

- What do you want to do?

- I still have to talk about that.

- Fancy a cup of tea or something?

- I would, thanks.

Jay left the interview room, returning a half-hour later with tea and biscuits.

- I thought you'd got lost, Ma'am.

- I had to make a call. I'll tell you something, Pearson; I see many

Infantry guys like you back from combat; no detraining - just paid off and left by the Army. There's a pattern that some of us are trying to highlight to the brass. If I said to contain your violence, you'd ignore me – right?

- I would, Ma'am.

- Can you give me an idea of what you think would help?

- Not really; everyone has their theories. Being made to feel part of something would go a long way.

- Will you miss your Infantry mates?

- More than you will ever know – Ma'am.

Jay sat back to take stock. He was a hard case, no doubting that, evident from the outset.

- You want to tell me what happened that day?

- I've told you, it was…

A knock at the door interrupted Pearson. An orderly entered and pointed to the telephone on the desk.

- Outside call for Lance Corporal Pearson, take it on that extension.

Pearson frowned.

- No one knows I'm here.

- Answer it.

Pearson pushed the receiver hard against his ear.

- Pearson.

Jay watched as his facial expression change from a smile of recognition to one of fear. He was ashen-faced as he replaced the phone, squaring the assembly on the table. His eyes remained fixed to the phone, then glared at Jay, then stared back at the phone.

His expression did not change when Rory opened the door opened. Jay and Pearson rose to salute.

- Sit down. Captain, have you completed your interview with my client?.

- Just bringing it to a close, Sir.

- Pearson, anything to tell me.

- I started the fight. I back-heeled that civvy first. I'll admit it all now, no need for witnesses. Get a statement written up, and I'll sign it. What will happen to me?

- We can keep it in house. If you co-operate, then we can help you, now and in the future. Agreed?.

- Yes, Ma'am, thank you, Ma'am.

Jay left Rory and Pearson. She smiled as she took her phone from her pocket and redialled the last number.

- Thanks, Bryce. You put the fear into him.

- No probs. How did you know he'd served under me in the Infantry?

- I read it in his record, what you did for him, and I reckoned that he owed you one. Thanks for making the call; I know you didn't have to. Coincidence eh?

- Naw, small world ours, Ma'am. I was surprised to hear from you. I was happy to do as you asked. By the way, can I ask what he did?

- Just what he's programmed to, just in the wrong place to the wrong person. What did you say to him?

- That's between him and me and the Infantry. Let's keep it that way, off the record.

- It is Bryce. Take care.

- You too, Ma'am

As Jay pushed the button to end the call, another came in. It was the hospital explaining what happened to her Mother. Panic set in; should she get Rory? Jay decided she was putting too much on him. May had added another problem to Jay's life. Nothing was easy.

JULIUS, MILTON AND …

-   What will happen to the soldier? May asked.
-   Rory will make a case; he'll get a dishonourable discharge and some time for actual bodily harm. Ben can sue the Armed forces for compensation if directed. All in all, it's a mess. The soldier is a victim of sorts. Who knows what would have happened to him if he had not joined up. Maybe being a soldier delayed the inevitable.
-   I've met my fair share of thugs and bullies. That's what put me in my state all those years ago, and now the same's happened to Ben. How is he? How long have I been in here?
-   You had your accident two days ago. I've been here and next door ever since. There is a guest room in this hospital; what would we have done if we did not have the resource to pay for this. It does not bear thinking. Ben has been under intense testing and evaluation; according to the Doctor, there is no response from his brain showing on the scan, although there is no change in the neuroimaging data.
-   It happened when I talked to him, and he was talking back to me through the lines on the screen. He was, honestly. Then all of a sudden, I told him something, and it just shut down. That's when I ran out of the room to get the Doctor and Nurse. I was in such a hurry. I did not see the trolley. All my fault; it's always my fault. Just when I find him, he's taken from me.

May's body rocked with sobbing. Jay called a Nurse to sedate her. Jay sat with her head in her hands while May was lay on her back, snoring.

-   Your Mother will be fine. The blood loss was contained; she'll be up and walking tomorrow. She needs rest, as do you.

The doctor arrived and put his hand on Jay's shoulder; she looked up, he saw the hurt and pain in her eyes.

- Can I call you a taxi; get you to your hotel.
- I'm okay, Doctor. I have to get it into perspective.

The Doctor smiled at her.

- What about my brother? Can you give me an update?
- I will say tomorrow morning first thing. Please get some rest, is there anyone with you?
- There is. Thank you, can you organise a taxi, please.
- I'll do it right now.

The doctor left Jay and her Mother. The silence of the room brought on the feeling of being alone, isolated and abandoned. She sent a text message to Rory, asking if he would meet her at the hotel for supper. The reply was immediate. He would get there before she did.

The cab ride to the hotel allowed Jay time to collect her thoughts. The series of events had become more explicit as she walked from the hospital's light to the dark of the waiting taxi. The cold rain on her face refreshed her, and she made the deliberate decision to stroll through it rather than concede to the instinct of running. Jay watched her reflection appear and disappear in the rain-spattered window as the lights of passing traffic marked their route. The cabbie tried to make small talk, but she cut him off. She raised both eyebrows to her image; the thought of the disparity of how easy she could resolve work-related issues compared to the current ones came to the for, a stark contrast to her newfound domestic life. She paid the fare without talking to the driver. Rory was waiting in the foyer. Jay's spirits lifted; his friendly presence was just what she needed. She resisted the urge to embrace and kiss him when she touched his sleeve, the pips reminding her that he was in uniform.

- Fancy a drink, Jay?
- Not here, Rory, let's go to the room. Minibar beckons.

They walked in silence to the lift and stepped straight in. Jay pushed the button then turned to Rory,

- Good day at the office, dear?

Jay burst into laughter.

- That wasn't good; we are some team. One-punch had no chance. Shame, as I liked him for what he was. A real soldier, I'm going to push to get something in place to help guys like him. None of it is their fault. They are the weapon, not the trigger puller.
- You're right, Jay. Use it as part of your Majors course; you have good experience of it. How did you get him to confess? That was genius.
- I'll tell you one day; you shouldn't know just now. Let's say it's the secret of telling a good joke.

As they reached the room, they both shouted "timing".

- Holy Moly Jay! Look at the size of this.
- It's May; she does nothing by halves. She booked suites, even though she's now paying to stay in the hospital. What is she like?
- I know that from when I met her.
- Ah, I have to talk to you about that.

Rory blushed; he tried to hide his embarrassment by opening the minibar door.

- What do you fancy?
- Don't try to bluff me, Rory. I'm going to take a shower; you relax and pour me a G'n't for when I get out.

Jay emerged from the bathroom in a hotel robe and slippers. Rory was lounging on one of the day room chairs, shoes off, shirt hanging outside his trousers, sipping a glass of red wine.

- You look relaxed.
- Listen, Jay, about May; she gave me a lift –
  Jay cut him off,
- I'm winding you up. I know what she's like. Remember you told me about your family, mine seems to be worse!

Jay walked toward him, kissed his lips and sat in the next chair. Rory smiled and passed her drink.

- I fancy a night in the room talking, shall we order room service – it's the least May can do for us. What do you fancy?
- You are bad, Jay. Can I take a shower - get the dirt of the day off me. I fancy a rare steak, with a nice red.
- Be my guest or May's, for that matter. I fancy one too, shall I order for say, in about an hour.

- You'll never let me forget that, will you? Order away.

- Never, you're my slave now.

Jay, enjoying the moment, laughed out loud and sipped her drink. She started to sing a long-forgotten tune.

The food came on time. Sat opposite at the small table, heads almost touching, they leaned forward to eat. Jay sat back,

- How do my new found family compare to yours? Both in hospital, one in a coma and one is recovering from a near-death accident! Can it get any worse?
- I told you about my family.
- You told me about your sister; I fell asleep when you mentioned your brother.
- Funnily enough, my father phoned me yesterday. This story will make you gasp in either laughter or wonder.
- Tell all.
- His son, Bertie and girlfriend, who I think are both twenty-one, persuaded him to let them go to London for a week break; they wanted to see a west end show. The boy insisted he be allowed to book train travel and hotel, and my brother had to agree on the proviso that his son phoned every day with an update of events. On the third day, my nephew told his father that he and his girlfriend had small red bites on their skin. My brother made them take photographs and send them on. It turns out they were bed bugs. My father laughed as he explained the rage my brother flew into, decreeing that

his house would never be home to such a parasite and that hotels that carried such things were a menace to public health. Believe this or not, he phoned the hotel and told the manager his inimitable way that his hotel was a disgrace and he would move heaven and earth to shut it down. He then phoned the Environmental Health agency in London to report this manifestation. They informed him any call out would be charged at fifty pounds an hour, more at weekends.

— Is he mad?

— What do you think?

— It gets worse.

— Please, Rory, how can that get worse?

— He then phones the local pest control for advice. They tell him what he must do to prevent a bed bug infestation in his home. He then buys the powder and sheets of polythene. On the day of his son's return, he lined his garage with the polythene sheets to make it pest-proof. He then tells Bertie to get a taxi from the airport as he does not want the risk of bugs in his car. The poor couple is ushered into the garage, made to strip to underwear and put on safety glasses and facemasks that cover the nose and mouth. My brother empties their luggage at their feet and throws their cases into the rubbish skip. He then douses them and their belongings with the powder supplied by pest control. They are then put into paper boiler suits and marched into the house, which has polythene sheets marking the way to the shower. They both have to shower and put on new paper boiler suit.

— That's nuts, Rory.

— I doubt anyone else would treat their kid like that. I wonder what the girl's parents thought when they heard what he had done to their child.

— He makes May seem like a saint. Talking of that, the Doctor wants to talk to us about Ben in the morning, will you come along with me.

— Of course.

— Mufti?

— Best to.

- I'm shattered, Rory, and I need an early night. I hope you understand.

Jay climbed into bed; she was asleep before Rory returned from putting the room service tray in the corridor. He put out the lights then slipped between the sheets.

May was sitting out of bed, eating breakfast and watching television when Rory and Jay walked in.

- Hi, you two. What a lovely looking couple!
- Can it May. Ordered Jay.
- Morning May, nice to see you again.
- You, you…nice to see you again. Want some tea, coffee – the breakfast here isn't half bad.
- I'm okay for now May, I've had mine. Jay?
- Not for me. The Doc will give us an update on Ben this morning. Has he been in to see you?
- Not yet. I wonder what he'll say.

Rory and May watched television and made small talk whilst Jay stared out of the window. The Doctor knocked and entered.

- Morning. How are you feeling, Ms Taylor?
- I'm grand Doctor, needed the rest. No pain to speak of apart from my dented pride for being so stupid.
- It was an accident, one we cannot have happening again. The hospital owners have their administrators doing a health and safety analysis on how it happened; those trolleys have no sharp edges, must have been a unique collision.
- I honestly cannot remember; I remember running out in a panic then waking up here. Tell me, Doctor, how is my son.

Jay turned from the window to listen.

- It's not good. Some of my colleagues are on their way, pulmonology, neurology, etc. they are going to gives us a detailed rundown on where things stand. All I can tell you, for now, is what we all know; it is the machine keeping Ben breathing. Ah, here they are now.

Jay, May and Rory listened whilst each specialist explained the tests, the outcome, and the prognosis in detail. The neurologist was last to speak; he explained the tests that determined whether brainstem reflexes were present to diagnose brain death. The Doctor waited a minute then spoke.

- We believe there is no brain function whatsoever. This will come as a shock but believe me when I say we have carried out the tests for brain activity levels many times. In brain death, there is no possibility of recovery.
- What options do we have? Asked Jay.
- In this case, where there is no advanced directive, we have to advise that support should be turned off.

May slumped back in her chair.

- No, this can't be right. We must have some options. Can we move him to a place to be looked after?
- I'm sorry, Ms Taylor; physicians are not required to provide futile care. We accept that once that person is brain dead, they are deceased. There is nothing more we could do.

We know you will be in shock. We have counsellors on hand to help. You can make the decision when you want it to happen.

- Can we see him? May asked.
- Of course, he's next door. He's still on a ventilator and ET tube inserted.

The three walked into the next room. The noise of the ventilator soundtracked emotions.

May surprised the others,

- That's no way for anyone to live. I have to go with the consultants; we should switch the machines off.

Jay embraced her Mother. They stood cheek to cheek, tears fusing their skin.

- You are right, May, but it seems such a cruel act. Almost murder.
- There's no brain scan monitor. Noted May.
- I doubt they think it is required now after all the tests they have done.
- We should say our goodbyes then tell the Doctors that we need to do this sooner than later. There is no point prolonging all of our agonies. What do you think, Jay?
- My heart says no, but my mind says yes. It all seems too final.
- I know, I know, but what else can we do.

Rory took the hand of both ladies.

- Put yourself in Ben's place, what would he choose to do; they call that substituted judgment in my trade. It can help you make the right decision.
- He's right, Jay. You knew the Ben I never, what would he want? To be like this, with no hope or to make a journey into the unknown, with our help.
- May, you've made the answer easy. He would relish an adventure. Rory, will you fetch the doctor? We'll say our goodbyes.

Ben was screaming,

- **Leave me alone. Leave me alone. I'm happy here. No one tells me what to do. I'm in a life I always wanted, and now strangers are taking me from it.**

Ben could hear May and Jay crying, each trying to say the same thing. How much they would miss him and how they would never forget him. How could they never forget a person they never knew? It was false, as false as all the promises made by philosophers. There was only one true line, Plant had told him, and he had found it. It came from the heart, and it was real and straightforward. And here they were spouting this esoteric mumbo jumbo.

The doctor entered the room.

-   You've made the decision.
-   We have. May answered with her head bowed.
-   Can we do it now?
-    I've called for the respiratory therapist; she will do what is necessary.
-   Are you sure now doctor, is there no hope? May asked.
-   None Ms Taylor, it may seem he retains some raw brainstem reflexes, but he has no higher function.

The therapist entered the room.

-   This is a difficult time for us all. Ben should only live for a couple of minutes once I turned the machine off. Have you said goodbyes?
-   We have.

Ben had no option, and he could not contain his fury; in his mind, his body was writhing and struggling, and he was screaming at the top of his voice.

-   **Stop, stop this is murder. I don't want this to happen.**

He heard the therapist's practised tones.

-   I'm going to switch the ventilator off first. Then I am going to move to the other side of the bed to remove the ET tube. You will hear Ben gasp and cough, and he may gag too. He may not die immediately, but, in his present state, it will be sooner rather than later.

He looked at May and Jay, who were sobbing; Jay was holding May's waist standing behind her, Rory was behind Jay in the same pose.

-   When you nod, I will begin the procedure.

Jay squeezed May.

 May nodded.

The therapist moved to the wall socket, flicked the switch, and then removed the plug. The Machine beeped loudly, then faded when the therapist hit the silence alarm button.

Ben heard the beep; he screamed again.

- **Fuckin' killers. I'm not going to let this happen.**

The therapist strolled to the other side of the bed, then began to peel off the retaining tape.

May turned her head into Jay's body as the therapist pulled the tube; the gurgling sound resonated through the white-walled room, a death rattle growing louder. The pipe's sound as it became free from Ben's throat caught all in the room by surprise; it was a membrane popping. They looked on in disbelief as Ben opened his eyes, pushed himself into a seating position and shouted at the top of his raw voice,

- **HARPO SPEAKS!**

ABOUT THE AUTHOR

Nothing of note. A large person with long legs, wide eyes and a big smile. Gluts on food, drink and conversation then worries about life's uncertainties.

Printed in Great Britain
by Amazon

57600203R10131